MALIGNED

Kathleen Papajohn

Martin Sisters Publishing

Published by

Sky Vine Books, a division of Martin Sisters Publishing, LLC

www.martinsisterspublishing.com

Copyright © 2012 Kathleen Papajohn

ISBN: 978-1-937273-26-2

Dystopian/Thriller

Printed in the United States of America
Martin Sisters Publishing, LLC

DEDICATION

For Stephen, who taught me that love truly is eternal.

Dystopian/Thriller

An imprint of Martin Sisters Publishing, LLC

Chapter One

Despite the searing Phoenix heat, the boy forced himself to keep running. As he raced past, he saw his sickly young image reflected a hundred-fold in the mirrored, solar-paneled walls of the city's buildings. The skin covering his thin frame was tightly drawn and almost translucent, his blond hair grimy and matted. Both his wrists were badly chafed. The skin around his right forearm was swollen, scraped almost to the bone, like someone had taken a cheese grater to it. In his fear, he barely noticed the cuff that was still attached securely to his left wrist. The thick chain that had originally connected the restraints now dangled freely from his arm and swung wildly as he ran, getting caught in his feet, causing the boy to stumble. The vile bracelet hung from its tether in ragged shreds, as if an animal had gnawed through it.

Terrified, the boy never turned around to try to catch a glimpse of who, or what, was chasing him. Without regard for his own safety, he didn't look left or right before sprinting across Washington Street and entering the park. Washington Street was empty of traffic, and like every other downtown Phoenix street, it had only rarely felt the tread of an automobile tire or heard the blare of a horn for over a century.

The boy's legs burned and began to cramp up. Gasping, he held his side. Pain overwhelmed him. Despair and horror filled him. He heard the footfalls getting closer and closer as he stumbled through the park's canopy of soaring trees. The thick foliage closed over his head like the ceiling of a cathedral, filtering the sun's harsh glare and providing a small amount of relief from high noon's burning heat.

Still holding his side, unable to catch a full breath, the boy lurched to the right where the park's trail turned. He prayed that the trail would lead him to safety. His eyes nervously jerked left and right, and he started to cry. The trail abruptly ended, and he found himself in the middle of the city.

In a full-blown panic, he broke from the park's camouflage, and his small legs pumped even harder as he dashed across an open plaza to where a handful of people were collected, some eating their lunch, others just lounging around.

***

Herman Blume opened his lunch pail, but he wasn't really hungry. Already disgruntled, his dark mood got even darker when he saw that there was no place for him to sit. He had fallen into the habit of going there every day at noon, not just to eat the tasteless lunch that his wife, Wilma, packed for him, but, more importantly, to temporarily flee Wilma's never-ending complaining. He went to look at the pretty women who gathered on the plaza at lunchtime.

Herman didn't think of what he did as leering, even when women deliberately avoided his gaze and quickly put some distance between him and them. His fantasies were fueled to even greater heights because he could admire his own burly, well-toned body in the reflective exteriors of the buildings without Wilma criticizing him, rolling her small mean eyes, and telling him he was no prize every time she caught him looking in a mirror, which was often.

In his mind, these pretty women, sometimes two or even more, returned his gaze with interest, asking Herman to follow them home where they would beg him to show them what it was like to be with a real man. That day, the plaza was more crowded than usual, and Herman resented the trespassers that were loitering in the one place he always counted on to forget about Wilma's harassment, even if just for an hour.

Herman found himself annoyed by the buzz of conversations around him, intruding on his own dream world, and he was just about to give up and go back to work when he saw a young boy dart out of the park and run toward the protection of the small crowd. Herman's mouth opened in bewilderment as the boy grabbed at him, pulling on Herman's brown shirt so hard that he thought the boy would pull it right off his back.

"Please help me, sir!" the boy cried.

Herman just stared as the boy fell to his knees on the hard concrete, pleading not only to Herman, but to anyone who might listen to him.

"Please help me! Someone is after me!"

A woman in the crowd, an especially attractive one wearing a long, sheer blue dress, whom Herman had seen there before, walked over to where Herman stood and looked sympathetically at the trembling child.

"What's wrong, boy?" she asked.

"Someone is trying to kill me!" wailed the boy, still shaking with fear.

The woman narrowed her eyes and examined the plaza. She looked toward the park where the boy had come from. "You're being silly," she said. "Look, the plaza is empty except for us, and we mean you no harm."

The boy suddenly stopped crying and looked up at the woman. He held his breath and turned around to look back at the way he had come. Herman followed the boy's gaze. There was no one. The boy cocked his head and listened intently for sounds of his hunter. There was nothing. The boy laughed out loud, lifted his arms in triumph and cried jubilantly, "I must have lost him. Yes!"

"Please, boy," Herman said, happy that the boy had released his hold on his shirt, "why don't you just go home? I'm sure that your parents are worried about you."

The boy looked up at Herman, his eyes still pleading. "Parents? Do I have parents? How can I go home? Do you know where I live?" he asked in a voice that was pitifully hopeful.

"Of course I don't know where you live," Herman said. "Just go away, please!"

Herman felt uneasy as he watched the woman in the blue dress shrug and walk away. He had enough problems of his own--at least he did according to Wilma. He didn't want any trouble from this strange boy. Still, the child would not leave his side.

Herman felt the muscles in his neck tighten with irritation. He looked around and asked, "Doesn't anyone know this child?"

A few people shook their heads indicating that no one knew the boy before drifting away.

"Wait just a minute," Herman called out desperately. "There must be someone who can help this kid."

A tall well-built man, wearing wrap-around sunglasses stepped forward and said, "I'll help the child. Leave him to me."

"Thank you," Herman said, embarrassed by the obvious relief he heard in his own voice. Still, he pushed the boy toward his new guardian.

The Good Samaritan looked down at the exhausted, grimy young boy and smiled. "Here, give me your hand. I won't hurt you."

The boy lifted his left hand toward the stranger.

"No, not that hand son, the other one."

Obediently, the boy raised his right hand.

The man removed his sunglasses, put them into his shirt pocket and carefully looked at the boy's outstretched arm. Herman was stunned as he watched the man's eyes turn from light blue to a sickly bright yellow. Herman's own eyes grew wide in surprise as he watched the man scan the boy's arm as if he were looking for something buried within the arm itself.

The boy screamed, "You're the one!"

Smiling down at the boy, the man stated clearly, "No, son. You're the one."

Lifting his lapel with his left hand, the man tilted his head to speak into a tiny communicator located under his collar. "Identification confirmed."

Herman felt paralyzed with shock and stood, frozen in place, as the boy vainly struggled with the man. The plaza was suddenly silent, and everything moved in slow motion. Herman saw the woman in the blue dress as she turned with an astonished look on her face to watch what was taking place between the boy and the man. People stopped whatever they were doing to gawk at the spectacle that was unfolding.

The boy tried to get away as the man pulled something from the small of his back. Still smiling, the man pointed his weapon at the boy. Herman recognized it as a sub-atomic disintegrator. He had not seen one of those loathsome devices since the war.

Before the boy had time to scream again, a blast from the weapon hit him squarely in the center of his chest. The intense flash was magnified in the mirrored walls of the plaza buildings.

Disintegration occurred fast. It started from the inside out. Major organs, heart, lungs and brain were the first to go. By the time the boy's skin began to blacken, he was already dead.

Before Herman knew what was happening, the small boy was gone, as if he had never existed. Total extinction. It was, after all, an execution, one that was much worse than mere death.

Slowly, the man took his sunglasses out of his pocket, put them back on, turned and calmly walked away, disappearing into the concealment of the park.

KATHLEEN PAPAJOHN

Chapter Two

"Call your office and tell them to send someone else," Nathaniel said, trying to keep his voice calm. "We'll watch retro movies and pretend we're on a date."

He didn't really expect her to stay, but, unreasonably, he felt irritated that she was leaving. He didn't like the stirrings of uneasiness he felt when he looked at her packed suitcase.

Realistically, Nathaniel knew that Kara was more than capable of taking care of herself. They had met when she helped him with a cyber-investigation that he had been involved in when he worked for a government agency a lifetime ago. It was not just her amazing computer skills that helped him catch the serial killer. Kara had saved his life.

Kara folded her arms across her chest and looked at her husband accusingly.

"Nate, you know I can't do that. Do you honestly believe that I could sleep knowing that one of the new analysts might misapply the software changes to a program that ensures the safety of everyone on the space station? No one on my staff has enough experience to deal with the complexity of this update. I wrote the original program, and I wouldn't feel comfortable letting someone else make the modifications."

Nathaniel started to open his mouth to protest, but before he could continue, Kara said, "Nathaniel, you're not being reasonable. You know that I haven't seen my mother in months, and the waiting list for flights to Alpha 33 is endless. This is a chance for me to actually go to the space station, see her, and get my assignment done at the same time. Would you deny me time with Velyn?"

Nathaniel knew by the set of Kara's jaw that any argument would be fruitless. Kara was a strong, determined woman. Little, if anything, scared her. Like him, she had survived the starving years.

"At least take Solis with you," Nathaniel said. He knew that Solis would keep Kara safe.

"If I could get another seat on the space plane I would take Solis just to keep you from worrying, but there are no available seats, and *tamen* aren't allowed to leave Phoenix until Quallou is found. No exceptions."

Quallou had already been identified as the Technological Alternative man who was responsible for the death of the boy. Yesterday's violent event had been captured digitally by several of the streaming video devices used by local government to monitor citizens of Phoenix, purportedly for their own protection. The local news media continued to air the scene, outraging everyone who watched the replay as if they had personally witnessed it.

The victim had been a child. Natural children were so rare, so precious, since the government had instituted a permit program for couples wanting a natural child. A permit to bear a human child was granted only when a vacancy in the population became available because a human had been killed. The law was unpopular, but was passed as an alternative when politicians threatened to set a legal limit on the length of a human life. Since genetic engineering halted the aging process, people only died from accidents, suicides, or rarely, as in the case from the day before, homicides.

Nathaniel couldn't understand how a unit like Quallou still existed. In the years since the war ended, most of the replica units that had been used in combat had been decommissioned, destroyed, or saved for reuse in other forms. The ones saved for reuse had been reprogrammed to serve rather than destroy. The current units did mundane or even dangerous work that had been previously done by humans. For example, exterior maintenance on Space Station Alpha 33 was done by these replicas, the very units that Kara was going to Alpha 33 to upgrade.

Despite their popularity, Nathaniel did not like being around manufactured replicas. His memories of their use in combat were still vivid, even after more than a century. He had never allowed one in his home until Kara found Solis. Kara's birthday gift had been a complete surprise for Nathaniel. She had reactivated and modified Solis herself. Knowing Nathaniel's distaste for new replicas, Kara had tracked down the serial number of the Destructor-4 *taman* that had served with him in the war. She found the decommissioned unit in an old, almost forgotten warehouse where outdated ordinance was stored.

Nathaniel was comfortable around Solis, who was now rated a Protector-2 *taman*, although with the customized programs that Kara had applied, the unit could easily have been given a dash-four rating.

First, Kara changed out the unit's older model body casing, using a newly developed material that more closely resembled human skin. Circuitry that sent signals to the central processing unit had been incorporated into Solis's realistic covering, much like nerve endings in human skin that send signals to the human brain. This new equipment gave Solis the sense of touch, rare even in units created using the latest technology available to *tamen* manufacturers.

Nathaniel still marveled at Solis's enhanced capabilities and skills. Kara had added seven additional processors to the primary processor in his storage rack. She expanded his memory chips so that Solis could process and store data that was equivalent to the amount of information that had been stored in pre-war Earth's complete Library of Congress.

Nathaniel knew that Kara hoped that her enhancements would increase Solis's learning capabilities and would give Solis the ability to acquire some level of human sensation, human feelings. She had even built an atrium for him.

Even with his obvious modifications, the first time that he had seen Solis, Nathaniel hadn't known whether to be pleased or to run. When he had learned that the unit did not even remember serving with him in combat, he accepted the gift graciously. Nathaniel had missed his friend.

Nathaniel crossed to where Kara was standing and put his arms around her.

"I feel like a piece of me is missing whenever we're apart. You must know that," he said. "But I know how much seeing Velyn means to you. I will just have to tough it out without you."

Kara laughed softly. "Thinking of you 'toughing out' anything is almost funny. You are the toughest man I have ever known."

"And you are the most beautiful and stubborn woman I have ever known. I guess that's what I get for falling for an older woman." To the day, Kara was one month older than Nathaniel, at least chronologically.

Laughing, Kara reluctantly pulled away from her husband and continued dressing. Nathaniel stood in silence, watching Kara as she brushed her long brown hair. She was pulling it up into a bun. He thought what a shame it was to hide that beautiful dark hair by confining it in a prim style, but he was also jealous that her long, graceful neck would be exposed for other men to see.

As he stared at her, Nathaniel remembered that it was the nape of her neck that first attracted him to her so many years ago. It still aroused him. He remembered last night, her hair spread across the pillow, her lovely eyes staring back into his as they made love. All he wanted now was to hold her again, to feel her lips on his, to smell the soft lilac cologne that she wore so sparingly.

As if she sensed his scrutiny, his wife put down her hairbrush, stood, turned and smiled at him. He walked over to her and took her by her shoulders. Kara had to tip her head back to look up into his eyes. As soon as he touched her, he felt her shiver slightly. Pleased with himself, he bent over and kissed her, lightly but teasingly. Nothing was beneath him if it would keep her from leaving.

Kara grudgingly pushed him away. He saw her desire for him struggle with her strong will and knew that her stubbornness, the one thing about her that so often frustrated him, was winning. She caught her breath and took a small step back.

"Nate, my love, there is nothing that I would like better than to return to bed with you, but now is not the time. The trip will be short. The units only need a small update to their software, and I know that Velyn misses me almost as much as I miss her."

Nathaniel knew he was defeated. Kara had not seen her mother in a long time, and a chance like this didn't come around too often.

Kara stood on her tiptoes and kissed Nathaniel on the mouth. "I love you, too," she whispered before disappearing into the cleansing chamber.

"Velyn must be counting the minutes until your arrival," Nathaniel said, loud enough to be heard over the soft hum of the chamber.

Velyn Stevens was currently performing in the most prestigious of the space station's many hotels.

Kara emerged from the cleansing chamber. She crossed the room to her closet and picked out a chic, tailored, jade-colored silk suit that made her eyes look startlingly green. When he looked at her, Nathaniel caught his breath.

"I'll get something to eat at the spaceport," Kara said as she walked over to Nathaniel and kissed him once more. "I'll call you tonight. Good luck with your court appearance this morning. I can't wait to find out if the Nualas will finally get their permit."

Nathaniel's eyes narrowed when he heard the sound of the shuttle's horn and watched as Kara hurriedly picked up her suitcase. Before Nathaniel knew it, she was out the door. He wasn't sure if she heard him tell her that he loved her.

Restless and unusually anxious by the emptiness he felt after Kara left, Nathaniel crossed to the kitchen wondering where Solis was.

"Solis," Nathaniel called. "Is there any coffee yet?"

Solis's answer came from directly behind Nathaniel's shoulder, as if he had been there all along, a ghost silently following Nathaniel without his knowledge.

"Of course there is, and I have prepared your favorite breakfast of desert peaches with native honey. What shade of coffee would you like? How about bright orange to stimulate you and prepare you for your appearance in court this morning?"

"Just the coffee."

Nathaniel still found it hard getting used to this competent, gentler version of the 'man' (at least that's how Nathaniel thought of him) that he had served with so many years ago. Dressed in a black turtle-necked sweater and dark green slacks, Solis looked like a well-toned athlete at his absolute physical peak. In spite of his superior strength, Solis wouldn't intentionally hurt a fly, yet Nathaniel knew that he could be lethal if either he or Kara needed protection.

"What would I do without you?" Nathaniel asked.

Nathaniel sat staring at the table, lost in his thoughts and puzzled by how deeply yesterday's incident had disturbed him. After all, he had seen this type of senseless violence often, but that was long ago in a world far different than today's.

He looked up at Solis, wondering if he could still be capable of the kind of bloodshed that took place yesterday. Nathaniel had a well-kept secret, one he had hidden even from Kara. Solis had been one of the most deadly destructor *tamen* deployed in the corporate war. Although this new incarnation of Solis couldn't remember it, he had reported directly to Nathaniel during the conflict.

Nathaniel was startled to see Solis returning his look, watching him intently. As he stood holding the breakfast tray, Solis looked down at Nathaniel, and, as if he knew what Nathaniel had been thinking, said, "Even though the *taman* was similar to me, I could never terminate a human life unless there was a direct threat to you or Miss Kara. I am a defender unit, not a destructor."

"When did you start reading minds?" Nathaniel asked as he took the tray from Solis and set it down on the table. He sat on the edge of his chair and started to eat. "I didn't realize just how hungry I was. This is wonderful."

"Here, let me heat up your coffee, Mr. Lamrock."

Nathaniel held up his cup. As soon as Solis touched it, the coffee began to steam.

"Not too hot, Solis," Nathaniel said. "I will never get tired of watching you do that. It's quite a trick."

"I have laid out a suit for you." Solis replied, not acknowledging Nathaniel's comment. "Today you are scheduled to appear in court to secure a child-bearing permit for Mr. and Mrs. Nuala. You must hurry. Artesia will be here within ten point two minutes to take you to the courthouse."

Nathaniel ignored the rest of his food, put down his cup, and went into the cleansing chamber, a windowless cubicle that resembled a shower stall, minus the water. A purplish light that started at the top of the chamber moved slowly down Nathaniel's torso to the stall's floor, cleaning and disinfecting every surface of his body. As the warm infusion of light and soft air enveloped him, Nathaniel began to relax and could almost feel the chamber removing dead skin cells. He emerged feeling vibrant and crossed to his bedchamber where he hurriedly dressed in the dark blue suit, white shirt and closely patterned dark blue silk tie that Solis had laid out for him. He was ready in less than ten minutes.

Nathaniel called his office to remind his secretary that he would be in court all morning and would be unavailable for the rest of the day. He said good-bye to Solis, grabbed his digital memory stick, and raced down the sterile hall's bleached white steps to the street just in time to see the Dash coming around the corner, floating on its cushion of air, only inches off the surface of the street. The morning was typical of Phoenix in July, bright and clear, already with more than a hint of the heat that would soon wash over the city.

The door to the Dash whooshed open. Nathaniel entered the vehicle and was greeted by Artesia's warm smile. It took Nathaniel's eyes a few seconds to adjust to the dimness of the Dash's interior.

Artesia blinked her lovely blue manufactured eyes at him. "Good morning, Mr. L. The Nualas are already on board, seated in the rear. It's going to take us eight point seven minutes to get to the courthouse. By the way, you look extremely nice today." Artesia's eyes scanned Nathaniel from head to toe, taking in every detail.

Nathaniel laughed. "If I didn't know you better, Artesia, I'd swear that you were flirting with me."

"Of course not. You know better than that," Artesia replied. "I am detail oriented, and I enjoy details, especially human details, and especially yours."

Nathaniel laughed again as he made his way to the rear of the Dash where the Nualas were patiently waiting.

Sha and Juan Nuala looked up expectantly as Nathaniel seated himself across the narrow aisle. For the time being, Nathaniel put aside the unfamiliar disquiet that made him try to keep Kara from going to Alpha 33. He expected a hard day and forced himself to concentrate on the task ahead of him.

***

Solis watched from the doorway as Nathaniel boarded the Dash. Once it was out of sight, Solis returned to his own chamber where he retrieved a small wooden box that he had hidden in his closet. Sitting on the edge of a chair, Solis opened the box and carefully took out the collection of toy soldiers that lay inside. He handled the box's contents with near-reverence. He polished each individual piece before replacing it back into the box. When he looked at the figurines, he felt stirrings of vague memories of warriors and comrades in arms, but these memories were buried deep within his circuitry, and he could not fully formulate them.

When he was done, Solis placed the box of soldiers back in his closet and went into the kitchen, where he prepared a mixture of milk and cereal in a small saucer. Careful not to spill a drop, Solis carried the saucer to the living room, placed the mixture at his feet and, with his toe, slowly slid it into the atrium. He backed up quietly and laid face down on the floor with his hands under his chin, his eyes focused on the exotic foliage. Patiently, he watched for movement.

Within minutes, his patience paid off. Solis heard a familiar meow. A small, furry figure emerged and began lapping the nourishment that Solis had prepared. The kitten was orange with a blaze of white fur on his nose and stomach. For the first time in his being, Solis smiled as he watched the tiny animal greedily lap up all of his breakfast. Solis softly spoke to him. "You are hungry this morning."

As if to answer, the kitten rubbed against him and purred. As a defender, Solis knew his job was to protect and serve Nathaniel and Kara. He had been programmed to obey their commands. Now, somehow on his own, Solis extended his capacity for protection to this small, helpless animal.

"If it's all right with you, I will call you 'Tandem.' My memory cells recall that my ancestors were named Tandem. Now you are also my family and I will protect and care for you. We must keep our relationship secret. At the proper time, I will introduce you to my controllers."

Chapter Three

In less than a month, Margaret Owning would captain Interglobal's space vehicle that would take the first group of colonists to Mars. As Kara waited for her flight in Sky Harbor's outbound Aquarian lounge, she watched Margaret speaking animatedly with a group of reporters on the lounge's holographic TV. Kara was engrossed in the interview. Not only was she entranced, imagining the adventures that would await those early settlers, she sensed that something about Margaret Owning was familiar, but Kara couldn't quite put her finger on what it was.

"After fifty-seven earth years, Interglobal's terraforming effort has turned Mars into one of the most beautiful places in our galaxy. As you know, fossil fuels have been prohibited on Earth for the last hundred and fifty years. In previous centuries, their output poisoned our atmosphere and destroyed much of Earth's ozone layer.

"Ironically, the very pollutants that contaminated Earth have been used on Mars to turn the planet from a barren caramel-colored desert into one capable of supporting a rich diversity of life. Carbon dioxide produced by Interglobal's huge terra forming plants has had the same effect on Mars as it did on Earth, only in a positive way. That is, those very same greenhouse gases that caused our own planet to heat have been used to melt Mars' polar ice caps. This has created ponds, lakes, rivers and even oceans.

"Over the past fifty years, *taman* units that manned the terra forming stations have planted a wide variety of trees, plants, and shrubs. This vegetation has produced an atmosphere rich in oxygen, making the planet very livable. The average surface temperature is currently a pleasant 68 degrees."

A reporter from the Eastern Zone's news network, EZZN, raised his hand. "Captain Owning, does Interglobal plan on instituting regular fights to Mars?"

"Yes, Interglobal will send a flight to Mars during the window when Mars is closest to Earth. This occurs every twenty-six months and is the optimal opportunity to undertake such a voyage."

The lounge was crowded, but there were still some empty seats and after the news conference ended, Kara moved to a seat nearer to the aquarium where she could relax. She kept thinking about Captain Owning, wondering what it was about the woman that made Kara feel like she knew her.

Kara couldn't think about that. Despite what she had told Nathaniel, the update was not going to be easy, and she was worried. She took out her notes and reread her project plan for about the twentieth time, looking for anything that she might have missed. No matter how hard she tried to concentrate, the image of Captain Margaret Owning kept creeping back into her consciousness.

What is it about this woman?

Then, like a gunshot, it came to her. It was the expression on Captain Owning's face, the look in her intelligent eyes. Kara remembered the last glimpse she'd had that very morning - her husband's eyes watching her as she ran out the door, rushing to make her flight. Margaret Owning's gray eyes were the same as Nathaniel's.

Margaret Owning is Rosemary!

Kara was engrossed in her revelation when an unkempt man approached her. His clothes had obviously never been within several feet of an iron, and he could only be described as rough looking.

"Excuse me, miss. Is this seat taken? I know it looks like there are a lot of other seats, but every time I go to sit down, the person next to the empty seat tells me that they are saving it for someone else."

Kara had been so preoccupied with her own thoughts that the man startled her. She looked around and saw some of the other people waiting in the lounge watching him warily. Kara realized that these people were acting as if poverty were contagious, and they were treating this obviously naïve young man as if he were a carrier. She did not often judge other people, but on that day, their attitude toward him offended her.

She smiled up at the man. "No, the seat's not taken. Just let me move my things." She moved her carry-on and was purposely friendly, almost as if by doing so she were defying the other travelers. Kara introduced herself. "Hi, I'm Kara Lamrock."

The man extended his hand. "I'm Leo Davis."

Kara accepted his hand and smiled again. "I'm pleased to meet you, Leo. Are you traveling on business or pleasure?"

"I believe that traveling is always a pleasure," Leo answered with excitement in his voice. He told Kara that, like his father before him, he was a miner.

"I'm on my way to see my girlfriend," Leo said. "Her name is Andrea Tustin. She works on Space Station Alpha 33. I plan on surprising her tonight. I can't wait to see her again. I'm going to ask her to marry me. I've even got the ring. Want to see it?"

Leo dug deep into his shirt pocket. He unwrapped an antique gold band that was tarnished and battered.

Kara smiled. "Oh, Leo, it's beautiful," she said kindly. "She's going to just love it."

"I know it's kind of old. It was my mother's. This is all she left me."

Kara watched Leo as he carefully put the ring back into his pocket. "Congratulations," she said. "I'm married myself. I hope you and your fiancée will both be as happy as my husband and I have been. We always say that we love each other as much as infinity times infinity. I have just gotten a surprise present for him. I can't wait to see his face."

"Can you tell me, Kara? I love surprises, especially happy ones."

"I'm bursting to tell someone, Leo. My husband is in court this morning and I can't get in touch with him." When she saw the stricken look on Leo's face she quickly explained. "He's not a defendant. He's an attorney."

Leo looked relieved, but also anxious to hear Kara's surprise.

"My husband and his sister were separated when they were children. He's spent most of his life searching for her. He's been looking for her for almost a century. He never gave up hope that she's alive. I can't wait to tell him that he's been correct all this time. I believe that I found her today."

Leo was as excited as Kara. "Really? You found her after all this time? Who is she?"

"I believe that his sister is Captain Margaret Owning. There is a family resemblance that is so overwhelmingly strong that it can't be a coincidence."

"Do you mean the woman who will be taking the first settlers to Mars?" Leo voice was starting to draw stares from other travelers as his excitement mounted.

Kara put her hand on his arm and whispered. "I'd like to keep it a secret until I see my husband in person. This is news that I want to give him face-to-face."

"Oh, of course. I'm sorry. I get carried away pretty easily."

"It's okay Leo. Your news is pretty exciting, too. I'll bet that Andrea will be so surprised and happy to see you."

Leo looked down, a concerned expression on his face. He appeared as though he wanted to tell Kara something, but she was inexplicitly distracted.

Suddenly, Kara felt a chill travel down her spine. She sensed that someone was watching her. She glanced around the lounge but everyone seemed to be occupied. She listened carefully, hearing the low murmur of conversations, the rattle of papers, and the clink of ice in the atmosphere-boosters that everyone was sipping. Despite her apprehension, she could see nothing out of place.

Kara said goodbye to Leo and moved to take her place in line when a soft female voice came from the tiny speakers that were discretely placed throughout the lounge. "Shuttle Flight 3777 to Alpha 33 is now ready for boarding. Please have your approval pass ready for the boarding agent. Have a pleasant stay at Space Station Alpha 33 and while you're there, be sure to visit the elegant Orbit Room, featuring the multi-talented Velyn Stevens."

Just after take-off, a three-dimensional image of Space Station Alpha 33 materialized in front of each passenger. Although she had seen the documentary many times before, Kara was still fascinated. It appeared to her that she was viewing the actual station from a vast distance. As Alpha 33 came closer, the hologram focused on a crystal band that surrounded the enormous station. The narrator explained that the band created artificial gravity using the latest in gyroscopic technology. An invisible electro-magnetic field that protected the space station from space debris, meteor showers and sun flares surrounded the station's outer core. Massive communications receivers and transmitters decorated the skin of the station like a forest of silver trees.

Alpha 33 was as large as a small moon. Some of its amazing features included its three fully stocked lakes for fishing and boating, and five mega-hotels that offered fine dining, entertainment, and gambling. Designers of the space station had been influenced by a romantic notion of old-Earth Las Vegas, which had been the world's entertainment capital before its destruction in the war.

The sleep time symbols that were visible throughout the cabin lit up. A light bluish mist came out of the space plane's ventilation system. Kara understood that the pilot was administering a sleeping gas that would ease each traveler's journey. Although the gas would put them into a deep sleep, it was completely harmless to humans and did not affect the *taman* units flying the space plane and serving the passengers. The flight attendants, all specially programmed, moved efficiently through the cabin picking up glasses and food trays and covering the sleeping travelers with blankets to be sure that they remained comfortable for the duration of the trip.

Just before she fell asleep, Kara noticed a man seated a few rows ahead of her who had turned around in his seat and was watching her. His scrutiny made Kara uncomfortable. When he saw Kara look his way, he straightened and closed his eyes, seeming to quickly succumb to the sleeping gas.

Chapter Four

Even before they turned into the corridor that led to Velyn's suite, Kara heard the familiar sound of her mother's laughter. The bellman knocked on the door and stood at attention as he spoke into the suite's hallway communicator. "Ms. Stevens, your guest, Mrs. Kara Lamrock, has arrived."

The door to the suite opened and a young, handsome *taman* instructed the bellman to leave Kara's bags. "You will find two barter credits in your account for your troubles. I will take Mrs. Lamrock's things from here."

The good-looking *taman* took her bags, bowed slightly to Kara and said, "Welcome, Miss Kara. My name is Apollo. Please follow me."

Kara smiled and followed the *taman*. Velyn's living quarters were incredible.

So, this is how famous people live, Kara thought as she entered the suite.

An astonishing view of Earth appeared through the living room's large picture window. A comfortable-looking couch and two retro armchairs sat across from the beautifully tiled fireplace. The most amazing feature of the room was the mural. Multi-colored plasma flowed continually within a framed visual rendering that covered an entire wall, shaping and reshaping the mural into different landscapes. At present, an old-Earth urban skyline at sunset was splashed across the wall. It was breathtaking.

Velyn was seated on the floor in the middle of the living room playing poker with three young *taman* units, each as handsome as the one who had opened the door for Kara. Her long, thick blond hair and regal bearing gave Velyn the look of a lioness. Even without makeup, her mother was one of the most beautiful women that Kara had ever seen.

Each time Velyn raked in a pot, she laughed at the consternation on the faces of her *taman* units.

"Kara, your programming skills leave something to be desired, dear. When you modified these units to be more docile, you took all the spunk out of them. In addition to protection skills, you could have at least programmed them to compete in a non-contact sport like poker."

Kara looked at her mother lovingly. "I didn't personally re-program the units, and they are quite capable of competing at card games. The problem is that they don't understand cheating."

"Well, they certainly keep me from getting bored," Velyn said, as she got to her feet. "I think I'll teach them strip-poker next."

Kara smiled, shook her head in amusement and put her arms around her mother. "It's so good to see you, Mom."

Kara caught their reflection in the hall mirror. Side by side they looked like a photograph and its negative. There was no mistaking the fact that they were related, although they looked more like sisters than mother and daughter. They shared the same large, green eyes, but Velyn's skin was pale, and her blond, straight hair hung free, reaching half way down her back. In comparison, Kara's complexion was olive and her own dark brown hair was pulled up in a severe style that was unmistakably businesslike.

Velyn glanced at the *taman* units who were anxiously waiting for her to deal the next hand.

"That's all for now, boys. Run along. I have an exciting new game that I will show you later."

Velyn turned to the *taman* that still stood holding Kara's bags. "Apollo, just a minute. Please run and get the best champagne you can find. It's not often I get to spend time with my beautiful daughter. Tonight, we celebrate!"

Apollo hesitated. "But, Madam, I am a *taman*-P2 unit. My job is to protect you. Can you not send one of the other units?"

Kara knew that Apollo was a higher model protector than the other *taman* units that cared for Velyn. His superior cognitive and organization skills allowed him to function efficiently as Velyn's secretary. Additionally, he had super human strength. If needed, he could defend Velyn from any attack. No mere mortal would be a match for him.

Velyn smiled up at Apollo and spoke in her sweetest voice. It was almost as if she were singing. "Apollo, you know that you are the only one I trust to do things right. If I send one of the others they could bring back a bottle of shampoo rather than a bottle of champagne. Now, please be a good boy."

As Kara watched the banter between Velyn and Apollo, she thought to herself, *Obviously, I have been stuck in the office and too engrossed in the bits and bytes. This fieldwork is just what I needed. Clearly, a class system is becoming established within the* taman *community. Apollo believes that his P2 rating certainly puts him in a superior status to the P1 units. What surprises me most, though, is that Apollo is so vulnerable to Velyn's manipulation.*

Kara was used to watching Velyn's human co-stars run around after her like little puppy dogs, just to get a glimpse of her fabulous smile. Apollo, however, had no testosterone running through his veins, yet Velyn's smile had the same effect on Apollo as it did on the human male actors that Velyn had worked with over the years.

Fascinating, Kara thought in amazement. She could not help but stare at the two of them.

As soon as Apollo left on his errand, Velyn turned to her daughter. Usually, her mother was carefree, but today, Kara saw that she was worried.

"That young boy was executed right in front of all those people. Is it safe to go out down there? What if there are other rogue *tamen* like that one roaming around? I remember the havoc that the *taman* units created on Mars when they were terraforming the planet. That was a violent and bloody mess! I always wondered if all of those units had been properly reprogrammed."

"Oh, Mother, you worry too much. Each unit is serially numbered and tracked, making it virtually impossible that one could have been overlooked. Even if someone wanted to alter a *taman* on purpose, it is highly unlikely that anyone would be able to do so. There are very few people within Interglobal, and virtually none outside the company, who understand the technology, including the exact sequence and unique process required for such a complex modification. I have to admit that I'm perplexed. The unit that killed the boy must have been an anomaly. As tragic as this incident was, the company will be absolutely sure that nothing like this will ever happen again. I'm convinced of it."

Obviously bored because the conversation had strayed from being about her, Velyn gladly changed the subject. "Whatever you say, dear. By the way, did you know that Digger is here? He called to say hello just before you arrived. I invited him to have dinner with us. Is that okay with you, Kara?"

Kara couldn't hide the joy that lit up her face. "Digger is here? I haven't seen him in decades."

Velyn glanced quickly at the clock, not noticing Kara's look. She nodded to the narrow passageway that led from her suite's living room. "I'm sorry, honey, but I have to hurry. Your room is at the end of the hall."

Kara stood in the doorway and watched as her mother left the suite. In the foyer, Velyn almost collided with a tall, well-built man that was getting off the elevator at the same time that Velyn was getting on. Kara stared at the man in surprise. She could swear that he was the man from the plane. Without even looking in Kara's direction, he turned and walked hurriedly the opposite way. Quickly, Kara closed the door to her mother's suite, double-checking to see that it was securely locked.

KATHLEEN PAPAJOHN

Chapter Five

Quallou checked his watch and saw that it was 6:37. Impatiently, he stood unmoving, listening intently. He knew that Kara, his target, was still inside Velyn's suite. Oddly, the thought of killing Kara Lamrock made him feel pleasantly aroused. He was actually anxious to kill her. For several seconds he analyzed the situation, then he turned and walked slowly back along the corridor inspecting each suite number that he passed.

He continued by the janitorial closet that was next to the elevators, and then counted three more doors until, finally, he found the one he was looking for. The door to the suite, of course, was locked. Quallou pointed to the knob. His finger emitted a low-level electronic pulse, and he heard a click as the pressure lock disengaged.

The electro-magnetic master key had done its job well. No alarm sounded as he walked into the suite. Quallou stayed low and moved quietly down the suite's hallway to the guest room where Kara was dressing for Velyn's show. He stood quietly in the shadows, listening for any sounds, preparing to ambush his prey when he abruptly sensed that he was not alone.

Making no more sound than a soft whisper, Apollo came up behind him. "May I help you?"

Quallou could see from the look on Apollo's face that his presence in the suite upset him.

He thinks I'm an infatuated fan, Quallou thought. *And, he thinks that he can make short work of me. He is so certain, that he has not even bothered to put down the bottle of expensive champagne that he's carrying.*

Apollo reached for Quallou's arm as if he intended to firmly escort him from the suite.

At Apollo's touch, Quallou spun around with such high speed that Apollo's central processing unit did not have the nanoseconds it needed to react. One of Quallou's massive hands encircled Apollo's neck and lifted him off the floor. Quallou's fingers dug into the spot that was equivalent to where a human jugular vein would be, ripping Apollo's fabricated skin.

Green fluid began to ooze from Apollo's neck. His arms and legs worked furiously, punching and kicking his attacker. Although a human would have been immobilized by Apollo's strength, his efforts didn't faze Quallou. Still holding Apollo off his feet, Quallou carried him to the door. Apollo's arms and legs continued to flail at Quallou with little effect.

Quallou's deadly grip cut off the circuit pathways that traveled from Apollo's processor rack to his central processing unit. Without electronic stimuli, the CPU could not issue commands to the rest of Apollo's body. He couldn't make a sound. Apollo's eyes rolled back, and Quallou knew that he could no longer see.

Quallou, with Apollo still dangling in his grasp, looked into the hallway. After ensuring that no one was there, he carried Apollo to the janitorial closet. He entered the closet with Apollo and locked the door behind him.

Quallou sneered as Apollo's eyes bulged with terror. He gave Apollo's neck a sudden twist and broke it. Still holding the champagne bottle, but no longer receiving instructions from his

CPU, Apollo's arms thrashed about wildly. As luck would have it, the bottle hit Quallou on the side of his head, knocking off his sunglasses. Without his dark glasses to hide them, Quallou saw his own naked, blood-red irises reflected back at him as he stared into the dying *taman*'s eyes.

Quallou's fingers worked their way through the skin covering Apollo's processor rack, which resembled human ribs. Each rib-shelf contained a specialized processor responsible for its own set of bodily functions and memory. The processors communicated with the CPU through a set of channels running through the *taman*'s electrical system and up through his spinal column. The rack itself provided protection for the unit's power supply, located slightly left of center in his chest, just behind the rack cage.

With a final, firm upward movement, Quallou thrust his hand deep into Apollo's chest and removed his power supply. The limp *taman*'s body dropped to the floor. Quallou calmly picked up his sunglasses, put them on, and stepped over Apollo's lifeless form. Instinctively, Quallou knew that Kara was no longer in the suite. With his left hand, Quallou lifted his lapel and spoke into the tiny microphone that was sewn into his jacket. "Mission aborted. Target no longer available. Awaiting new orders." Disappointed, Quallou knew that he would have to be patient. There would be other opportunities to satisfy his blood lust.

***

The wall clock read 6:40 when Kara thought she heard a noise outside her bedroom door. "Apollo is that you?" she called. When she didn't get a response, she shrugged.

It must have been the guest in the adjoining suite, she thought.

She left the bedroom and headed straight for the living room communicator. "Mother, it's me. I know I'm late, but I'll be there before the curtain goes up."

Kara sped out the door into the hallway, slipping on green liquid that had been spilled on the floor.

Tomorrow, I need to take a look at the janitorial program in the station's taman-S units. Someone spilled something in this hallway and the units have not even cleaned it up, she thought, as she hurried past the janitorial closet and stepped into the open elevator.

The audience was already seated when Kara arrived at the Orbit Room. A beautiful female *taman* wearing a short orange mini-skirt with a matching halter top and knee-high boots escorted Kara to her table. The auditorium was large and beautifully decorated. The tables were set with crystal goblets and fine linen tablecloths. The chairs were upholstered in a rich dark red velvet.

Kara looked around the room, taking in the lavish setting. She wanted to remember every moment of her experience.

Just as she was about to sit down, Kara spotted Leo Davis. Without hesitation she called over the hostess and whispered, "Would you kindly ask that man over there to join me?"

Leo was sitting at a single table where the stage was hidden from view by a massive column that stood between his table and the stage. He had changed his clothes, but he still looked like a ruffian, out of place with the rest of the elegantly dressed audience. When the hostess delivered Kara's message, Leo looked baffled but got up and walked uncertainly to Kara's table. "Hello, Leo. I'm lost at this big table. I was hoping that you would do me a favor by sharing it with me," Kara said with a smile.

Kara recognized that Leo was preoccupied. He stood there for several seconds as if he wasn't sure what to do. Finally, he pulled out a chair and sat, dropping the small bouquet of flowers he was holding. Kara leaned over, picked up the flowers and handed them back to him.

"Are these flowers for your fiancée?" she asked.

Leo lowered his eyes. "I bought them for her, but I can't give them to her looking like this." He grabbed the lapel of his well-worn suit, obviously embarrassed that he was caught in this condition. He blurted out, "My girlfriend, Andrea, thinks I'm a big shot because I told her that I hobnob with movie stars and famous people. Andrea comes from a good family. She's very educated and refined. The truth is I don't know anyone famous. I don't plan to always be just a regular guy barely getting by, working the remote mines. One day, I'll be something. One day, I'll own my own mines everywhere throughout the established planet system. But right now, heck, I'm so afraid that when she learns the truth she won't want to see me again, or worse will laugh at me. I just don't know what to do."

Kara's heart went out to him. "If your fiancée is as fine a woman as you paint her to be, I'm sure that she won't care about your financial status or your circle of friends – or your clothes. She'll love you for yourself." Kara looked as though she was struggling with a decision. "What's your fiancée's name again?" she asked.

"Andrea Tustin. She plays the piano here in Haley's Lounge. I don't plan to let her see me, though. I just need to have that one last look at her."

A waiter, dressed entirely in black faux leather, approached to take their drink order. "White wine for me," Kara said. When Leo looked as if he didn't know what to say, Kara leaned over to him and whispered, "The white wine here is superb, and it's on the house. Would you care to try it?"

Leo looked gratefully at Kara and then nodded confidently at the waiter. "White wine for both of us, please," he replied.

After the waiter left, Kara looked over at Leo and asked to be excused. Leo quickly jumped to his feet and pulled back her chair. She got up from the table and went out into the lobby where she found the maître d'.

"Do you have something I can write on?" she asked.

The maître d' begrudgingly handed her the small pad of paper that he used to take nightly seating reservations. Kara wrote quickly and then handed the folded note, along with a generous tip back to the maître d'. "Would you please see to it that Ms. Stevens gets this before her show?"

The maître d' looked at the large amount of barter credits that Kara had given him. His attitude immediately changed and he bowed slightly to her. "Of course, Madam, consider it done."

Kara thanked him and returned to her table where a nervous Leo had already finished his wine and was starting in on Kara's. He kept looking around as if he were a felon on the run, expecting to be caught at any minute.

The sound of kettledrums rumbled, the showroom went dark and multi-colored lights played across the stage.

"Ladies and Gentlemen, please give a warm welcome to the most exciting entertainer in our solar system. Here, in our very own Orbit Room, Miss Velyn Stevens!"

The crowd applauded, the curtain opened and the orchestra began playing *Till the End of Time,* while Velyn descended from the ceiling, appearing almost magically center stage. She truly looked like a goddess. Her long blond hair hung past her shoulders. Her entire body glistened as the spotlight played along the sequins that covered her gold, form-fitting gown.

Once again, there was enthusiastic applause from the audience. Velyn's sexy, husky voice filled the room as she began singing her signature song.

When the song ended, the applause was deafening. Kara was struck by how fresh her mother's performance was. Velyn had been performing for almost 90 years. She was known all around the world and was even famous on the Moon colonies and in every space station in Earth's orbit. When the show ended, the crowd was on its feet.

The hostess walked over and discreetly handed Kara a note. Kara read it and smiled to herself. She turned to Leo and asked him if he would join her and Velyn for dinner. She explained that her mother had made reservations in the Satellite Steak House and that she had requested that both he and Andrea join her party.

"Velyn has already spoken with Andrea and she's agreed to join us," Kara told him.

Leo was astounded. "Velyn is your mother?"

With Kara's affirmation, he could only nod in mute acceptance.

Kara was about to leave a tip, when Leo reached into his pocket and took out a wad of money, the size of which staggered Kara. He placed an extremely generous tip on the table. Kara was perplexed because she had assumed that Leo had little, if any, money.

Just who is this guy? she thought. She gave him directions to the restaurant and told him that she would meet him there.

As Kara was leaving, she received a text from her mother. The unexplained anxiety she had been feeling all day returned as she read the message: *Is Apollo with you?*

KATHLEEN PAPAJOHN

Chapter Six

Digger Rooney stepped off the elevator into the corridor that led to Velyn's suite. He was so nervous about seeing Kara again that he could hear his own heart thumping loudly. In spite of the way he felt about her, Digger hadn't seen Kara in decades. It had taken every ounce of his willpower to stay away from her, and he wondered if she was still as lovely as he remembered.

A *taman* answered Digger's knock on the door. "Velyn is expecting you, but you just missed her and her guest," the *taman* told him. "They will be back as soon as Velyn's show is over. Velyn said that you were to wait here for them. Please come in." The *taman* led Digger into the living room. "Is there anything I can get for you? Maybe a cup of tea?"

"Nothing to drink, thank you. It's been a long trip. I need to freshen up."

"Certainly, sir. The bathroom is just down the hall."

Digger started walking toward the bathroom, but before he reached the door, he froze. The floor leading past the guestroom was spotted with droplets of green liquid that he recognized as the fabricated serum used to lubricate *taman* units.

Digger returned to the living room to find the *taman* who had answered the door. "How many *tamen* work for Miss Stevens?" he asked.

"There are four of us. Three, including myself, are *taman*-P1 units. We wait on Miss Stevens and make sure that the suite is clean. Apollo, our supervisor, is a *taman*-P2. He is very smart and very strong," he said proudly.

"Where is Apollo right now? I'd like to speak with him," Digger said.

The *taman* looked concerned. "Apollo went out to get some champagne for Miss Stevens and her guest about an hour ago. I'm afraid that he's not back yet."

"Does it usually take this long to get a bottle of champagne?" Digger asked.

"I don't think so," the unit answered. "But Miss Stevens did tell Apollo to get the best champagne he could find. I assume that he's still looking."

Digger asked the *taman* to follow him into the hall. He pointed to the spill on the floor. "Can you tell me how long this has been here?" he asked.

"Oh, my!" exclaimed the *taman* in surprise. "We would never allow a stain like this to remain," he said defensively. "This could not have been here for more than a few minutes."

Digger pulled his personal weapon from his waistband. "Go back to the living room and stay there," he told the *taman* quietly. "Don't make a sound."

Digger slowly pushed open the bathroom door. The room was empty. He began searching all the rooms in the suite. Finally, satisfied that they were alone, Digger reholstered his weapon and returned to the living room where the *taman* anxiously waited.

"Are you fitted with a discretion chip?" Digger asked him.

"Oh, yes, sir. It would never do for any us to repeat anything that is said by Miss Stevens, or by anyone else in her entourage."

"Good. Then let's keep this between us. I don't want to bother Miss Stevens or her guest."

Digger followed the trail of droplets out the door and into the hallway. They led to the janitor closet at the end of the corridor. Once again, Digger opened his jacket and put his hand on the handle of his personal laser. He listened at the closet door for sounds of any movement. *Nothing.* Slowly, he opened the door and looked inside. A severed arm, with its hand still clinging to a champagne bottle, sat in a pool of green liquid.

It was hard to believe that this thing on the closet floor could ever have been an S2 unit, but Digger knew that it must be the *taman*-S2 that was assigned to Velyn. No one would have been able to recognize it with such damage.

Digger flipped open his communicator. "Rooney here. I need to speak with Martina Brainly, immediately!"

"Hey, Digger. How's the vacation?" Marty's voice dripped sarcasm.

"Not now, Marty," Digger said impatiently. "Is there an I-team on Alpha 33? I need a clean-up crew at the Cosmos. Twenty-fifth floor. West-wing janitor's closet. Right away. I can't wait for them to get here. I'll explain when I get back."

Digger closed the door to the janitor's closet and hurriedly walked back to the elevator. His gruesome discovery confirmed what his informants had told him. Kara was in danger. He would wait outside the Orbit Room to make sure that she was all right. Digger wouldn't let her out of his sight until he found out what was going on.

***

"Digger!" Kara shouted and flung open the door.

Digger pretended to stagger back under Kara's assault. He gently pushed her away and held her at arm's length. "You look as good as ever, young lady." He had waited so long to see her again. He should have been elated but the look on her face made his spirits plummet. Her eyes were filled with love--*brotherly* love. He didn't really expect anything else, but, unreasonably, he was still disappointed. "Are you still married to that bum, Nathaniel?"

Kara's beautiful eyes flashed in anger.

Before she could berate him, or even slap him, Digger held up his hands in mock surrender. "You know I'm just kidding."

Kara sighed resignedly. "You know, Digger, I think that you and Nathaniel get on each other's nerves because you two are actually so much alike."

Digger let his eyes widen in exaggerated horror. "Me? Like Nathaniel? I'd rather be dead!"

"Oh, you'll never die," Kara laughed. "You like your wine, women, and song too much to ever let that happen, and you love that so-called magazine of yours. Besides all that, you fit right in with those political zealots you work with. At least Nathaniel was smart enough to get out of the Internals."

She turned her back on Digger. As far as she was concerned, their conversation was over the minute Digger had insulted Nathaniel.

Kara's words had stung, as Digger knew she intended. She didn't really know much about the Internals, and the only thing she knew about Nathaniel's involvement was that he had left the organization, purportedly because he no longer subscribed to their secretive political agenda. On the other hand, Digger got an adrenaline rush from his work. He loved the excitement and even the danger associated with undercover assignments. That's why he had agreed to run that appalling rag. His magazine, *Galaxy Gossip,* reported things that celebrities did not want their fans to know about. It was more than the perfect cover. Digger actually took pleasure in exposing secrets about public figures.

Digger was already frustrated about the way his meeting with Kara was going. He had purposefully stayed away from her because it was too painful to see her with Nathaniel. He told himself that the only reason he had come now was because he believed that she was in danger.

Digger had actually been the one who introduced Nathaniel and Kara shortly after the end of the final corporate war. He had borrowed her from Interglobal as a temporary computer consultant on a domestic Internals case. He never forgave himself. The saddest day of Digger's life was the day that he realized that Kara and Nathaniel were in love.

Digger had met Nathaniel in the war. After the war, they had worked together in a special unit whose mission consisted of covert activities and black operations. The Nathaniel that Digger had known was a brooding, sometimes violent, individual. A hands-on lieutenant, Nathaniel had a reputation as a strong and capable combat leader, even though he often employed extreme measures to fulfill his mission--measures that Digger often disagreed with. Digger was still not convinced that Nathaniel had so completely changed from those days when they had served together.

Velyn finally intervened. "Are you two ever going to stop bickering? You've been at it since you were children!" She kissed Digger on the cheek. "I'm so pleased to see you. I made reservations for the five of us at the Satellite Restaurant."

"Five?" Digger asked.

"I was surprised when Kara told me that Andrea's boyfriend was here. Andrea and I have been friends since she first came to Alpha 33. As close as we've become, she never told me that she had a boyfriend. She plays the piano in Haley's lounge--beautifully, I might add. She comes from a very fine family. Her father was a professor at Harvard before the war and her mother was a doctor. Andrea speaks several languages. The other day, I caught her reading a book, yes, an old-time paper book. It was poetry, no less. I think what most embarrassed her was that it was written in Latin, of all things."

Kara looked confused. "Andrea certainly doesn't sound like Leo's type. Oh, well. They say that opposites attract."

"That's certainly true of you and Nathaniel." Digger said.

Velyn immediately changed the subject before they could start squabbling again. "It won't take me more than two minutes to wash off this greasepaint so that we can go down to dinner."

The maître d' showed them to the restaurant's best table. Digger held out the chair for Velyn and then quickly walked around the table to hold out Kara's chair. Absently, he nodded to the two strangers who were already seated. The male, who must have been Leo, was staring adoringly at the woman, Andrea.

Before turning her attention to Digger, Kara introduced Leo. Andrea continued to stare at her lap, looking grim.

"What are you doing so far from home, Digger? Have you ever married? Why should I forgive you for not getting in touch with me for so long?" Kara sounded indignant, but Digger knew that she was glad to see him.

It had been years since they had last seen each other, and Digger hoped that Kara had at least wondered about him. Before she had married Nathaniel, Digger made it a point to see her whenever he could. He always had an adventurous tale to tell her. She never knew that he left out the truly dangerous parts of the stories.

Digger chuckled, "I'm here for a little R&R. And no, I've never had time to get married. While I was in the neighborhood, I thought I'd drop in to say hello to Velyn, but I really came up here to get away from some of the lawsuits that are being filed against *Galaxy Gossip*, and me in particular. I don't need any more excitement in my life right now."

Kara looked surprised that Digger had so little to say. Usually he would entertain her for hours with his tall tales.

The silence was becoming uncomfortable when Leo finally spoke up. "Andrea said, 'yes'," Leo said, hardly able to keep the surprise out of his voice. His face was the picture of pure joy.

Digger saw that Andrea's hands were folded, but that she wore a tarnished ring on her left hand that seemed out of place with the tastefully classic dress she was wearing.

Velyn's face lit up as she gestured excitedly for their waiter. "How about a 2131 Lafitte Rothschild?" She addressed all the members of her party, "My treat, of course." She motioned to Andrea and Leo, who had not taken his eyes from his new fiancée since they arrived. "We have some wonderful news. Let the celebration begin!"

The talk was light as they ate the wide variety of exotic delights. Every course consisted of food that had been cultivated right on the space station. No one would ever have guessed that most items were tofu-based renditions of everything from escargot smothered in a delicious garlic butter sauce to medium rare filet mignon that literally melted in the mouths of those enjoying it. Dessert was crème brûlée covered with a raspberry-sugar topping that had been fired to a crisp, delicious shell.

After the last plate was cleared and the waiter had served steaming cups of hot, traditional coffee, Digger looked over at Kara. "What brings you here? It's certainly a pleasant surprise that I get to see both you and Velyn at the same time. Are you here on vacation?"

"Only partly," Kara answered. "I'm here to upgrade the *taman-C3* engineering units that work on the space station's exterior, and of course, to visit my mother." Kara smiled over at Velyn.

"The work part of the trip shouldn't take very long. The new program modifications will be sent to me remotely by way of transmissions similar to e-mail." She looked over at Digger.

"Please stop me if I'm boring you."

Digger smiled. Kara could never bore him.

Since there were no objections, Kara continued. "Before I load the updated program, the old program is deleted so that the units will not get their new instructions confused with their old instructions. The sequence is really the key. It's very easy and very fast. The engineering units won't miss a beat."

The waiter was about to ask if anyone wanted more coffee when the maître d' approached and handed a communicator to Kara.

"There is an urgent communication from Earth for you, Mrs. Lamrock. It's from the Company. A Mr. Brader."

Kara frowned, took the communicator, excused herself, and walked away so that she could talk without disturbing the rest of the table.

When Kara returned to the table, Digger noticed the concerned look on her face. "Something wrong?"

Kara looked at Digger and then at her mother. "Something's come up at Interglobal, and they need me to come back right away. It's nothing to worry about, but I need to get back immediately. I'm sorry, Mother. They've got me booked on the 11 o'clock shuttle."

Velyn smiled, but her disappointment was obvious. "Well that's okay, honey. I know how work can be. The show must go on. Remember, I wasn't always a glamorous superstar!"

"Want some company, Kara? I planned on getting back to Earth tomorrow anyway," Digger told her.

"Digger, you were never a good liar. I appreciate your very generous offer, but no. I don't want to spoil your vacation too. I'll be back in a few days, as soon as this matter is cleared up."

"It has something to do with the *taman* that killed that young boy, doesn't it?" Velyn asked, looking frightened. "Aren't the local authorities launching their own investigation? Why does the Company have to get involved? The reports we get up here say that this case is open and shut. Security cameras recorded everything."

"Mother, I didn't say that it had anything to do with the boy's murder," Kara replied evasively. "I'll probably be back here in a couple of days."

Digger sat like statue, ominously quiet.

Kara started to get up from the table. "I really have to get going if I'm going to pack and make the 11 o'clock shuttle." She turned to Digger. "Please don't think that I don't appreciate your offer. Anyway, I have the last available seat, so you wouldn't be able to return with me, even if you really wanted to."

Digger stood and hugged Kara. She put her arms around him, kissed his cheek, and held on to him like he was a long lost brother.

Velyn picked up her purse and took Kara's arm. "Let's go, Baby. You need to call Nathaniel and let him know what's going on.

"Andrea, I'm so sorry that we have to break up the party. Please, you and Leo stay and enjoy yourselves. I'll see you tomorrow."

Digger was silent as he watched Kara and Velyn leave the restaurant and head up to Velyn's suite. He was going back with Kara, no matter what he had to do to get on that shuttle.

Chapter Seven

Malcolm Godfrey was internally fuming as his chauffeur-driven limousine approached Interglobal's headquarters. Usually, he appreciated the aesthetics of the sweeping terrain alongside the four-lane private highway leading to the building. The scene was fiercely beautiful with bowling-ball-sized oranges hanging from enormous fruit trees next to the headquarters' main entrance. Saguaro cacti, some up to eighty feet tall, stood like sentinels in the oasis-like landscape. A twelve-foot wall, skillfully designed to blend in with the topography of the rolling desert hills, surrounded the main structure.

In contrast to the natural beauty leading up to Interglobal, the massive headquarters building hidden behind the wall looked like an ugly apparition. Heat waves shimmered from its plain gray concrete face. It would look like a small prison had it not been for the unique domed structure rising from the north end of the building like an incompetent architect's afterthought.

Malcolm entered the building's main entrance and walked past the rabbit warren of cubicle work areas. Fifteen hundred of Interglobal's loyal, highly-skilled employees toiled within the seemingly endless maze. Each of Interglobal's many enterprises was overseen from the complex: agriculture, communications, medicine, genetic engineering, entertainment, transportation, architect engineering/terraforming, artificial intelligence development/micro mechanics, and inter-planetary construction and maintenance.

Interglobal's endeavors, in one way or another, affected just about every aspect of daily life. Often referred to as simply the "Company," Interglobal was by far the largest, wealthiest, and most complex corporation in the world. Like all business, including the government, Interglobal was a for-profit corporation. The Company employed more than three million people throughout the world, extending its reach to remote settlements on the moon and the many space stations surrounding Earth. Soon, the Company would open an office on Mars. It had taken sixty years, but the Company was finally about to celebrate completion of its largest and most successful terraforming project.

The moon had been the Company's first success. Huge, terraforming industrial plants that released large amounts of carbon dioxide into the atmosphere were built in key moon surface locations. Within thirty years, emissions from the industrial plants had caused a greenhouse effect that warmed the sphere's temperature to an average 45 degrees Fahrenheit. The byproduct of hydrogen power plants, which were also established on the moon's surface, provided enough water to supply the work crews, colonists and genetically engineered vegetation. Everything necessary had first been transported from Earth to the moon until the settlers developed their own self-sustaining systems that produced food, oxygen, and whatever else they needed to survive. In less than forty years after the first colonists landed, the moon had become a hub of commerce that supported over two million human lives and an equal number of technological alternative units.

Malcolm passed offices that looked exactly like the next, with secretaries and assistants busily answering communications from all over the world. Unlike the small but efficiently designed cubicles, the offices in executive row were spacious and appealing. Only one office was unique--his own, the office of the Company's CEO.

A beautiful, exotic young woman sat at a workstation in front of the door that led to his cavernous suite. Malcolm had personally recruited Palya. Interglobal's employee roster listed her nationality as "Lunarite," a second-generation moonchild. Palya's grandparents had worked for the Company in the construction of the moon colony. Her father had been one of the first children actually born there.

Palya's presence outside Malcolm's office was his self-congratulatory reminder of Interglobal's sweeping terraforming success. Born and raised on the dark side of the moon, Palya's long straight hair was the color of milk; her skin was like cream, and her eyes were so light, their color was a soft pink. Her neck was long and swan-like. The moon's weak gravity during her formative years was responsible for long, long legs that carried her slim body. Palya stood just over six and a half feet tall and carried herself with the grace of a gazelle.

Unlike the plain offices in the main building, the suite where Malcolm Godfrey ran Interglobal with an iron fist consisted of three large, tastefully furnished rooms sharing space beneath the domed ceiling.

Godfrey, the only son of wealthy parents, was extremely intelligent. As a child, he had been introverted and sickly, and he had found it difficult to make friends. Even his parents' money could not buy him the companionship he craved. Other children picked on him, and he was often the butt of his classmates' cruel pranks and jokes. Unable to respond physically, Godfrey had learned to take revenge by underhanded methods. For example, he would secretly add his own saliva (he often had a cold) to an adversary's lunch, or he would insert deliberate mistakes into a classmate's homework before it was turned in. Revenge had always been sweet.

These days, Godfrey commanded, and received, respect from his entire executive staff. Only a very small circle of friends was allowed to address him as "Malcolm." Even his mother did not dare to call him "Mal." Behind his back, although he knew everything that was said in secret or otherwise, some of his employees referred to him as "God," a nickname that he did not find offensive. To everyone else he was "Dr. Godfrey."

Twenty or so hologram monitors surrounded Godfrey's desk on three sides. These monitors were shielded from full light to prevent distracting reflections on the holographic images. His personal workstation provided Godfrey with everything he could possibly need to run the mega-conglomerate that was Interglobal. His desk was a voice-activated command center. A single word from Godfrey could turn the domed ceiling into the black sky of a planetarium that depicted the cosmos and graphically identified the Company's many inter-planetary projects.

Malcolm Godfrey entered his office with his head down and slammed the door behind him with such force, that his framed awards swayed on the walls. Today, even the beautiful rainbow of light from the domed crystal sunroof that poured into his office could not improve Malcolm's dark mood.

Godfrey snarled into one of the tiny communicators positioned throughout the room. "Palya, have Brader come to my office."

Simon Brader burst into Godfrey's office without knocking. The brightness from the skylight made him squint. He did not venture more than a few steps into the office before Godfrey's glare pinned him to the spot where he stood. Godfrey inwardly smirked as he watched Brader literally shiver in fear. Even after all these years in command, Godfrey still took pleasure from the fright he instilled in the people who worked for him.

"What the hell happened out there?" Godfrey hissed.

Brader stammered, "There was a malfunction in the *taman*'s central decision system. It's all been taken care of; the *taman* unit has already been modified. The bug has been corrected."

Godfrey was mad at himself for trusting this complete idiot to do anything correctly.

"And you think that makes everything all right? Not only were there sixteen witnesses in the plaza in person, every second leading up to the boy's death is on digital surveillance footage. By morning, everyone with eyes and ears will be an eyewitness to the murder."

"I have marketing working on an explanation to be distributed over the news media, but you're right. There will no doubt be a formal investigation. I've already headed it off. I thought you would want me to be pro-active, so I recalled one of our lead programmers in the Artificial Intelligence Division from another assignment. We'll claim that she modified the unit without the Company's knowledge. The Artificial Intelligence programmer, a woman by the name of Kara Lamrock, will be blamed. I was hoping that perhaps it would appear as if the unit had turned on her, but as of the last communication I received, that idea didn't work out. What a shame! That would have ended it.

"Anyway, all is not lost. Our main objective was still successful. The boy was destroyed, and no one knows who he was or where he came from. The *taman* unit did as he was instructed. Unfortunately, his discretion chip malfunctioned. It must have reverted back to its original version. That was my fault, sir. When you told me it was a rush job, I cut a few corners in the rebuild sequence to save time."

Godfrey frowned as he considered Brader's plan. He barked into his command console, "Give me all the information we have on Mrs. Lamrock."

A holographic image of Kara Lamrock materialized on the wall opposite Malcolm's desk. Kara's biography was presented alongside her likeness. Her resume indicated that she had received several degrees in computer science. She was married, no children, and had worked for the Company for over fifty years, progressing from an entry level programmer to her current position of lead programmer in the Artificial Intelligence Division.

"What is her genetic alteration date?" Godfrey asked. Immediately, *GAD: June 19, 2031* appeared. Beside her generic alteration date, her chronological birth date (CBD) was displayed: *September 29, 1999.*

There was additional information. Her background check indicated that during her college years, Kara had protested the government's attempts at mass sterilization in the days that followed the first genetic alterations. Geneticists had discovered a means to successfully block the human aging process. When science actually succeeded in reversing aging itself, a feat that promised to keep people alive indefinitely, the government had set up a program of mass sterilization in an attempt to keep the world's population under control. Many people, including Kara, believed the government program to be unjust and excessive.

Kara's husband, Nathaniel Lamrock (*GAD: April 30, 2030, CBD: October 29, 1999*) was an attorney with a lucrative legal practice. He was currently representing a couple trying to obtain government permission to bear a natural child. He had previously been employed by: "*CENSORED* (past position information classified)."

The displayed information indicated that Kara's father had died in 2029, but her mother was still alive and was currently active in the entertainment industry.

Mrs. Lamrock's background sounds all too familiar, Godfrey thought uncomfortably. He considered what he had just learned. *Surely, this can't be a fluke,* he told himself.

"Who is her mother?" Godfrey asked.

A life sized 3-D holographic image of Velyn Stevens appeared on the wall. For an instant, Godfrey felt like he had been punched in the stomach. He gasped. "I knew this couldn't be a coincidence. It's her and she's still as lovely as ever." He cleared his throat and pretended to cough when he realized that he had spoken his thought aloud.

Velyn Stevens' personal information was displayed on the screen next to her beautiful face. *GAD: September 12, 2029; CBD, February 21, 1964.* Family: Husband deceased. One child: Kara Lamrock. Profession: Entertainer, actor.

"Her image doesn't do her justice," Godfrey remarked. "I was acquainted with Ms. Stevens many years ago. She's as elegant as she is sexy."

Godfrey shook his head, trying to shake memories of her from his thoughts. "When she speaks, her voice sounds like the tinkling of crystal chimes, so sexy that it sends shivers down a man's spine."

Godfrey was startled to hear the sound of his own voice. He had not meant to share his thoughts about Velyn with anyone, but staring at her image had left Godfrey mesmerized. Learning that she still had this effect on him after all these years only fired his anger until his rage was white hot. Godfrey reached over, switched off the hologram viewer and turned his ire on Brader.

"How can we blame Mrs. Lamrock when her mother is so famous, you fool? The publicity and resulting scandal would surely expose us."

"On the contrary," Brader answered confidently. "Velyn Stevens has taken extreme measures to ensure that Kara is not linked to her fame. There's not even one photograph of them together. Kara might just as well be Jane Doe, and that's how I propose we handle her."

Godfrey was silent as he pondered this course of action. It was remarkable that a good idea had come from Brader, and more remarkable that it just might work. Brader's plan could serve two purposes. First, it would settle the mess created by the boy's very public execution, and second, it would help settle an old score with Ms. Hot-shot Velyn Stevens.

"I like it," smiled Godfrey. "Excellent job, Brader."

"Thank you, sir. I thought it to be a masterpiece, if I do say so myself."

"Don't push it Brader," Godfrey snarled. "You don't know the half of it. Get Mrs. Lamrock back to Phoenix as soon as possible. I want her to meet my special welcoming committee. Keep me personally informed on this one."After Brader left, Godfrey sat down at his desk and softly whispered, "Close." The verbal command instructed the overhead ceiling panels to close, plunging his office into near-darkness. Millions of tiny lights representing stars and planets appeared in the black-domed ceiling. Some of the holographic planets and moons were illuminated brighter than the others because they represented Interglobal projects.

Godfrey closed his eyes and remembered how he had felt when Velyn rejected him after her husband had died. The emotion he had experienced all those years ago had changed, but it had never completely gone away. His feelings for Velyn were the closest he had ever come to experiencing love. He had never married because he had never met anyone who could live up to the original object of his affections. Over the decades, his one-sided love had turned to hate.

Godfrey sat brooding in the darkness of his office. Abruptly, he looked up and said, "Palya, come in here."

As she had done many times before, the beautiful young girl came slowly into his office, locking the door behind her. The resigned look on her face betrayed her knowledge of what his command portended. She stood behind Godfrey, leaning over him so that her long, blond hair fell over him like a veil.

He pulled her to him and kissed her small mouth brutally. Before he took her, he thought gleefully that if she ever got with child, it would provide his research team with a new specimen to analyze. As he kissed her again, he closed his eyes, but instead of Palya, it was the beautiful face of Velyn Stevens that floated across his mind.

Chapter Eight

There were only a few spectators in the courtroom where Nathaniel stood and confidently began his argument.

"In accordance with my duty as their counsel, I hereby swear to the integrity of my clients and petition the court to grant Juan and Sha Nuala a permit to bear a natural human child in accordance with global law.

"This is the fifth petition filed with this court on behalf of the Nualas. Each previous filing was denied.

"I anticipate that this filing will be different because of the tragic incident that took place yesterday at 11:55:45 p.m. The Nualas' petition was filed at 11:56:00, fifteen seconds after the terrible incident. The world population clock automatically decreased by one, reporting the population vacancy that was caused by yesterday's death. Although sad, this tragedy has provided these good people with the potential to have a natural human child and to bring the population back to its maximum number as proscribed by Global Law."

The 3-D image of the Honorable Mologor Graph was silent for several minutes as he reviewed all the documents before him. Although, to everyone present, Judge Graph appeared to be physically presiding over the Phoenix courtroom, his image could have been transmitted from anywhere in the world, from an office in the Phoenix courthouse itself or from an office somewhere in the Western hemisphere. Finally, the judge spoke, "Counselor, there's one problem with your brief. The Population Clock has not changed. There was no population decrease yesterday."

The small group of spectators in the courtroom, present mainly as a means to relieve the boredom that was their everyday lives, burst out in laughter and began taunting Nathaniel and the Nualas. Sternly, the clerk, who was physically present, ordered the crowd to be silent.

"I'm sorry, Your Honor," Nathaniel replied. "There must be a mistake. A young boy was terminated in Phoenix yesterday at 11:55:45. Local digital surveillance cameras recorded the incident. Thousands witnessed the occurrence on their personal hologram monitors in real-time, as it happened. Tens of thousands more have seen the tragedy continually replayed on the news. If it would please the Court, I can place a copy of the recorded event into evidence."

Judge Graph hesitated a moment before he turned his communicator off. The courtroom monitor went black as he turned to whisper something to his law clerk. After several minutes, Graph came back on line. "I would like to speak privately with counsel in my chambers. Counselor, would you please step into the booth on your right."

Nathaniel turned to the Nualas and reassured them that he would get to the bottom of the mistake.

Once again, the hologram monitor displaying the image of Judge Graph was blank. Nathaniel opened the door to the small booth, stepped in and closed the door behind him. The booth was airtight and soundproofed. Oxygen was pumped in through the booth's ventilation system. Nathaniel never liked tight spaces and began to feel claustrophobic. A display screen located inside the booth finally displayed Judge Graph's image.

"Counselor, I understand that this may come as a shock to you, but the World Population Clock has not changed."

"Your Honor, I don't mean to disagree with the Court, but thousands of people witnessed the termination of a young boy in downtown Phoenix yesterday. There must be a mistake."

"Attorney Lamrock, I need to contact someone at Interglobal. As unthinkable as it may be, if what you say is true, the clock must have malfunctioned. This has never happened before. Please wait there in the booth until I get back to you. I don't want this information to go beyond this room. Do you understand?"

Once again, the screen went blank, leaving Nathaniel in semidarkness. Nathaniel grew extremely anxious. He felt as if the walls were closing in on him. It brought back memories of hours spent in a cold, damp closet when he was a child, his court-appointed foster parents' favored form of punishment for even the most minor transgression. This current discomfort only served to make him angry with himself. He had let the Nualas down.

Nathaniel had grown to respect both Juan and Sha Nuala. Despite his chronic bad luck, Juan Nuala was a positive, honest, and hard-working man. He was determined to provide a good life for his wife, but a series of poor investments and unfortunate business ventures had taken most of the couple's financial assets. It was as if Juan's last vestige of good fortune had been used up when Sha agreed to marry him.

Nathaniel knew that Juan's lack of monetary success meant nothing to Sha. She loved him for who he was and she wanted nothing more than to have a child with him. Nathaniel had rarely seen a man so determined to make his wife happy, and if a child is what Sha wanted, Nathaniel knew that Juan would to do everything in his power, within the law, to make it happen. But, Juan's run of fiscal bad luck seemed to spill over into his personal life. Up until now, the court had assigned him a series of incompetent attorneys, none of whom had been able to secure a child-bearing permit that was required before Juan and Sha could begin their family.

Finally, Juan's luck started to change for the better, and the turnaround came when he least expected it. On their fifth attempt, the court had once again denied the Nualas a child-bearing permit. Frustrated and overwhelmed by disappointment, Juan argued loudly with his latest attorney in the hallway outside the courtroom door. Just by chance Nathaniel had stood within hearing range, conferring with his own latest client, a wealthy businessman seeking a building permit for a new sky mall. Nathaniel could catch only a few words and phrases but he heard Juan's lawyer say, "It's not my fault that the judge didn't read the petition in time." To which Nathaniel heard Juan respond, "But you didn't bother to file the petition before the time limit was up!"

Nathaniel turned to see that Sha, standing beside her husband, was quietly weeping.

"Please, excuse me," Nathaniel said to his well-healed client, quickly walking away before the man could protest.

Nathaniel approached Sha and asked her what was wrong. She looked up at him but was too grief-stricken to respond. Nathaniel's heart went out to her. He handed her his handkerchief, asking if there was anything he could do. When Juan turned to look at Nathaniel, his bungling attorney used the interruption as his chance to escape the unpleasant consequences of his ineffectual representation.

Juan watched his attorney disappear down the courthouse stairway, thinking that if the man had not run away, Juan may have decked him there on the spot. He took Sha's arm and also began to walk away, but Nathaniel stopped him.

"I couldn't help but overhear your conversation," Nathaniel said. "Perhaps I can help." Nathaniel reached into his pocket and pulled out his business card, holding it out to Juan.

Juan half-heartedly looked at the card Nathaniel proffered and shook his head in dismay. "Thank you, sir, but we don't have the means to retain your services."

Nathaniel could see from the look on Juan's face that his own perfectly tailored suit accurately depicted his success, and this fact was not lost on Juan. His look told Nathaniel that Juan couldn't afford even a bargain basement suit, much less have the funds to hire someone of Nathaniel's caliber.

Nathaniel pulled back his card, turned it over and wrote something on the back. Holding it out to Juan once again, he said, "Here, take my card. My fee is on the back. Think about it, and if you want to retain my services, please contact me." Nathaniel smiled kindly at Sha, turned and walked back to his current impatient client.

Juan had later told Nathaniel that although he had placed Nathaniel's card in his shirt pocket, he had intended to throw it away when he got home. He had been concerned that Sha would have been unrealistically encouraged by Nathaniel's offer. He didn't want her disappointed again. Juan told Nathaniel that later that day, alone in their pod, Sha had been overwhelmed with hopelessness.

Juan had gone to the kitchen to brew some tea for her, thankful for something to keep him occupied. Before serving it to her, he placed a mild sedative in the tea to calm her. Returning to their living room, he had said, "Here, my love, take this. It will help you relax."

After she finished the tea, Sha told him that she was feeling a little tired and that she'd like to lie down for a while. Putting down her cup, Sha walked to their bedroom, quickly undressed and got into bed. Juan followed and sat on the edge of the bed next to her, stroking her hair while the sedative took effect.

"I needed to sleep myself," he had told Nathaniel.

Juan said that when he began to remove items from his pockets, he found the card that Nathaniel had given to him earlier that day.

He pulled the card from his pocket and placed it face down on the nightstand. He looked with astonishment at the card. On the back, Nathaniel had written the number "0." Suddenly, Juan's fatigue vanished. For the first time in a long time Juan had smiled as he reached for his communicator.

It was hard for Nathaniel to believe that a year had passed since he and the Nualas had first sat down to map out a strategy. Nathaniel knew that this was as close as they would ever get to getting official permission to have the precious child they both so desired and so deserved. Nathaniel had been so sure that he could obtain a permit for them that he had recommended against the purchase of a *taman* infant as an alternative.

The wait inside the booth was making Nathaniel ready to jump out of his skin. He had been so deep in thought remembering what had brought him to this point, he jumped when the judge finally reappeared on the monitor.

"I've spoken with Cushman Sellers at Interglobal," Judge Graph told him. "He remembers you and has instructed me that he will work with you to get to the bottom of this as quickly as possible. Please return to the courtroom."

Nathaniel gratefully opened the door to the booth took a long, deep breath and went back to stand before the courtroom's bank of display screens. Judge Graph's image was already on the main monitor.

"Counselor, Mr. and Mrs. Nuala, it is hereby the decision of this court to continue this matter until a formal investigation into the functioning of the world clock can be conducted. This does not affect your case in any way, and you will not forfeit your petition fee. The petition shall remain active. I have spoken with a representative at Interglobal, the manufacturer of the world clock. Mr. and Mrs. Nuala, Interglobal's agent, Mr. Cushman Sellers, will be contacting your attorney with a full briefing. I will reexamine your petition after this matter with the clock has been resolved to the Court's satisfaction. The Court has spoken."

Abruptly, Judge Graph's image disappeared. The Nualas stood in a state of shock because, after months of preparation and precision timing in filing their petition, their fate was still undecided. The future of their family was still unresolved, as if a book was slammed shut before final page was read.

KATHLEEN PAPAJOHN

Chapter Nine

Cushman Sellers was terrified. For him, fear of any kind was a strange and unfamiliar sensation, but if it were true that the Population Clock had malfunctioned, then the situation could turn into a disaster of indescribable proportions. Governments all over the world relied on the accuracy of the clock to ensure that Earth's population was under control. The absolute accuracy of the clock was taken for granted. This knowledge had kept the world free from war for over a hundred years. If there were the slightest hint that such reliance was misplaced, there was no way to predict the consequences.

Midnight had come and gone hours before, and still he sat at his desk. He had not left his office since he had received Graph's call. Trying to sleep with such an enormous problem on his mind would be fruitless. He gazed out the large window that took up an entire wall of his luxurious penthouse office to watch the sun come up over Camelback Mountain. He looked down and realized that he had been holding his distinguished service medal so tightly that his hand had begun to cramp up. He had come to the realization that, even during the war, mortal fear had never affected him like this, not even during his darkest days when danger was his constant companion, hovering over him like a fog that invaded his every pore.

Framed awards and citations attested to the fact that Sellers had been the brains that secured capital backing for Interglobal's major successes, the first of which was implementation of the genetic engineering process that so dramatically increased human life expectancy. Cash generated by this first triumph had allowed The Company to begin inter-planetary exploration and terra-forming. Eventually, under Seller's financial guidance, Interglobal became the most successful for-profit company in the world.

In order that the wildly beautiful but delicate planet that human beings called home would not be overwhelmed by a population that would never be reduced by natural death, Interglobal had developed a mandatory under-skin implant that could identify all human, carbon-producing life forms and transmit the existence of each and every human life to the Company's world population clock.

The device tracked the total number of existing human lives and had correctly recorded each death and birth since its inception, ensuring that the world's population never exceeded the ever-constant number of 10,456,352,909 lives, which, according to sound empirical scientific evidence, indicated the number of lives that planet Earth's resources could safely sustain.

It took decades after the devastation and casualties caused by the final corporate war, but eventually the population count hit the maximum number of people that the planet could support. At that time, a permit system had been instituted that allowed new births to take place only when a vacancy occurred in the existing population.

Unlike most of Interglobal's other executives, Cushman Sellers possessed a social conscience. He was most proud of the portrait showing him shaking hands with the current political leader of the Western World, a beautiful and genuinely brilliant African American woman, taken when she had been appointed CEO of the

Western Sector after the termination of her successor, Ikabod Ice. It had been she who signed the Natural Child Permit Act. Passage of this act had eliminated the need for mass sterilization. No one disagreed that the new law was preferable to governmental specification of a legal limit that would have determined the maximum age of a human's life span.

In spite of Cushman's objections, he had agreed to a compromise that had been necessary to get the law passed: non-compliance with the act's reproduction laws would be punishable by death. The same punishment had been used for decades to control human cloning, a process which had become a reality, but was quickly banned in the first quarter of the twenty-first century.

Cushman sat perfectly still in the early morning light filtering into his well-appointed office. He stood and began pacing the room. Frustrated, he couldn't figure out what could have happened to the population clock. The clock, with its many backup and safety processes, was virtually indestructible. In its long history, it had never malfunctioned.

I don't know how, but I see Brader's blundering handiwork in this mess, Cushman thought.

He looked at his watch and saw that already a new workday had begun. In a voice that, although demanding, sounded a lot calmer than what was going on in his turbulent mind, Cushman spoke into his communicator.

"Esther, tell Simon Brader to come to my office immediately."

Chapter 10

Digger flipped open his communicator, attached a scrambler device to conceal the signal and hit his speed dial. His call was answered immediately.

"How can I be of assistance Agent Rooney?"

"Book me on the next flight out of Space Station Alpha 33 to Phoenix Sky Harbor. It's essential that I be on tonight's shuttle. Seat me next to passenger Kara Lamrock. This is a Priority One request."

"Acknowledged. Reservation confirmed."

Digger raced up to Velyn's suite, hoping to catch Kara before she left for the shuttle. To his relief, Kara answered his knock. She stood with her suitcases next to the door, packed and ready to go.

Digger grinned at her. "It must be my lucky day! There was a cancellation, and I got the last seat on your flight."

"Digger, you're impossible!" Kara smiled.

Digger and Kara got to the gate with less than five minutes to spare. There was no time to enjoy the amenities of the station's lavish outbound chamber. The other passengers had already boarded. They proceeded to the space plane where they were instructed to place their hands, palm down on the scanner. Digger made sure that Kara placed her hand on the scanner first. The overhead monitor displayed passenger information, "Identity: Mrs. Kara Lamrock, V.I.P seating, Interglobal Corporation."

Digger was impressed and joked with Kara about being a corporate big shot. A V.I P. ticket cost 5,000 barter credits, almost Digger's monthly salary. He laughed to himself when he thought that what he was paid each month made the value of his life the same as the cost of a V.I.P. seat on Interglobal's space plane. Kara looked so serious, almost embarrassed, as she explained that Interglobal owned the space plane shuttle service and that she could never afford such an expensive ticket if she had to pay for it herself. Taking for granted that Digger's seat would be in the back section, Kara kissed him on the cheek and headed for first class.

Digger looked over his shoulder to make sure that the ticket agent was the only one around; then, he reached up and switched off the overhead monitor so that his identifying information would only be displayed on the lower monitor that was hidden from public view. Digger placed his hand on the scanner. "Identity: CLASSIFIED, V.I.P seating, Official Business."

Digger winked at the *taman* ticket agent who was monitoring the scanner and said, "Let's just keep this between ourselves."

The expression on the unit's face didn't even change. It was as if this was an everyday occurrence. He simply read the display, nodded his head, and replied, "I see nothing, sir."

Kara was already seated and covered in a blanket when Digger appeared carrying a sports magazine. He plopped himself down next to her.

"Now, what are the odds of this happening to me?" Digger laughed. "I was told that there were no more economy seats so the flight attendant said to sit here."

Digger tried to look absorbed in his magazine's article that questioned that advisability of firing the manager every time a baseball team did not live up to fans' expectations. In reality, he was trying to savor every minute that he was with Kara. He knew that his mind would replay the sound of her voice saying his name over and over. He had already been through it before. He knew the pain that would remain after she was gone, but for the time being, he would live in the moment. That would be enough. His left arm grazed hers on the armrest that separated their seats. The feel of her skin against his was all that should have filled his mind, but still, the gears were turning like the inside of a finely tuned watch. He could see that she looked disappointed, but also he could see that she was exhausted. Even though he knew that he should let her sleep, he couldn't help himself from trying to find out what was on her mind.

"What's wrong, Kara?"

"I was just thinking about Nathaniel."

"Naturally," said Digger, trying to keep the edge out of his voice

His tone made Kara give him a puzzled look. Digger thought that she would call him on it and prepared for another of their normal "sibling" squabbles, but she was evidently too tired to fight.

She shrugged and said, "It's the Nualas. They've applied for a child permit five times, and Nathaniel has filed their most recent petition. Over the last ten years they have been continually questioned, evaluated. Every aspect of their lives has been exposed to public scrutiny. They have never complained about this intrusion into their privacy."

Kara laughed derisively. "In fact, they have no privacy. Nathaniel told me that in forty years of practicing law, he has only seen a handful of permits granted and only when someone had been killed in an accident or when a criminal had been executed. I can't remember the last time that a human being died from natural causes. Sha and Juan are just so *nice*. Sometimes I think that all these so-called "protection" laws are a mistake. If society could pick a perfect couple to be parents, it would be the Nualas. Don't get me wrong; I do believe that it would be a mistake to put a time limit on someone's life span, but I still remember when a family meant a mother, father, and children, or at least one child."

"What about you, Kara? Would you want to have a child?"

"Of, course," she answered. "Children are precious. Wouldn't you want to have a child?" She looked directly into his eyes. "A little, Digger?"

Although it was rare that anyone could outlast Digger in a staring contest, he broke their gaze first without answering.

If the child was yours, he thought, *there would be nothing that could ever be more precious.*

Kara continued to watch him as if waiting for an answer, but Digger was suddenly completely engrossed in his magazine again.

Kara's communicator buzzed, indicating a new text message. Out of the corner of his eye, Digger saw that it was from Nathaniel.

Will meet you at our favorite restaurant near the courthouse.

Once again, Digger felt irritated because Kara's face immediately brightened. The message continued.

I love you infinity times infinity. Nathaniel.

Kara was so exhausted from all of the night's excitement that, as soon as the pod that protected travelers from the strong G-forces associated with take-offs raised, she fell asleep even before the blue sleep mist was released from the shuttle's ventilation system.

Unlike Kara, Digger did not have the luxury of taking time to sleep. Ever watchful, Digger had already noticed someone suspicious. The passenger was seated several rows in back of them. He looked like he was watching Digger and Kara, even from behind his dark sunglasses.

Upon landing, Digger escorted Kara to the spaceport exit and watched her head off down the moving walkway. He began to back-track their route as soon as she was out of sight and out of immediate danger. No surprise to Digger, there was the suspicious-looking man in the dark sunglasses whom Digger had observed seated a few rows behind Kara. He was headed in Kara's direction.

Digger started after him but swiftly lost sight of him in the crowded terminal. He hurriedly followed the walkway that the man had taken, but there were so many people that Digger couldn't see him. Another shuttle had just landed, and people were just stopping in the middle of the walkway to hug each other in greeting. Digger was actually being pushed back by the throng. The man was getting away, and worse, he was getting closer to Kara.

Then, suddenly, Digger spotted him. The man saw Digger at the same time and hastily turned, attempting to hide his face, but it was too late. Pretending to be a lost tourist, Digger approached the man, not caring whether or not he, Digger, would be in danger. He purposely bumped into the subject. A tiny tracking device that the man was carrying fell to the ground.

"Excuse me," Digger said. "Let me help you get that."

Digger got so close to the man that he would have felt his breath if the man had needed to breathe. Digger shoved his gun into the man's ribs and growled, "Move a muscle and I will blow you into the next galaxy."

Digger assessed the situation in less than a nanosecond. He knew that this *taman* could have crushed him like an insect. He also knew that the unit was smart enough to recognize that there was an anti-matter plasma pistol aimed directly at his internal power supply. Digger knew that the gun was capable of disabling the *taman* without destroying any of the data that was stored in the unit's memory banks.

Digger wasn't surprised when he felt no pulse as he gripped the man's arm. "So what do we have here?" Digger asked. "You're a *taman* unit aren't you? I should have known. I can smell your kind a mile away. Why are you following Kara Lamrock?"

The *taman* remained silent as he looked back at Digger with disdain. Digger was vaguely surprised that the unit did not resist. He knew that units such as this one had the technical capability and training that would allow him to end Digger's life.

Digger realized just how precarious his own position was. Still, he continued to bait his subject.

"You should know that spying on humans is punishable by immediate decommissioning. That's total destruction in your case, you bag of digital blips."

Digger grabbed for his own communicator, "Get someone to Sky Harbor Terminal Four immediately. I have a rogue *taman* unit in custody, and I need a wagon."

Digger was still standing close to the *taman*, with only his weapon separating them. With his free hand, the unit slowly removed his sunglasses, gritted his teeth, smiled, and looked directly into Digger's eyes.

"My name is Quallou."

Digger was startled that the unit had even spoken, let alone that he had admitted to be the *taman* that every law enforcement agency was looking for. Still, Digger knew that Quallou's instinct was to destroy him. He undoubtedly intended to crush Digger's skull, but just before Quallou could strike, Digger recognized that something strange was happening. Quallou's new program began to execute, overriding his original CPU programming.

Immediately, the *taman*'s movements stopped. Then, moving in slow motion, he lowered his hand, stared at Digger and said defiantly, "Self-destruct mode initiated. Executing."

Digger smelled a slight hint of metallic corrosion. Instinctively, he let go of the *taman* and jumped backed. He couldn't believe what he was seeing. A *taman* unit was incinerating itself with acid in order to destroy all evidence of its mission. It stood there with no fear, smiling, its eyes wide open, and then just ceased to function. Within less than a second, the unit had destroyed itself.

Digger had never seen this type of behavior from any *taman* before, regardless of model. He was sure that this one had been modified and instinctively knew that he was somehow connected to the boy's death and to Kara, but how and why?

Just as the *taman* ceased functioning, backup personnel arrived at the scene. "What happened here, Agent?"

"I don't know. Take this one back to headquarters. We need to pop its cork to see what made this thing tick."

Additional support personnel dressed as emergency medical technicians arrived. It took six of them to lift Quallou onto a stretcher and roll him out of the spaceport to an awaiting transport. They were all amazed at how heavy the unit was.

Digger needed to get to Kara immediately. The *taman* had confirmed what his sources had told him. Kara was a target.

Chapter 11

Suddenly, Kara heard a noise that made the hair on the back of her neck stand up. She looked closely into the shadows beside the pathway.

"Who's there?" she asked, her voice quivering.

When there was no answer, she quickly continued down the path. Within minutes, she reached the park's halfway point and she lost sight of Washington Street behind her. Kara thought, *How strange. The park's lights are out.* Darkness was falling fast.

Although she couldn't get the broadcasted images of the young boy fleeing through the same park the day before out of her mind, she thought, *I'm just being silly.* Still, she began to walk faster. Suddenly, she heard another noise. This time, it seemed to come from right behind her. She turned, but all she could see was darkness. She began to run.

To Kara's relief, the lights from the restaurant came into view. She ran out of the park and stopped running only after she crossed Jefferson Street. She walked up to the restaurant's door and went in, out of breath. The artificial cool air of the restaurant gave her a slight chill, making her damp blouse feel clammy against her skin.

The restaurant was filled to capacity. Nathaniel was already there, seated in the back of the restaurant at their favorite table. Nathaniel rose from his seat as soon as he saw Kara, and she rushed into his welcoming arms. For the first time since Brader had told her to return to Earth, Kara felt that she could finally relax.

Nathaniel held her close. "Kara, what's wrong? You're shaking," he said.

"It's nothing," Kara replied. "I'm just so happy to see you."

Kara was surprised that the Nualas were not present. That could only mean one thing: they had not received their permit. *Oh, no!* she thought. She had so wanted to tell him about Rosemary, but she wanted the occasion to be one of joy. She decided to wait until later. She would wait until some of the day's disappointment began to fade. She started to console Nathaniel when he stopped her by putting his finger to her lips.

"We didn't lose," Nathaniel explained. "The hearing was temporarily postponed because of a malfunction of the World Population Clock. Judge Graph appointed Cushman Sellers to determine the cause of the malfunction and report back to him directly. Once the judge finds out what went wrong with the clock, he'll proceed with the Nualas' petition. There's no doubt that Judge Graph will look very favorably at our petition as soon as Cushman clears up the Population Clock matter."

Kara and Nathaniel finished their dinner in a comfortable silence. Kara could hardly wait until they were home alone to tell him about Rosemary. As they stood to leave, a uniformed *taman* police officer approached their table. He was followed by another and then another.

"Are you Kara Lamrock?"

Bewildered, Kara responded, "I am. What can I do for you, officer?"

Before the officer could say another word, Nathaniel stepped between him and Kara. "Excuse me, officer, what is this all about?"

Other diners turned to stare.

The officer reached around Nathaniel trying to grab Kara. "Mrs. Kara Lamrock, please come with me. You are under arrest for murder."

"This must be a joke," Kara answered. She looked back at Nathaniel, confused and a little frightened.

Nathaniel's jaw dropped. "What did you say? Murder? You must be talking about the boy that was killed by the rogue *taman*. That's preposterous! I am Mrs. Lamrock's husband, and as an attorney, I am also an officer of the court. Under what authority do you arrest my wife?"

"I have in my hands, a warrant issued by the Regional Board of Governors for Mrs. Kara Lamrock. Here it is, sir. Read it carefully. Now please step back, I will not repeat my request. Mrs. Lamrock is under arrest for conspiracy to murder."

Nathaniel grabbed the officer by his arm. "This is unfounded. She's not going anywhere."

Without warning, one of the other uniformed officers punched Nathaniel in the stomach, knocking him to the floor. Nathaniel lay there, gasping for air. The officer pulled back his foot, preparing to kick Nathaniel. Kara screamed.

"Just what's going on here, gentlemen?" Digger Rooney had entered the restaurant and pushed his way through the crowd to see what the uproar was all about. He gently moved Kara so that she was standing behind him, and then helped Nathaniel to his feet. He flashed a golden badge with a black "I" engraved through the center, commanding instant respect.

"We are on the board's business," stated the first officer. "Please move back. Do not make me use force."

A unit came up behind Digger and took Kara by the arm while another held Nathaniel back. Kara unsuccessfully tried to free herself from the unit's grasp.

Digger smirked and flashed his credentials again. This time he also drew his weapon. The *taman* units backed off, finally deferring to Digger's authority. "I know these people," Digger said. "There's been a mistake." He turned to the unit who held Kara's arm. "Take your hands off her immediately!"

The officer released Kara without hesitation. He backed away and saluted Digger. "As you say, sir." He seemed to be waiting for Digger to give him directions on how to handle this situation.

Digger obliged, "Stand down, you fools!" Digger barked.

"Yes, sir. Sorry, sir. But what are we supposed to do about the warrant for Mrs. Lamrock?"

"I would tell you where to file that warrant, but there are ladies present. Return to your station for further instructions. Let your controller know that Kara Lamrock will not be coming in just now, and that she is in my custody. I will personally transport Mrs. Lamrock to the station so that she can be interviewed."

"I'm sorry, sir," said the second officer. "My superiors have just communicated to us that the strength of the warrant overrides your authority in this matter." Other uniformed officers began to arrive.

Nathaniel lunged toward the officer that had hit him, but Digger stepped between them.

"Nathaniel," whispered Digger, "this is not the time for action. We will pick our own time and place. For the time being, I believe that we should let Kara go with them. I'll follow them to the station to make sure that she's all right. I'll call you as soon as I find out what's going on."

Unable to control his anger, Nathaniel made one more attempt at the officer who held Kara, but Digger restrained him. Nathaniel, fury evident his eyes, stared at Digger for what seemed an eternity, then reluctantly stepped back.

"If anything happens to my wife …"

KATHLEEN PAPAJOHN

Chapter 12

Digger downloaded every piece of information that he could find relating to Kara's indictment. Interglobal had evidently accused Kara of reprogramming the *taman* unit that had executed the boy. It was information that Interglobal gave to the authorities that led to Kara's arrest.

What am I missing? he asked himself.

He knew that Kara would never intentionally reprogram a *taman* unit to become an assassin. The very idea was preposterous. Why would Interglobal accuse her of doing such a thing? Why were the authorities so dead-set on keeping her away from everyone?

I've never had a problem working with the local authorities before, Digger thought. He couldn't understand why he was having problems now. *There's no favorable percentage in this for Interglobal. Even if Kara did do what they say she did, which I know she didn't, Interglobal would still be financially responsible to the boy's family. With all their money, Interglobal wouldn't even blink at a settlement, no matter how high. Another thing I don't understand, why haven't the kid's parents or guardian come forward? Who was this kid anyway? Was he just a random target?*

Digger's head was still spinning trying to make sense out of all this when his communicator buzzed.

"Digger, this is Nathaniel. Where the hell is Kara?"

"She was booked into the Jefferson Street Holding Facility for Women, but they've moved her and they aren't saying where. Because I'm not officially 'family,' they wouldn't let me in to see her. I tried calling in some favors, but almost everyone I tried to get in touch with was conveniently unavailable. If I did get in contact with someone, he clammed up. Either they truly don't know what's going on, or they're too scared to say anything."

"Don't tell me that you actually trust those misfits that you call friends," Nathaniel said.

"I'm still old school, Nathaniel. These contacts have come in handy more than once. I'm not ashamed that I made my living in some questionable ways before joining the Internals. You were no angel yourself. Remember, I stuck with the Internals when you decided you'd had enough. You're lucky I stayed with the team. If I weren't an agent, I couldn't help you now. You'd have no one and neither would Kara."

"Sorry for landing my plane on your head, Digger. It's just that I'm going crazy with worry about Kara. I appreciate everything you're doing."

"Let's get one thing clear. I'm not doing it for you, Nathaniel."

"Okay, I understand. So what do we do now, Digger?"

"Since they're not admitting where Kara is being held, we can't get to her. I'm going to the office to see if there is something I can dig up there. I'll get back to you as soon as I find anything."

Nathaniel turned to Solis as soon as Digger hung up. "Solis, contact Cushman Sellers at Interglobal Corporation. Cushman was my commanding officer during the war and he's the one who got Digger to recruit me into the Internals. I heard that he retired from the Internals several years ago. I believe that he's currently the chief financial officer for Interglobal.

"I need to see Cushman right away. Use the population clock malfunction as an excuse for the meeting. Who knows, he just might be delighted to see an old combat buddy. I don't expect him to tell me everything that's going on, but at least I'll be inside Interglobal's facility. Maybe I can spot something that can help Kara."

Just as he expected, Cushman Sellers agreed to meeting with Nathaniel right away. The quicker he could get the population clock problem put to rest, the better. Cushman was also anxious to see Nathaniel for personal reasons. He had helped raise him, and Nathaniel was the closest thing to a son that Cushman would ever have.

Every year, around July 4, there was an exodus from Phoenix. Even die-hard Arizonans headed north, taking a break from the hellish summer heat. When Nathaniel and Solis arrived at Interglobal on July 4, it was evident from the scarcity of workers that it was vacation time in Phoenix.

A security guard met them in the lobby. He wore a name tag that identified him as George Max, Supervisor of Security for Interglobal. After checking the visitor's log, he directed Nathaniel and Solis to Cushman's office, but only after giving them both a quick and thorough once-over.

"Are you getting all of this Solis?"

"Yes sir, recording structural supports, security camera positions, entrance and exit locations. Mapping names and locations of all doors facing each hallway, management offices, location of filing room and laboratories.

"Keep track of the number of steps it takes to get to Mr. Sellers' office and how long it takes to get there. Get it all Solis. We need as much information about this place as possible. I also have a strange feeling that we haven't seen the last of Mr. George Max."

Cushman Sellers stood up with his hand outstretched when his secretary, Esther, admitted Nathaniel and Solis, Nathaniel saluted Cushman as if they were still back in the military.

Cushman smiled. "None of that, Nathaniel. Those days are long over, thank God."

Nathaniel extended his own hand in a friendly and respectful manner, but before they could actually shake hands, Cushman grabbed Nathaniel and embraced him.

"You look great! It's been too long. You don't look a day older than the last time I saw you. That was on Tuesday, June 15 in 2157, I believe."

Nathaniel smiled, "I can see that you haven't lost that phenomenal memory of yours, Colonel Sellers. I bet you even remember what I was wearing."

"Actually I do, son. You had just opened your law practice. You were wearing a blue pinstriped suit, white shirt, and an awful bowtie. Everything matched but that damned tie."

Nathaniel was amazed at Sellers' powers of recall.

"You're absolutely correct, sir." Nathaniel was pleased to see that Cushman was still as vibrant as ever. "You look fit, Colonel."

"You know how it is. I just eat right and keep chasing young women. Nathaniel, forever is a long time, and I plan to stay fit so that I can keep up. I still enjoy every day to its fullest."

Solis looked on silently as Nathaniel and Cushman got reacquainted.

"Sorry. I'm being rude," Nathaniel said. "I'd like to introduce my associate. Cushman, this is Solis."

Cushman nodded to Solis. "Nice to meet you, Mr. Solis. Any friend of Nathaniel's is a friend of mine.

Solis smiled and shook Cushman's hand.

"Now this guy is in shape!" Cushman said. He peered closely at Solis as if trying to place him.

"Have we met before? What kind of work are you in, Mr. Solis?"

Solis glanced over at Nathaniel as if asking him what he was supposed to answer. Nathaniel hadn't anticipated that anyone would ask Solis any questions. His mind raced. He didn't want Cushman to know that Solis was a *taman*. He especially didn't want him to know that Solis was the destructor that had been assigned to Nathaniel during the war.

Nathaniel knew that Solis was incapable of lying. Nathaniel started to answer for him, but before Nathaniel could get a word in, Solis replied, "I work for myself. I am a health consultant."

It took all Nathaniel's self-control to hide his astonishment at Solis's answer. *How did Solis come up with that response?* Nevertheless, Nathaniel sighed with relief.

I guess you are capable of telling a white lie after all, he thought. *What else can you do that I don't know about?*

"So, I guess that this mess about the clock does have a bright side. At least I get to see you again." Cushman said, waving Nathaniel and Solis to seats across from his expansive desk.

"Yes, sir, that's part of it." Nathaniel hesitated. "It's also about my wife, Kara Lamrock."

Cushman frowned. "I assumed that it wasn't a coincidence that you both have the same last name," he said.

Nathaniel explained that he had met Kara shortly before he left the Internals, and that they had been married for over 50 years.

"Cushman, I'm hoping that you can help me understand what this is all about. There's no way that Kara could be remotely associated with anything that contributed to that boy's death. Why is your company accusing her?"

Cushman sat stone-faced until Nathaniel finished. It took him several seconds to collect his thoughts. He looked concernedly at Nathaniel and said, "What do you think I can tell you? You know that the law clearly states that the programmer is responsible for a *taman*'s actions. As an officer of the court, you know I can't discuss an open case with anyone, even if I knew anything, which I don't."

"Come on, Cushman. You're the chief financial officer for Interglobal. Nothing goes on here that you don't know about. Anything you can tell me might help Kara."

"Nathaniel, there's nothing I can tell you that you don't already know," Cushman answered.

"I'll get to the point, Cushman. Something doesn't smell right here. Why is Interglobal accusing my wife? Are they trying to use Kara as a scapegoat? Jasmine always said that you were a good man. You were the closest thing I ever had to a father!"

Sellers stood up abruptly. "Nathaniel, how can you bring Jasmine's name into this? Do you think that reminding me that Jasmine was your aunt will change my mind? I don't want to hear you utter her name again in my presence. This meeting is over!"

Cushman spoke into his office communicator. "Esther, please have George Max come to my office to escort my guests out of the building. Good day, gentlemen."

"Cushman!" Nathaniel pleaded. "You must help me. There's no one else that I can turn to. During the war I did everything you asked of me. I would have traded my life for yours at any time. You owe me."

Cushman motioned for to Nathaniel to walk with him to the door. "I'll get a message to you letting you know where we can meet again. There are eyes and ears everywhere," he whispered, indicating his own office. "Be careful, son."

Chapter 13

Kara could hear cries and screams from the other cells. Foul-mouthed guards yelled back at the women. The whole fetid cellblock reeked.

This is no place for any woman, Kara thought.

Bypassing normal booking procedures, Kara had been taken to the lowest cellblock in the Jefferson Street Holding Facility for Women and placed in a cell alone.

Kara had been jeered and taunted by everyone since she arrived. Her beauty only made her a bigger target because the women were jealous of her and the men resented her because they knew that she was the kind of woman they could never have. By the time she was brought something that they tried to pass off as food, her emotions had run the gamut from confusion, to fear to anger.

"Guard, come here," she demanded angrily. "I demand to see my husband! I'm allowed one call. At least bring me a communicator."

The guard only glared at her through the bars, and then walked off.

Frustrated, Kara sat on the cold bunk. She was starting to shiver. *Nathaniel*, she thought. *Where are you?*

Seconds passed like days. When it was lights-out, the predators began to circle. One guard after another entered Kara's cell. They were like sharks on a feeding frenzy. The first ripped her clothes off and ran his hands over her body as if he were her lover rather than her brutalizer. The others watched. A second guard's foul smell assaulted her even before he did. Finally, the third guard took his turn, hitting her with his closed fist. Kara's eyes and mouth swollen, they left her to lie there, moaning in pain.

"Want another phone call, Princess?" The first guard laughed as he left her cell.

The next day, Kara was brought before the magistrate to face the charges brought against her. In spite of the indignities she had suffered the night before, she squared her shoulders and stood ramrod straight. She stared back at the magistrate as he read the charges against her. Unaware of her night of torture, he misinterpreted what he saw on her face to be defiance--to be proof that she was the cold-blooded killer they said she was rather than evidence of the inner strength that had allowed her this display of dignity.

"Kara Lamrock, you will be held in this facility until a trial date is set by the Manager of Court Cases. At that time, you will be transferred to a Maricopa Courthouse holding cell to stand trial for first-degree murder. Do you have anything to say?"

Kara tried to form words to communicate a plea for help, but the only sound that she could pass through her bruised lips was one slurred word that she repeated over and over, "Nathaniel."

Chapter 14

Just off Interstate 10, about twenty miles west of the old nuclear generating station, Abacus Publications sat among a dozen other rundown buildings, each one seedier than the next. Gray paint was peeling from every wall, and vehicles obviously past their prime sat at the building's open truck bays.

Digger Rooney entered the building by the main door. A bored, gum-chewing receptionist was filing her nails at the rickety front counter. She answered the switchboard with a yawn, "Abacus Publications, home of *Galaxy Gossip*. Please hold."

She nodded to Digger as he walked briskly past the counter to a door located at the back of the lobby. The door looked like it was about to fall off its hinges. Behind the door, Digger's office sat amid cubicles filled with agents posing as reporters busily writing their less-than-truthful articles for the scandal sheet. In fact, these "reporters" could easily physically repel anyone who attempted to enter the facility.

Digger placed his hand on a glass plate that sat on top of his desk. The back wall of the office opened, revealing an elevator. Once again, Digger placed his palm on a plate next to the elevator. The door opened and Digger stepped in. The door closed behind him, and the elevator descended four floors to the Internals' Phoenix branch office.

Digger flopped, exhausted, into his chair and said, "Messages."

The perturbed voice of his female *taman* assistant came from his computer speaker. "These messages came in while you were out having fun at Space Station Alpha 33, leaving me here to do your reports. There are to-dos, can't-waits and must-sees."

Digger turned off the recording and spoke into his communicator, "Marty, please come in here and give me the fifty thousand foot level of these messages."

Marty was a well-organized artificial unit with a memory like super glue. To her, details were like food. She digested them the way most people did a good meal. Her chassis was short and appeared slightly overweight. She had hazel eyes and nondescript light brown hair pulled back severely into a bun at the back of her head. Marty walked up to Digger's desk and started reciting the list to him without even a hello.

"One: All personal passwords must be changed by 12:00 hours today or security will revoke system access. Two: The Quallou analysis you requested has been loaded onto your drive in the common access area."

"Anything else important?"

"That about covers it."

"Great. Now I want you to do something for me."

"Sure, like I'm not busy".

"This is an emergency. Get me everything on the Kara Lamrock case. I want the information in my computer before you go home tonight. Clear?"

"I'm on it."

The next time Digger looked up, Marty was standing there, looking thoughtful.

Digger looked at the screen and began scrolling through what seemed a myriad of binary information.

"Marty, it will take me forever to get through this. Just tell me what you found."

"Okay, first, there is Interglobal's public security system's digitized recording of the boy's termination with something quite unusual on the digital record. Second, several interesting recordings at Interglobal's headquarters. Third, more recordings at Interglobal's headquarters--nothing important. Fourth, system modification programming entries."

Agent Rooney looked up at Marty. "Details, please."

"Here you see a copy of the digital record of the boy's termination. There is nothing really out of the ordinary that I could see at first. A destructor *taman* in military tracking and destructor mode locates target, validates target, and terminates target. No abnormalities with this sequence of events, except for the fact that no *taman* unit has been placed in destructor mode for over 55 years. This was a special modification job. According to the lab's report, the *taman* unit you ran into at Sky Harbor was probably this same, specially modified unit. The lab found a partial logo we tracked down to the Interglobal Corporation.

"Now, look again at this display. If you look closely, you will see something quite unusual. Stop. Right there. The destructor unit scans the boy's arm. Notice the *taman* unit's image. It's light blue-cold just like any *taman* would register on video. Now, look at the boy's image. It's red-hot. At first, I thought that maybe the boy might have been another *taman* unit, but he was definitely human. I didn't know what the *taman* unit was looking for so I decided to run the record through the lab's enhanced imaging infrared identification system. I zoomed in on the identification label beneath the skin on the boy's forearm. Now this part gets strange. The boy's ID number doesn't match any identification sequence established by all known sources synchronized to the World Clock Tracking system. According to Council records, this boy was never born, and the identification tag is a forgery. As far as the World Clock knows, the boy never existed."

"Marty, how could that be?" Digger asked, flabbergasted by the implications.

"Since the boy registered red on the scan, and that is the only information that is available, I believe that he was human. The World Clock registers all humans, yet the boy was not registered. The only conclusion is that the boy must have been an illegal clone."

Startled, Digger looked up at Marty. "Do you know what this means? Cloning is an expensive and complex process that requires an enormous amount of scientific resources, not to mention significant financing. Someone with access to these resources has violated the Council's sanctions against clones. Since clones are not registered, the World Clock will not track their existence. If your conclusions are correct, then the Council cannot track and manage all human life on this planet."

Marty looked worried. "It gets worse."

"I was able to tap into Interglobal's security system's digital backup. Knowing that most companies save history on digitized disk servers, I decided to search all security records by the keyword 'Lamrock.' Most of the information yielded no peculiarities, except for this one excerpt."

Marty leaned over Digger to reach his computer keypad and selected an entry marked, "July 3, 2195. 15:14:36 Audio record, Interglobal." The rest of the description had been erased.

"It looks to me like someone was in the process of deleting this entry. They had already scrambled the voice patterns, so I can't tell who is speaking. Also, they made it part way through the data tag and some of the conversation, but I got a little of it before they deleted the entire record. Listen to this:"

"There was a malfunction in the destructor's central decision system. It's all been taken care of. The taman unit has already been modified. The bug has been corrected."

"And you think that makes everything all right? Not only were there sixteen witnesses in the plaza, every second leading up to the

boy's death is on surveillance footage. By tonight, every citizen will be an eyewitness to the murder."

"I have marketing working on an explanation to be distributed over the news media, but, you're right. There will no doubt be a formal investigation. In fact, I've already headed it off. I recalled one of our lead programmers in the Artificial Intelligence Division from another assignment. We will claim that she modified the unit without The Company's knowledge. The Artificial Intelligence programmer, a woman by the name of Kara Lamrock, will be blamed. I was hoping that perhaps it would appear as if the unit had turned on her, but as of the last communication I received, that idea didn't work out. What a shame! That would have ended it.

"All is not lost. The boy was destroyed and no one knows who he was or where he came from. The unit did as he was instructed. Unfortunately, his discretion chip malfunctioned. It must have reverted back to its original version. That was my fault, sir. When you told me it was a rush job, I cut a few corners in the rebuild sequence to save time."

The recording abruptly stopped. "This is all I could get before the record was deleted."

"I can't believe what I'm listening to. Marty, isn't there some way that you can make out who's having the conversation?"

"Sorry. No reverse reference to my keyword search within this segment. However, I was able to check their employee roster to see who is in charge of Interglobal Security. The Security Chief's name is Mr. Simon Brader. He may have some idea of who was speaking."

"That's good work, Marty. Have you got anything else?"

"More digital records recorded at Interglobal but nothing relevant, except this other one."

Again, Marty reached over to Digger's keypad and brought up a record titled, "System modification programming entries, July 2, 2195. 13:16:45."

"This file has obviously been doctored and I'll show you why. This is a close up shot of Kara Lamrock's hands supposedly keying in 'SN: 493A0744,' which is displayed on her monitor. The next thing she types in is 'OPEN FILE, BEHAVIOR AYX19.' She is supposedly opening the *taman* unit's memory bank that controls its behavior module. Now she keys in the following command: 'REPLACE FILE Z:\BEHAVIOR AYX19 with Z:\BEHAVIOR FILE DESTROYER.'"

"Marty, this is really damning evidence. Why would Kara do such a thing?"

"I don't believe that this record is real. First, the primary key required by law to identify all *taman* units is a highly kept secret. It is made up of both the Model and SN number. Whoever attempted to modify this record was not aware of how the system works. Their policy is that anytime a system modification is made, no record is made that would openly display the model and serial number of the *taman* unit. The model and serial number entries are always keyed under a hood, shielding them from all cameras. This is the law, and it assures *taman* unit security integrity. Do you want me to show you their security manual?"

"That won't be necessary, Marty."

Marty continued with her report. "These aren't human hands you see keying in data. They emit no infrared heat. This is a *taman* unit that is keying in the entries."

"You truly are the best."

"I had a great teacher." For the first time that day, Marty smiled at Agent Rooney.

While Marty went back to see what else she could find, Digger made a mental list of questions that he knew had to be answered: *What could be so important that someone would risk reconfiguring a taman to a destructor unit? Who was having the conversation on the digital record that Marty found? Who doctored the records framing Kara?*

The question of why the boy's family had not come forward had been answered already: *Clones don't have families.*

Digger had to do something.

His office suddenly felt like a dungeon. He was not helping Kara, and he was becoming more and more worried about her as each minute passed. Pulling on his jacket he headed off to the women's detention center. He told himself that if he didn't get some answers fast, he'd make sure that someone would be eating his meals through a straw.

KATHLEEN PAPAJOHN

Chapter 15

"Nathaniel, this is Digger. I just found out that Kara will be going to trial in two days. I've also found out that someone at Interglobal doctored records to make it appear as if Kara modified the *taman*."

"What? Two days! Have you seen her? Is she all right? What do you mean someone 'doctored records'?"

"Look Nathaniel, I can't talk about it right now. I haven't been able to communicate with her. She's being held in the Women's Detention Facility all right, but in a remote cell isolated from the other detainees."

"Why is she being isolated? I need to get to her as soon as possible. I need to find out what she knows about all of this if I'm going to be able to represent her."

"Nathaniel, they won't let you see her."

"They can't keep me away from her. Not only am I her husband, I'm also her lawyer."

"They can and will keep you away from her. Remember those old topographical maps that we used in the military? Do you still have them?"

"No, I don't think so. Kara threw out most of those old relics. She thinks they caused my flashbacks, so she got rid of them."

It's good to hear that I'm not the only one who hasn't had a good night's sleep in years.

"Nathaniel, I still have copies of the old maps. I'm sending you a flash copy of some of them. Download the files into Solis's memory and then delete it from your flash memory immediately."

After a few seconds, Digger asked, "Do you have them now?"

"I've got them Digger." Nathaniel turned to Solis, who nodded at him. "They've been downloaded and deleted. Now what?"

"You have to assume that our communicators are not secure. I'm going to scramble the next communication I send. Solis can interpret it for you. The key to translate the code is part of the information that you just loaded into his memory."

Nathaniel looked at Solis who appeared to be concentrating hard. Solis picked up a pen and wrote down, "Go to Grid 14, sector 22, Delta site Echo. Meet me there at 1:00 A.M. tomorrow morning. Enter from the rear security gate on the southeast side of the cooling tower. Bring Solis and make sure no one follows you."

"What's going on here Digger? You're not telling me everything."

Once more, Solis's pen flew over the paper. "I've seen surveillance records of Kara that have obviously been falsified. Just meet me at those coordinates tomorrow at 1:00 A.M. If I'm not there, you'll have to proceed alone because I will either be dead or incarcerated. It's imperative that when you get there, you and Solis go directly to the control room vault located on the third floor. Inside, you'll find a cache of weapons that I've been stockpiling for some time. In the warehouse, there's a fully-functional destructor battlewagon that only Solis or another dash-three *taman* unit can operate. I know that you remember those systems. They caused us more casualties than either of us wants to remember."

"I'll be there," Nathaniel said. "Solis will be with me."

Nathaniel had no sooner hung up the communicator than it buzzed again. "Hello, Nathaniel, this is Cushman Sellers. Can you meet me for a cup of coffee, alone?"

Nathaniel wanted to trust Cushman. He agreed to the meeting, but he would not go alone. Solis would be with him.

Nathaniel and Solis arrived at the diner before Cushman. The North Central Diner was a seedy establishment that served food, drinks, and just about anything anyone's imagination could conjure up. It was the only all-night diner still operating in downtown Phoenix. The establishment catered to society's lower elements. It was frequented by older-model female *taman* units working as ladies of the night.

The smoke-filled room was packed, and retro music blared from the ancient speakers that lined the grimy walls. Nathaniel smirked inwardly as he watched a pickpocket try to lift Solis's wallet as he and Solis pushed their way through the unruly crowd to the only open table.

Without turning around, Solis grabbed the man's testicles, causing them to heat up as if they were no more than a cup of morning coffee. The pickpocket moaned in pain, but no one could hear him over the deafening music. Slowly, Solis turned around to the thief. He grabbed the man's hand and held it tightly, crushing its bones and then shaking it as if he were greeting an old friend.

"Hello, it's so nice to see you again." Solis smiled and gripped the man's injured hand even harder. In agony now, the man fell to his knees.

"Oh, let me help you up, sir." Solis plucked his wallet from the man's good hand and placed it back into his own pocket. "Have a nice day."

Solis continued with Nathaniel following him. Everything had happened so fast, Nathaniel knew that no one else had even noticed the exchange between Solis and the pickpocket. Solis didn't say a word as he and Nathaniel approached the cluttered table. Before he sat down, Nathaniel swept his arm across the table, pushing the filthy glasses and overflowing ashtrays to the floor.

"There. That's better."

Nathaniel and Solis didn't have to wait long. Nathaniel saw Cushman, dressed in a leather jacket and jeans, pushing his way through the crowd. As soon as he spotted Solis sitting with Nathaniel, Cushman turned and began heading back through the crowd. Nathaniel darted after him and grabbed his arm before he could reach the door.

"I told you to come alone, Nathaniel! I knew I should have never tried to help you, or for that matter, trusted you."

"Cushman, Solis is my protector unit. I trust him with my life."

Cushman stared at Nathaniel as he wrestled with his decision. Finally, he nodded at Nathaniel and followed him back to the table.

"I've prepared a certified statement explaining that the boy's identifying serial number was misread by the clock's scanning mechanism. That's why the clock's population count did not decrease when the boy died. The malfunction has since been corrected. Present this signed report to Judge Graph and the Nualas will receive their childbearing permit. That's one thing that I can take care of for you, Nathaniel."

Startled, Nathaniel just looked at Cushman. "What happened, Cushman? You don't really expect me to buy the old 'clock malfunction' story, do you? And why are you dressed like that? Whom are you hiding from?"

Cushman started to deny any fabrication, when Nathaniel interrupted him. "I don't care about the clock. I want to know why Interglobal is framing my wife."

Cushman leaned over to Nathaniel and said in a whisper, "I did find documentation, but it won't help Kara. In fact, it's a record of her actually modifying a unit. It shows her loading the destructor sequence into a common worker unit's memory bank."

"That's a lie! I know someone who has seen surveillance records that have been altered. Why would someone at Interglobal falsify records about my wife? Answer that for me!" Nathaniel's voice was so loud that some of the diners heard him over the blare of the music and turned to stare.

Solis put his hand on Nathaniel's arm to calm him down.

Nathaniel looked at Cushman and said quietly through clenched teeth, "I'll kill you if you have anything to do with this."

Cushman stood up and turned to leave. "Nathaniel, I certainly didn't doctor any surveillance video. I realize that you're upset, but you know that I wouldn't do anything to harm you or Kara. I'll try to find the surveillance records that you say are falsified. I can't make any promises, but if they're at Interglobal, I'll find them."

Nathaniel started to stand, but Cushman waved him back to his seat. He leaned over and put something in Nathaniel's hand. Nathaniel looked down at the proton pistol that Cushman had given him.

"Watch your back. You're in danger. I'll contact you by morning to let you know what I've found," Cushman said and quickly walked away through the crowd.

Just then, Solis looked at Nathaniel and nodded his head toward three husky uniformed men who had just walked into the diner. He whispered in Nathaniel's ear, "Detention guards, from the women's facility."

Nathaniel shrugged. "They have no authority outside of the detention center." Still, he watched them in disgust.

The three men pushed other customers out of the way as they headed for the bar. The tallest ordered a drink as his partners laughingly groped the nearest women, not caring whether they were human or *taman*.

There was something about these brutes that made Nathaniel keep watching them. He got up and made his way to the bar. *Maybe they know some information about Kara.*

"Buy you a drink?" Nathaniel asked the short stocky one. Nathaniel could smell the man's bad breath from two feet away.

"We don't drink with pretty boys," the tall one answered.

"Wait," said Bad Breath. "We're celebrating. Anyone with a barter credit can buy us a drink."

Nathaniel smiled menacingly. "What are you celebrating?"

Bad Breath looked at his friends and smiled, showing his rotting teeth. "We've been fondling a pretty good piece of ass. What's even better, the bitch actually likes it. I bet her wimp of a husband could never turn her on the way real men like us do."

"And just who are you talking about?" Nathaniel asked.

Of course, he didn't believe that these ruffians could get any woman, but he let them brag. Already, he was looking forward to the beating he was going to give these blowhards. That should release some of the tension that Nathaniel felt building inside him.

Unfortunately for him, this particular thug did not know when to shut up. He smiled his sickening smile and said, "That bitch murderess that they brought in yesterday, that's who. She might have been the best piece of tail we've ever had, but she packs a whale of a punch."

One of the other guards laughed and nodded his head at Bad Breath's black eye.

Bad Breath rubbed his swollen cheek and said, "Yeah, but she paid the price. Her eye doesn't look any better than mine."

Nathaniel held his breath. White-hot rage washed over him. Only his military discipline kept him from killing the brutes on the spot. Solis had just come up beside him and could feel the heat coming off Nathaniel's body from a foot away.

"Nathaniel, we must get going if we're going to meet Digger on time," he whispered.

Nathaniel shook off Solis's hand and glared at him. Without a word, he burst out the door. Puzzled, Solis followed Nathaniel, who led him to the alley beside the diner, where the empty Dash car was stored for the night.

After twenty minutes, the three unruly bullies emerged, drunk and staggering into the dark moonless night.

"Hey look, there's the Dash. Let's get on and have some fun with the driver."

The lights inside the Dash were off, but there was no "Out of Service" sign displayed, so they boldly walked up to the Dash's door.

"Hey, there's someone hiding in there."

One of the men hollered, "Come out of there, or we're coming in to kick your ass."

The only response was the rustle of someone moving even further back into the Dash's dark interior.

The taller bully said, "I'll bet it's that good looking blond that I see tooling around in this thing as if she thinks she's the queen of the May."

Bad Breath sneered, "Come out of there, you bitch. We've got something for you." He groped himself and laughed.

A proton blast lit up the night. It hit one of the men dead center. There was a second blast, and the tall guard exploded. The molten metal that came from the weapon burned into both of the guards' torsos. Blood splattered all over the Dash's windows. The guards were dead before they hit the pavement. The third guard, Bad Breath, tried to run back into the diner when a laser beam cut across his pant leg and deep into his left calf. He screamed, grabbed his leg in pain and fell to the pavement.

A solitary figure emerged from the Dash. The man held a shiny titanium, sixty-caliber hand-held proton pistol with a laser barrel and a guided tracking sight. The figure stood over the detention guard and pointed the weapon directly at his groin.

The assassin looked down. "It's your turn to moan like a little girl."

The blast hit the guard directly between his legs. He didn't have time to moan. He was dead before he even realized what was happening to him.

The Population Clock clicked down by three.

Another figure emerged from the Dash and together, the two men melted away into the night, leaving the smell of burning flesh behind them.

Chapter 16

Marty had been at work for over 16 hours and needed regeneration if she were to put in a full day the next day. *Anything for tamen automatically gets to be last on Interglobal's 'to-do' list. They've been promising a battery that never needs recharging for decades*, she thought.

The street where Marty lived was dark and full of shadows as she made her way back to her living pod. It was a moonless night and the streetlights were out. Marty had lived alone since her reprogramming. She had only one companion. It was her TMP (Totally Manufactured Pet: Animal), a white-haired miniature terrier canine unit that she had named Bunker. Every evening, when Marty got home from work, she would take her pet for a late night stroll to the park, just the same way that her human neighbors walked their dogs.

It was about 12:10 A.M. when she opened the door to her living pod. Bunker was seated on the sofa with his leash in his mouth. He was waiting patiently for Marty to come home and take him for his walk. The park had always been a safe place. At least every one thought it was safe until the young boy was murdered right in front of a crowd of people.

Marty patted Bunker and then went into her bedroom to change into her jogging suit and walking shoes. Bunker watched her every move. "Okay, Bunker, it's time to go."

Bunker bounced up and down and squealed with joy. He stopped to let Marty attach his leash to his collar, even though he had no intention of running away. When she was done, the *tapet* immediately raced to the door, pulling Marty behind him.

As they exited the pod, Marty looked around. *Strange*, she thought. *There isn't a soul on the street.*

It was darker than usual, and Marty felt uncharacteristically uncomfortable. She really didn't want to go for the walk, but she didn't want to disappoint Bunker. Marty laughed at herself and asked Bunker, "Will you protect me?"

Bunker looked up at Marty and turned his head slightly as if trying to make out what she had just said. He turned and headed for the park as fast as he could. Marty laughed again, engaged the retractable wheels on her walking shoes and allowed Bunker to pull her along after him.

When they got to the park, Marty reached down, removed Bunker's leash and retracted her sport shoes' wheels. Bunker headed for the grass and began rolling over and over. All of a sudden, Marty sensed that they were not alone. She thought that she'd seen movement in the shadows over by the park benches up ahead. Marty's first instinct was to run, but she wouldn't leave Bunker.

"Whoever is there, I have a guard dog trained to kill at my command! Bunker, come!" she commanded.

The shadow took shape and began moving towards her. She started walking slowly backward until she found herself backed up against a large tree. She knew something very bad was about to happen.

"Bunker, help me! Attack!" Bunker kept rolling in the grass as if he were at a picnic. Marty braced herself.

She heard a voice behind her. "Marty, is that you?"

"Digger!" Marty's relief was evident. She looked back toward the park bench where she had seen the shadow, but it was no longer there.

Had it ever been there at all?

Too proud to let Digger see that she was afraid, Marty turned and called, "Bunker, come here."

This time Bunker came immediately and began sounding off. Digger laughed as Bunker lapped him and rolled over and over in the grass.

Trying to hide her shaking voice Marty said, "Bad dog, Bunker! You must come when I call you!"

"Digger, what are you doing here? You scared me half to death. Some guard dog you are, Bunker."

Unconcerned, Bunker continued to roll over in the grass. Marty walked over to Bunker, picked him up and shut down his power supply. "I should trade you in for a new model." Bunker looked frozen in time.

"Marty, what happened to the files that you downloaded?"

"What do you mean, what happened to the files? I loaded them onto your hard drive just like you asked me to do. I found some more information after you left and I put that into your computer also."

"Marty, there's no information on my hard drive. Someone must have gotten to the files and erased them. Can you remember anything?"

"How about if I can remember everything, Digger?"

Digger smiled and handed Marty his handheld digital stick. "Dictate everything you remember. Please try to hurry, Marty. You can come with me. I've got to get across town to another meeting. You can get this all recorded on the way there. This could mean life or death for someone very close to me."

Chapter 17

Solis and Nathaniel strapped themselves into their cylinders and waited for the countdown. Solis keyed their point of disembarkation into the Bullet Tram's destination grid. It would place them less than half a mile from their final destination, approximately 90 miles away.

A G-force deflector protected them from the fast acceleration rate, from zero to the tram's cruising speed of 250 miles per hour. The trip would take 38 minutes. This would give them plenty of time to walk from the drop-off station to the meeting place. Nathaniel looked down at his watch. It was 12:15 A.M.

As they stepped out of their cylinders, Nathaniel and Solis found themselves in the middle of the desert. This was the last stop in the Bullet Tram tunnel system. It had been built to accommodate power plant workers but had remained largely unused since the plant was decommissioned. The remote drop off station was deserted, and there was no sign of civilization for miles in any direction. Adding to Nathaniel's sense of other-worldliness, there was no moon and Nathaniel had to put on his night-vision goggles to see the power plant.

"Even with these damn goggles, I can't see a thing," Nathaniel said.

"Stay close behind me, Nathaniel," Solis said. Nathaniel knew that Solis could see clearly, day or night, because Kara had fitted him with the latest infrared *taman* sight technology.

Nathaniel had just fallen in line behind Solis when he was startled by a rattling sound to his left.

"What's that?"

Solis turned in time to see a rattlesnake, coiled and ready to strike. "It's only a rattlesnake," he answered. Solis moved Nathaniel aside and knelt down by the reptile. The rattler coiled back and then struck at Solis. Solis's reflexes were so fast, he caught the snake in mid-air. Looking at the snake with curiosity, Solis carried it about 15 yards and released it back into the desert.

When he returned to Nathaniel, he said, "This is the reptile's home. He is only defending his small area. We are the intruders here and must respect his environment."

Nathaniel was puzzled. Even though Nathaniel knew it was not possible, Solis seemed to understand what the snake was feeling. *Taman* units did not understand things such as feelings. Solis was becoming unlike any *taman* unit that Nathaniel had ever seen before. He was acting almost human. Almost.

When Solis and Nathaniel got to the site it was 12:56 A.M.-- four minutes ahead of schedule. Nathaniel decided to wait until exactly 1:00 A.M. before entering the facility. He noticed that there were bright yellow "Radioactive" warning signs posted everywhere.

Not a very healthy place to be, he thought.

Like so many other ancient nuclear plants, the utility had simply put a fence around the plant and closed it down when it had outlived its purpose.

Nathaniel saw and heard nothing, but Solis indicated that he saw a vehicle with no headlights approaching the station from the west and nudged Nathaniel. Two figures got out of the vehicle and walked to the station's doorway.

"Digger, is that you?"

"Where are you Nathaniel? I can't see you."

Nathaniel and Solis moved out from the shadows. Digger told them that Marty had accompanied him. He led the way to the freight elevator. When he turned on an old lamp, the sudden illumination showed just how old and dirty the station was. The tiny band entered the elevator. Digger shut the sliding door and hit three.

When they reached the third floor, Digger opened the door and led them into an apartment that was in stark contrast to the station's exterior. It was so clean, it looked almost sterile. Digger had converted the third-floor control room into a living pod. The apartment was complete with full living quarters, including a medical room and a kitchen.

As soon as Digger entered, the lights in the main room came on. Two walls were lined with weapons and ammunition. The third wall was covered with hologram monitors and communication equipment. The final wall contained a steel door that led to a gigantic vault.

Nathaniel was not surprised that Digger had this hideaway. Digger had never been one to leave anything to chance. Digger showed them a room filled with medical supplies, food, and water. He explained that the walls were eight feet thick, with two inch reinforced rebar imbedded every twelve inches on all sides of the apartment. The one-way windows were made of bulletproof glass. This was the safe house he had been secretly stockpiling over the years, ever since he had been recruited into the Internals.

From the astonished look on Marty's face, Nathaniel knew that she was seeing Digger's safe house for the first time.

"Digger, what are you getting me into? Does anyone at the office know about this?" she asked.

"Marty, you can't tell anyone anything about what you see here. Someone inside the Internals has been compromised. How else did the information you put into my computer disappear?"

"You got it, boss," Marty answered without hesitation. "But, where did you get all this?"

"When the Council ordered all old ordinance destroyed, I quietly liberated some weaponry that I knew wouldn't be missed, especially since so much had been destroyed toward the end of the war without being inventoried."

Digger took them downstairs and over to a large bay door. He keyed a combination into a keypad, and a foot-thick steel door groaned opened to reveal another service elevator. They took the elevator to a first-floor warehouse. There, suspended by mini cranes, was a fully loaded destructor battlewagon ready for action. The twelve-foot-high suit, weighing over three tons, was developed toward the end of the last war for use solely by destructor *taman* units.

Digger showed the suit off. "The suit is made with the strongest material known to man and incorporates an IMLS, or Intelligent Missile Launch System, a Round Gun, and a visual analyzer. This last toy automatically adjusts its ordinance to deliver the perfect combination of firepower to destroy any target, whether human, *taman,* or structural. There's also a battle evaluator that anticipates the enemy's movements, creates a red zone, then destroys everything within that zone. In addition, the suit allows its *taman* operator to relocate by increasing the speed that he can run to 68 miles per hour."

Nathaniel had been silent ever since Digger led them into the elevator. "They're torturing Kara," he blurted out as soon as he could get Digger alone.

Digger paled. "How do you know that?"

Nathaniel had seen Digger in some very dicey situations, but he never saw him so rattled that his voice broke, like it was doing now. The desperation that Nathaniel heard in Digger's voice made his own heart race even faster.

Nathaniel cleared his throat before he spoke. He needed a few seconds before he could make himself tell Digger, make himself say the words that described Kara's current desperate situation. "I ran across some of the bastards that were doing it. Believe me. They won't be hurting anyone else. But we need to get her out *tonight*! We need to get her out *right now*!"

Digger was visibly shaken, but his jaw was set in determination. "Nathaniel, I wish there was something that we could do, but there's no way to get to Kara tonight. Tomorrow they plan to transfer her to the courthouse. Once she's at the courthouse, there will be so much media coverage, no one will be able to touch her. I've already seen Interglobal documents that prove her innocence. We need the originals to use as evidence in court. Marty and I plan on breaking into Interglobal tonight."

Nathaniel stopped him. "Solis and I have already been to Interglobal's headquarters. I've had two meetings with Cushman Sellers. I told him that a friend of mine had seen surveillance records of Kara that had obviously been falsified. He's promised to search Interglobal's records and get the originals to me. He'll have a much better chance of locating the records than you and Marty. Cushman knows the company inside and out. Besides, we can't take the chance that you might be caught. That would compromise you and prevent you from helping Kara. Kara needs both of us right now."

"Okay, we'll have to act as if everything is normal. You continue representing your clients as usual, but be sure to submit a formal application to serve as Kara's counsel. They'll use any technicality they can come up with to keep you away from her. If Cushman can find the originals of the records that I saw, the documentation will certainly exonerate her. Once you get your hands on it, we can free Kara."

Nathaniel was reluctant to leave Kara in jail. He would die to get her out.

Digger could read his mind. "Think about it, Nathaniel. You said that you took care of her tormentors. No one is hurting her right now."

Digger paused as his stomach churned when he thought about Kara being tortured. He took a deep breath. "Our best chance to get her back alive is to prove that she's innocent. You know I'm right. Tell him, Solis!"

Solis looked at Nathaniel a long time before he finally nodded in agreement.

Chapter 18

Nathaniel's heart skipped a beat when he opened his door and saw that his in-mailbox was illuminated. A flash-mail from Judge Graph was waiting. "Received documentation re: Clock from C. Sellers. All is in order. Nuala hearing rescheduled for July 6, 2195 at 07:00 hours. ID: AZ2765."

It looks like Cushman was at least true to his word about the permit, Nathaniel thought.

As soon as Nathaniel finished reading the flash mail he dialed the Nualas. Juan answered on the first ring.

Although exhausted and preoccupied with Kara's safety, Nathaniel was still a professional who cared deeply about the interests of his clients. "Juan, this is Nathaniel Lamrock. I'm sorry to be calling you so early this morning. Can you and your wife meet me at the courthouse at 06:30? Your hearing has been rescheduled for 07:00."

At precisely 7:00 A.M. Nathaniel stood beside the Nualas and watched as a holographic image of Judge Graph filled the main screen.

The judge spoke. "I have your petition before me Counselor. Please proceed."

Disheveled and obviously preoccupied with something else, Nathaniel stepped forward and spoke to the judge.

"Your Honor, the court has been provided with Interglobal's certified explanation for the Clock's malfunction. Do the findings meet with the courts approval?"

Judge Graph responded, "The paperwork is all in order. Please proceed with your petition."

Nathaniel was finding it difficult to concentrate. Images of Kara, alone in a dark cell, haunted his thoughts. He forced himself to focus on the case at hand.

"Your Honor, let the record show that Juan and Sha Nuala have been legal, law abiding life partners for forty-three years. They are good citizens, loyal to the governing hierarchy. There is nothing criminal in either of their backgrounds. In accordance with my duty as their Counsel, I hereby swear to the integrity of my clients and petition the court to grant them a permit to bear a natural human child in accordance with global law GL4752."

Nathaniel recited his presentation by rote. After watching Nathaniel's disappointing performance, Juan Nuala didn't believe that there was a ghost of a chance that their petition would be approved.

Judge Graph shuffled the documents before him and indicated that he was ready to rule. Nathaniel turned and motioned for the Nualas to stand at his side.

Judge Graph finally spoke, "Attorney Lamrock, Mr. and Mrs. Nuala, I hereby approve your petition for a Child Bearing Permit. May God bless you both and grant your family health and happiness. Clerk, please see to it that a permit is drawn up and sent to me for signature before the end of today."

The joy on Sha Nuala's face said it all. She hugged Nathaniel. "How can we ever thank you? God has sent you to us. If there is ever anything, anything at all that we can do for you, we will do it."

Juan got Nathaniel in a bear hug as soon as Sha released him. "You have my word, too. My life is yours from this day forward."

KATHLEEN PAPAJOHN

Chapter 19

The Manager of Court Cases was startled out of a deep sleep when his private communicator buzzed. *Who the hell could be calling me at 05:00?* He leaned over and was about to shut off the annoying sound when he saw the Interglobal caller ID. No one ignored a call from Interglobal.

"Hello, Cilio. This is Malcolm Godfrey. How have you been? How's your reappointment coming along?" Malcolm's voice dripped pure honey.

Cilio rubbed the sleep from his eyes and turned on the nightstand light. "Things are going well," he stammered. Cilio couldn't understand why the CEO of Interglobal would be calling him since Cilio was so low down the judicial totem pole. He regained his composure and said, "Thank you for Interglobal's large contribution, Mr. Godfrey."

When Malcolm didn't answer, Cilio continued, "Mr. Godfrey, the hour is very early. Is there something that I can do for you?"

"Well, since you mention it, I do need a small favor."

Cilio knew that without Godfrey's generosity, his reappointment was far from assured. "Of course, Mr. Godfrey, just name it."

"I would appreciate it if you would assign Judge Langston to the Kara Lamrock case. You're an intelligent person, so you understand how important this case is to Interglobal and to me personally, don't you?"

"Mr. Godfrey, I'm sure that you are aware that judges are assigned to cases randomly. If anyone ever thought that I manipulated the system to assign a particular judge to a specific case, I would be immediately dismissed. Criminal charges could even be brought against me."

"Come now, Cilio. Do you think that I would allow that to happen to a friend of mine? By the way, today I am having lunch with the president of the governing council. Should I put in a good word for you?"

Cilio was well aware that Godfrey's offer was, in actuality, a veiled threat. He knew that Malcolm would never consider someone of Cilio's lowly status to be a friend of his. Still, if he could gain Malcolm's friendship by doing him this favor, Cilio knew that his future would be assured. On the other hand, if he didn't comply with his request, Godfrey would make sure that Cilio would not be reappointed. Cilio was no genius, but he didn't take more than a second to make up his mind.

"Of course, Mr. Godfrey, I'll be happy to see to it that Judge Langston is assigned to the Lamrock trial."

"That makes me very happy, Cilio. Oh, one more thing. The trial must begin in two days. No sense letting something like this drag out."

Cilio took a deep breath. "Two days! That's unheard of in a capital case."

The silence on Malcolm's end was palpable.

"All right. Let me check the calendar." There was a drug case scheduled to begin on Monday, but Cilio could reshuffle the docket to accommodate Malcolm's request. He made a note on his calendar. "The Lamrock trial will begin on July 8th. Is there anything else?" Cilio asked resignedly.

"Only one thing. Nathaniel Lamrock cannot be allowed to represent his wife. The court needs to appoint counsel for her. I believe that this would be a good chance for one of the newer barristers to get some experience."

Cilio was almost in tears. This would be the ruin of him. What little integrity he had left was evaporating like a lone raindrop falling on the Sonoran Desert. "Of course, Mr. Godfrey, I understand."

"I knew I could count on you, Cilio."

KATHLEEN PAPAJOHN

Chapter 20

By mid-afternoon, Trey Thrasher, along with every other news reporter in the Western Zone, was broadcasting that the trial of Kara Lamrock, the Patriot Park Murderess, would begin in two days. After fifty years of covering neighborhood news stories, Trey was still a local reporter. He longed to cover the national and international scene. This story could be his big chance to be spotted by one of the large national news chains.

On July eighth, the first day of trial, Trey stood with the mob of other reporters on the Maricopa Courthouse steps. He looked from face to face and knew that the other reporters had the same doubts that he did. *How could everything needed for a case of this magnitude be made ready in such a short time?*

Unable to accommodate this throng of reporters and paparazzi, the Manager of Court Cases decided that all but one of the reporters would have to leave. Because of space considerations, only the local news agency would be allowed in the courtroom. Trey Thrasher felt like his lottery number had been drawn when he learned that his would be the reports that would be instantly transmitted to the other reporters that hung around the front of the courthouse, and from there, they would be broadcast around the globe.

Trey Thrasher was ready for his debut on the national stage. His face was appropriately somber as he and his crew stationed themselves right outside the courthouse door. The assistant producer was standing next to their cameraman and intently watching Trey.

"Go to live feed. Trey, you begin in 3, 2, 1 . . ."

"This is Trey Thrasher reporting live from the Maricopa Courthouse in downtown Phoenix. As you can see behind me, hundreds of people have filled the courtroom, and others are waiting in line all the way to the outside stairs trying to get a glimpse of the infamous Kara Lamrock, the 'Patriot Park Murderess.' Previously, Lamrock was a lead programmer in the Artificial Intelligence Division for Interglobal, where she allegedly modified the *taman* unit that killed a young boy in the plaza just west of Patriot Park. She is the only person indicted for this bizarre execution-style slaying. The footage we are about to show is pretty graphic, so if you have any small children, you may want them to leave the room."

Although it had been broadcast almost continually since the boy was killed, Trey Thrasher ran the video of the events leading up to the boy's murder once again.

"This is the child, with outstretched arms pleading for help from someone in the crowd. Look closely, as a large man moves forward, smiles, then brutally vaporizes the boy."

The video ended, and Trey Thrasher deliberately made his face into a mask of phony sincerity as he reported the cover story that had been planted by Interglobal security.

"Later that day, Interglobal security forces cornered, captured, and destroyed the *taman* unit responsible for this murder."

Trey used all of his acting ability to look as though he were on the verge of tears. He shook his head sadly and said, "That poor kid never had a chance."

In his own mind, Trey was picturing the head of the national news agency watching his stunning performance, and planning how to get rid of their current head broadcaster in order to offer Trey the anchor chair for the national evening news.

Thrasher pretended to struggle to get his emotions under control and then continued. "It is alleged that Kara Lamrock purposely modified the *taman* unit by loading a destruction sequence into the unit's memory. Last night, I recorded this conversation with Mr. Simon Brader, Chief of Security for Interglobal."

The taped record of Brader's serious face filled the screen. "It is still unknown what motivated her to do such an extreme act. My guess is that this is just a gruesome game that she engaged in to discredit Interglobal. I believe that she wanted to embarrass The Company because we were investigating her for misuse of corporate funds. There is no other reasonable explanation.

"Interglobal has taken every step to ensure that something like this can never happen again. All old destructor programs have been erased, and the backups have been destroyed."

Trey Thrasher's face returned to the screen. "Stay tuned as this reporter will bring you exclusive coverage of the events as they unfold in the courthouse behind me."

Nathaniel arrived at the courthouse just as Thrasher was signing off. Reporters mobbed Nathaniel, pushing him so that he had to fight for each forward step. He felt a sharp pain in the back of his head where a reporter had deliberately smashed a microphone against his skull. Nathaniel was completely surrounded but kept moving forward. He felt the wave of reporters suffocating him. Microphones were stuck in his face making it even harder for him to breathe.

"Why did she do it?" a reporter yelled. "Did she have help?" yelled another. "Did you help her?" yelled still another. Onlookers that could not get into the courthouse held signs that read "Baby Killer" and "Fry the Bitch."

Solis moved in front of Nathaniel to block the sea of reporters and photographers trying to get at him. The crowd was in a frenzy, but Solis made sure that Nathaniel got into the courthouse.

A security guard stopped Solis at the security gate. "I'm sorry, but *taman* units are not permitted in the courthouse as long as the trial is in session."

"What?" Nathaniel erupted. "This is unheard of! I'm the defendant's lawyer, and this is my assistant. I will not stand for this."

Solis laid his hand on Nathaniel's arm. "Nathaniel, we do not need trouble right now. Your first and only job is to take care of Miss Kara. You will not need me. I'll wait here until you return."

Reluctantly, Nathaniel said, "No, Solis. There's no need for you to stand out here all day. Go home. I'll see you there tonight."

Solis nodded, and Nathaniel proceeded through the security gate alone. He looked back at Solis just before he turned down the corridor that led to the courtroom. Nathaniel felt stirrings of fear creeping up his spine.

Expecting to be by himself, Nathaniel was startled by a young man who had followed him into the courtroom and was pulling up a seat beside him at the defense table. Nathaniel was out of patience. "Who do you think you are? This is the defense table, so please take a seat in the gallery."

The young man looked at Nathaniel quizzically. "I'm Kimp Jennings, Mrs. Lamrock's court-appointed attorney. Just who are you?"

Nathaniel thought, *If this were not so absurd, it would be funny.* He looked hard at Kimp and said, "I'll get this straightened out immediately."

Nathaniel was glad that the judge for the trial would not be a hologram. He needed to speak with a live person. Nathaniel found the clerk standing by the door to the judge's chambers.

"I'm Nathaniel Lamrock, attorney for Kara Lamrock. There's been a mistake. Another attorney has been appointed as her counsel. As you can see, that's not necessary, as I will be representing Mrs. Lamrock."

The clerk looked Nathaniel up and down, and then said, "Wait here. I'll check with the judge's assistant."

It seemed like an eternity before the clerk returned. "There's been no mistake. The court has no record of your request to serve as counsel for Mrs. Lamrock. Attorney Jennings has been appointed to represent her. You will have to go back to the gallery."

Nathaniel was outraged. "That can't be. Let me in to speak with the judge."

"Sorry, Mr. Lamrock. The trial is about to commence. There's nothing to be done."

Nathaniel started to push his way past the clerk when a security guard came over. "Is there a problem, Afton?"

"This man is claiming to be Mrs. Lamrock's attorney. I told him that Jennings was her attorney, but he doesn't want to believe me."

"This way, please." The guard took Nathaniel by his arm.

"I'm not moving until I speak with the judge," Nathaniel roared.

Two other guards came running over when they heard the commotion. "Throw this man out," said the clerk.

Nathaniel's anger was turning into white-hot rage. He knew that if he were thrown out, he would be no help to Kara. With visible effort, he forced himself to remain calm. Shaking off the guard's hand, he said, "Never mind. I'll sit in the gallery."

As he passed the defense table he hissed at Jennings, "I want to see you at the first recess."

Nathaniel took the last empty seat at the back of the gallery.

"Please stand. Court is now in session. The Honorable Judge Langston presiding."

Judge Langston sauntered through the door and climbed to his seat on the bench.

Nathaniel groaned inwardly. Judge Langston was known to be the most incompetent member of the judiciary. Rumors had been flying for years that he was not averse to taking payola. *What absolute rotten luck that it's Langston who was randomly selected for Kara's trial*, Nathaniel thought to himself.

"You may all be seated."

Judge Langston looked toward the prosecutor's table. "Please identify yourselves."

"Your Honor, representing the Southwest Division, I am Assistant District Attorney James Newton and these are my associates." There were five other attorneys seated at the prosecutor's table and like pre-*tamen robotons*, they nodded in unison to Judge Langston.

Langston smiled at Newton, obviously impressed by the sheer number of prosecutors. "Thank you, Attorney Newton," said Langston.

"Defense, please identify yourself."

Kimp Jennings was busily trying to locate a paper from one of the stacks that he had haphazardly pulled from his brief case.

"Defense," bellowed Langston. "I will not ask again. Please identify yourself."

Jennings looked up as if he had just realized that the judge was talking to him. "I'm Kimp Jennings," he stammered. I'll be representing Mrs., uh, Mrs..."

"Mrs. Lamrock," Langston, annoyed, completed Kimp's sentence for him.

"Yes," replied Kimp. "Mrs. Lamrock. We plead 'not guilty.'"

"I haven't asked how you plead yet," said Langston, obviously running out of patience with Jennings. "Now, sit down until I tell you to come forward."

"I will hear opening statements now, please."

"Objection, Your Honor." Kimp was on his feet. "I haven't had a chance to offer a plea."

Nathaniel could not believe his ears when Langston said, "Overruled. Mr. Newton, you may proceed."

A hologram appeared along the west wall of the courtroom. Twelve jurors were present to hear the case. None had been questioned by Jennings as to their prejudices prior to being seated.

A door on the east side of the courtroom opened to reveal the accused. Nathaniel felt his heart stop when he saw her. His lungs fought for air and he had to remind himself to keep breathing.

The spectators gasped as Kara was brought, literally dragged, into the courtroom. Her hair was matted and her gray, loose fitting prison garb hung on her like a sack. Her left hand was wrapped in a dirty bandage. Her bruises could only be seen by those sitting close to her. She stared blankly straight ahead as she was marched to the prisoner's dock where a clear tube-like cage descended around her, capturing her as if she were a lab specimen on display. She stood with her head hung down looking at the floor.

Nathaniel's heart was breaking. If only he could get close enough to Kara so that she could see him. She needed to know that he was here, that she was not alone.

The twelve jurors eyed Kara closely. His experience told Nathaniel, that, to a man, each juror would interpret her blank look to be the cold-eyed glare of an unrepentant murderess.

Assistant District Attorney Newton sneered condescendingly at Kimp as he stood and walked to the center of the courtroom. He looked coldly at Kara and then turned, smiling, to the jury.

"Gentlemen of the jury, this is an open and shut case. What you will see is hard evidence proving that this murderess, Kara Lamrock, did knowingly modify a *taman* unit for the sole purpose of turning it into a killing machine. She did this to embarrass her employer because she was being investigated for misuse of corporate funds. We will show that Mrs. Lamrock, infuriated because she believed The Company was conspiring against her, committed this act to discredit them. The evidence you will be presented here is so compelling that it will leave no doubt in your mind as to the defendant's guilt.

"Look at Mrs. Lamrock. You can see for yourself that the defendant shows no signs of remorse. I'm sure that you twelve good citizens will do your duty and return the only verdict possible--guilty with the penalty of death. Thank you."

Judge Langston smiled and looked as if he were about to applaud the prosecutor's opening remarks. He nodded his congratulations to Newton and then turned to Kimp. "Is the defense ready to give its opening remarks?"

Kimp got up from his seat and reluctantly walked to the middle of the floor. He didn't even look at Kara. People in the courtroom had to strain to hear him.

"Your Honor, gentlemen of the jury. I am here today to prove that ..." Kimp looked down and read from the paper he was holding, "Mrs. Kara Lamrock is being tried for a crime that she did not commit. I've spoken with the defendant several times by telephone, and I'm certain that she is innocent. The accusations you have before you are false. The prosecution can produce no motive, and does not have witnesses to this crime. With no hard evidence, you will have no choice but to find the defendant innocent. Thank you, Your Honor, and members of the jury."

Nathaniel thought, *Is that it? This attorney might just as well have said he has no evidence of Kara's innocence. He practically gave up before he even started.*

Despite what he saw as grave incompetence, Nathaniel wasn't overly concerned. Cushman would get his hands on documents that would clear Kara. Nathaniel looked at his watch. Cushman should have been here by now. Nathaniel walked to the courtroom door to see if Cushman had been kept waiting in the hall.

Two men whom Nathaniel had never seen before walked up and stood beside him as he waited outside the courtroom door for Cushman. Engrossed with the thousands of thoughts running through his mind at once, Nathaniel ignored the men until one of them shoved a gun hard against Nathaniel's ribs.

"Don't say a word. Just walk straight ahead into that men's room."

Nathaniel looked down at the gun, and reluctantly did as he was told.

"Get out," the first man snarled to someone who was washing his hands at one of the three waterless sinks. The man didn't even turn around before he went scurrying out the door.

The second thug threw Nathaniel against one of the stalls. "Don't speak one word to Kimp Jennings if you value your wife's life. Is that clear?"

The first man smiled sickeningly at Nathaniel, then put something that was wrapped in gauze into Nathaniel's hand and closed his fingers around it. In an instant, both men were gone.

Nathaniel opened his hand and gagged when he unraveled the gauze and saw what he knew was the tip of one of Kara's fingers. Nathaniel's red hot rage threatened his already thready self-control, causing him to smash into a man attempting to enter the men's room as he raced out the door after the two hoodlums.

KATHLEEN PAPAJOHN

Chapter 21

The two thugs that had accosted Nathaniel had vanished. Nathaniel's mind was in turmoil. *Kara's finger?* He was close to panic but his years of combat training helped him regain control.

He would take her fingertip to Judge Langston to show him just what kind of danger his wife was in. Surely, even Langston would have to do something when he saw what had been done to her.

Nathaniel reached into his pocket for the grisly reminder of Kara's abuse at the hands of her captors. The finger was gone. The face of the person in the men's room that Nathaniel had "accidentally" bumped into flashed into his mind.

Son of a bitch! Nathaniel raged at himself. *How could I be so stupid? I should have known that they couldn't allow me to have any physical proof of Kara's mistreatment.*

Nathaniel made his way back to the courtroom and resumed his seat in the gallery. It took every ounce of willpower he had to keep him from running to where they held Kara. He knew that if he disrupted the proceedings, it would only get worse for her.

The prosecution was just beginning their case. "Your Honor, members of the jury, the prosecution would like to call Mr. Simon Brader of Interglobal Corporation to the stand."

Brader stood before the clerk. "Mr. Brader, repeat after me. Do you swear to tell the truth and nothing but the truth, so help you God?"

"I will."

"Please be seated and state your name and address for the record."

"My name is Simon Brader. I am currently the Chief of Security for Interglobal Enterprises, Incorporated. My former position was Chief Detective for the Denver Police Department in the Central Division, Sector Three. Your Honor, I do not wish to provide the court with my home address for obvious security reasons."

"Why, of course, Mr. Brader," Judge Langston answered deferentially.

"You may proceed with your witness, Mr. Newton."

"Mr. Brader, were you acquainted with Mrs. Kara Lamrock?"

"Why, yes I was. Well, everyone knew Kara around the office. She was a personable, very attractive young lady. Rumor had it that she was way over her head, and she was derelict in her duties as a lead programmer. It was reported to me, verbally of course, that she was always going on trips, using corporate funds for her personal travel."

Kimp jumped in, "Objection, Your Honor. That's hearsay as to the character of my client. There's no proof to substantiate that allegation."

"Overruled, Mr. Jennings. You may proceed with questioning the witness Mr. Newton."

"Mr. Brader, you stated, and I quote, 'She was way over her head and she was derelict in her duties as a lead programmer.' Is that correct?"

"Objection!" Jennings was out of his seat.

The judge asked Newton if the prosecution was going somewhere with this line of questioning. The prosecutor indicated that he was providing the jury with a motive. The prosecution would show that Kara had a grudge against her employer. This line of questioning was to point out her character and state of mind.

"No, Mr. Jennings. I'm going to allow this line of questioning as it relates to character and motive. Objection overruled."

Newton continued, "Mr. Brader, were you personally aware of Mrs. Lamrock's misuse of corporate funds?"

"Yes, I was. It was brought to my attention by one of the secretaries in the Artificial Intelligence Division. Very recently, Kara charged a first class round trip to Space Station Alpha 33 to Interglobal. She went there to visit her mother."

"Mr. Brader, did you investigate these allegations?"

"I did. I activated our personal security tracking cameras in Mrs. Lamrock's office and was tracking her movements throughout Interglobal. She was considered a high risk because the projects she was working on were highly classified."

"I see. What did you do next, Mr. Brader?"

"I confronted Mrs. Lamrock about her using corporate funds for her personal benefit. I told her that Interglobal planned to take her to court to recover the money that she stole."

"What did Mrs. Lamrock do after you confronted her?"

"She called me a few names that I would not like to repeat in mixed company. She said that she thought someone at Interglobal was conspiring against her. Then, she stormed off to her development laboratory. Our security cameras tracked her every movement. We recorded her modifying one of her *taman* units. It was unit SN: 493A0744."

"Mr. Brader, what is so significant about that serial number?"

"Well, if you recall, it was Interglobal's security team that cornered and destroyed the rogue *taman* unit that killed the young boy in the plaza. After we captured the unit, the remains were recovered and taken to our lab for analysis before they were destroyed. The killer unit's serial number was SN: 493A0744. It was an exact match. It was the *taman* unit that we observed Kara

Lamrock modifying just after I told her that Interglobal was going to sue her for misuse and return of corporate funds."

Newton was gloating at this point. "Mr. Brader, you are under oath. Are you sure this was the same *taman* unit that Kara Lamrock modified?"

"Yes. It was an exact match to the serial number of the killer *taman* unit. I am one hundred percent certain of it."

"In your opinion Mr. Brader, why did Kara Lamrock do this?"

"Objection, Your Honor." Kimp finally emerged from his stupor.

"Objection overruled."

Brader continued as if there had been no interruption. "Mrs. Lamrock refused to take responsibility for her larcenous actions. She believed that there was some sort of conspiracy against her and that Interglobal was behind it. I believe that she tried to punish the company by modifying one of the *taman* units. She knew that Interglobal would be blamed if the unit broke the law."

"So, Mr. Brader, it's your belief that Kara Lamrock's poorly planned retaliation on Interglobal is what brought us here today?"

"Yes, sir."

"Thank you, Mr. Brader. I'm through with this witness, Your Honor."

As Newton sat down, he was handed a memory stick that had been delivered to the prosecutor's table while he was interrogating Brader. He inserted the digital stick into his personal display monitor.

"You may cross-examine the witness now, Mr. Jennings," said Judge Langston.

Before Jennings could begin, Newton jumped up. "Your Honor. I have just come into possession of evidence that I will require this witness to explain. I need to reopen my questioning."

"Objection. Newton has completed his examination. He'll have to wait for cross-direct." Even Jennings knew that court protocol would not allow Newton to reopen his examination until rebuttal.

"I want to see both of you up here now," ordered Judge Langston.

Nathaniel had to strain to hear what was being said.

Judge Langston whispered to the prosecutor, "What's going on Mr. Newton?"

"I have just taken receipt of information from Interglobal that supports Mr. Brader's testimony. It's the recording made by the security tracking system at Interglobal that recorded the events that occurred in Mrs. Lamrock's office and laboratory."

"Your Honor, I demand that a copy of this evidence be provided to me immediately. This is outrageous."

Langston sighed, "All right, Jennings. For once, I agree with you."

"Mr. Newton, what are you trying to do here? Mr. Jennings would have sufficient grounds for a mistrial. I don't believe that either of us wants that to happen. Now both of you return to your seats."

When the attorneys had resumed their seats, the judge spoke. "Mr. Newton, please provide Mr. Jennings access to all evidence that was just delivered to the prosecution. We will take a two-hour recess."

"Jennings, be prepared to cross-examine the witness when we return."

Attorney Kimp Jennings jumped to his feet. "Your Honor, I cannot possibly review all of this material in such a short time."

Judge Langston smirked. "I agree that you will have your work cut out for you. Nevertheless, two hours is what you get."

As soon as Judge Langston left the bench, the prisoner's dock where Kara was being held went dark. It was impossible to tell if she was still there or if she had been taken out of the courtroom.

In the back of the gallery, Nathaniel was desolate. He knew that he would have to get dramatic proof of Kara's innocence if she were to be acquitted. Why hadn't he heard from Cushman yet?

Chapter 22

Velyn was as nervous as a cornered cat. She waited impatiently as the stampede raced off the shuttle. It was if, on arrival, the captain had said, "Gentlemen, start your engines."

When the last passenger left the cabin, she stood, grabbed her one, small overnight bag and walked quickly to the space plane's exit. She stepped onto the moving sidewalk that would carry her to the mandatory welcome chamber.

Velyn was so anxious about Kara that she absently walked right past the virus scan. Lights went on and alarms sounded. Embarrassed, she looked around and then quickly got back into line. She hadn't seen any news since she left Alpha 33, and she was starved for information. She passed through the virus scan and stepped onto the moving walkway that would take her to the disembarkation lounge. The walkway was just moving too slow. Velyn began walking quickly, almost running, passing passenger after passenger.

Velyn's manager had not been happy that she had abruptly left the Orbit Room on such short notice. He was going to have to hustle to find a replacement for her quickly, especially if he wanted to keep the Cosmos Hotel as a client. After Nathaniel's call, Velyn left Alpha 33 so quickly that she didn't even take the time to have her *taman* unit make hotel reservations for her. Once she was in Phoenix, she would have to find her own accommodations. She didn't want to stay with Nathaniel because the news media might connect her with Kara. As soon as she got to the welcome lounge, Velyn took out her communicator and placed a call to her favorite Phoenix hotel.

That taken care of, Velyn called Nathaniel. Solis answered, telling her that Nathaniel was not back from court yet. Velyn instructed Solis to tell Nathaniel that she would be staying at the Biltmore Hotel, and that Nathaniel should contact her there.

Velyn hadn't slept since she heard from Nathaniel. She was exhausted. Fortunately, the few sips that she had taken of the cactus cocktail that she'd been given in the welcome lounge was starting to wake her up. When she walked out of the spaceport, she saw the Biltmore limousine already waiting for her at the curb and sighed with relief. As usual, the Biltmore was practicing discretion. The driver was holding up a sign that read, "Ms. V. S."

Not more than fifteen minutes after she checked in, there was a knock at her door.

"Nathaniel," she cried when she opened it. Velyn reached out and literally pulled him into her suite.

Before she could even close the door, Nathaniel said, "Velyn, you had better sit down."

Nathaniel told Velyn everything that had happened since he met Kara at the restaurant. Of course, he left out what he knew about Kara's physical condition and his own fears about her safety.

"Velyn, you used to know the CEO of Interglobal, didn't you?" Nathaniel asked.

"Yes, Nathaniel. Malcolm Godfrey and my husband worked closely together for several years. Malcolm's a very eccentric man."

"I'm at a dead end. I believe that someone at Interglobal is framing Kara. Ever since she was arrested, I've been trying to find something, anything that will prove her innocence. I believe that someone from Interglobal has to be behind all of this. Interglobal is the only company that employs computer scientists with enough know-how to break through *taman* access codes to actually reprogram a unit.

"Do you think that you could get Malcolm to speak with you? Maybe you can convince him that Kara had nothing to do with this. Perhaps, with his connections, he can stop this circus before Kara gets ..." Nathaniel hesitated. He didn't want to use the word "convicted."

"It's been years since I've spoken with Malcolm, but if you think it will help, I'll try to get him to see me. I'll do anything for my daughter."

Chapter 23

As Judge Langston's two-hour recess came to an end, Nathaniel regained his seat in the gallery and continued to watch helplessly as the evidence against Kara mounted. He was at his lowest point of despair when his communicator vibrated. He stood up and walked out into the hallway before he answered.

It was a relief to hear Cushman's welcome voice.

"Nathaniel, I believe that I've found it. I located the original of Brader's surveillance record of Kara. This must be the same footage that your friend found. The most damning evidence against Kara is a visual image of her altering the *taman*'s program. I've analyzed the record, and I agree with your friend. I believe that this image has been doctored. According to our policy, all modifications such as this one can only be made under a protective hood. There's no hood displayed in this visual record. It's evident to me that this record was made in haste, and whoever made it left out several important details."

Cushman hesitated then asked, "Nathaniel, does Kara wear a wedding band?"

"Of course. She never takes it off," Nathaniel answered.

"I thought so," Cushman said. "Then where is Kara's wedding band in this video? She's not wearing one in this record. Also, why would a woman with Kara's experience openly type in a *taman*'s identification when she knows that information is always kept secret? Nathaniel, I believe that an independent analysis of this evidence will be more than enough to introduce a reasonable doubt as to Kara's guilt."

"Cushman, do you have the original of the visual record?"

"Unfortunately, I only have read access to Interglobal's secure records, but I believe that I can get the original tonight, after every one has left for the day."

Nathaniel was adamant, "Cushman, you've got to get the original of that record over to the court as soon as possible. Without that evidence, Kara will be convicted."

Tension was evident in Cushman's voice. "You're asking a lot, Nathaniel, but I'll do everything in my power to get it and bring it to the court. I'll contact you later this evening, after I leave Interglobal."

At last, Nathaniel felt hopeful as he made his way back into the courtroom. Cushman had come through. Nathaniel regretted that he had yelled at him the last time they met. He knew that Cushman was putting himself on the line. As Nathaniel took his seat, Brader was just resuming his testimony.

"Mr. Brader, I remind you that you are still under oath," admonished Judge Langston.

Prosecutor Newton addressed the bench. "Your Honor, I'd like to resume my questioning of Mr. Brader and get his views on this latest evidence that I've received. These records were given to the defense before the break, so I'm now offering them into evidence."

"Objection!" stormed Jennings. "There's no way that I could have reviewed that evidence between the time I received it and now! I formally request that this evidence be disallowed."

"Overruled." Langston was almost yelling. "The rule of law was satisfied when you accepted the records. It's not the prosecution's fault that you didn't review them in a timely manner. Please proceed, Mr. Newton."

"Thank you, Your Honor.

"If I may, I'd like to have Mr. Brader review the visual record of Mrs. Lamrock's actions at Interglobal just prior to the *taman destructor's* assault on the boy." Prosecutor Newton was smug.

"Objection, Your Honor. These records have not been scientifically authenticated. There is no proof that they are valid."

"Objection overruled. The evidence was given to you in good faith, Mr. Jennings. You could have had the records verified yourself. Please proceed, Mr. Newton."

Jennings was desperate. "Your Honor, may we at least have you review the visual record in closed chambers?"

Langston was becoming impatient. "No, Mr. Jennings. The public has a right to see what makes up the case against Mrs. Lamrock. Bailiff, please start the image viewer."

Newton was almost gleeful as he continued his examination of Brader. "Mr. Brader, please tell us what we're looking at."

Brader looked serious as he studied the pictures that were being displayed on a large hologram monitor, located where everyone in the court could see it. "You can see the date, time and the office location in the bottom right hand side of the image. This record was taken just a few hours before the fatal assault on the boy."

Satisfied that the jury was well aware of the implications of the date and time that the record was made, Brader continued. "Mr. Cushman Sellers, Interglobal's Chief Financial Officer, had contacted me earlier in the day and asked me to track Mrs. Kara Lamrock on our security system. This is standard operating procedure whenever there is a complaint against an employee or there is suspicion of fraud."

When Nathaniel heard this part of Brader's testimony, he clenched his teeth. *I can't believe that it was Cushman who started this mess by having Kara tracked!* he thought. *What was he thinking, and why didn't he tell me? Is he really helping or is he trying to set me up?* Nathaniel didn't know what to believe or who to trust.

Brader continued. "As you can see here, Mrs. Lamrock is placing her palm on the access reader for authentication. She then proceeds to her work area, where she removes the central processing unit from an immobilized *taman* and plugs it into her software modification drive. I employed several cameras in order to take pictures from different angles. To get a closer look, I zoomed in from the overhead camera to see what she was keying into her computer. This is a close up shot of her hands keying in 'SN: 493A0744,' which you can see displayed on her monitor. The next thing she types in is 'OPEN FILE, BEHAVIOR AYX19.'"

Even Newton was mesmerized by Brader's account. "What is Kara Lamrock doing now, Mr. Brader?"

"She's opening the *taman* unit's primary memory bank that controls its behavior module. Now she's keying in the following command, 'REPLACE FILE Z:\BEHAVIOR AYX19 with Z:\BEHAVIOR FILE DESTROYER.'"

There was a collective gasp from the courtroom. Almost with one voice, the spectators began chanting, "Guilty! Guilty! Guilty!"

Judge Langston's gavel almost shattered as he slammed it against his desk. "Order in the court! I will clear this courtroom if order does not resume immediately!"

Newton smiled. "The prosecution has no further questions, Your Honor."

"Your witness, Mr. Jennings!"

From the look on his face, Nathaniel thought that Kara's lawyer might as well have admitted out loud that he himself believed that his client was guilty. Nathaniel watched as Kara's lawyer made a half-hearted attempt to discredit Brader's testimony.

"Mr. Brader, have these records been modified or tampered with before they were sent to this courtroom?"

Brader smirked, "Absolutely not. I'm a man of integrity. I would put my reputation up against anyone's, including yours, Mr.

Jennings. I'm an honest, peace-loving man, and I resent your implication to the contrary."

Kimp Jennings knew when he was beaten. "No further questions, Your Honor."

Judge Langston looked down at Jennings and asked, "Mr. Jennings, do you have any defense witnesses to testify at these proceedings?"

"No, Your Honor."

Even Judge Langston looked incredulous, but he called for closing arguments in spite of his own misgivings concerning Kara's defense.

"Mr. Newton, You first."

Newton stood up and faced the jury.

"Thank you, Your Honor. Gentlemen of the jury, I'll be extremely brief because the evidence speaks for itself. I have no words to express my outrage over the senselessness of this crime. The evidence that you have been presented is clear, accurate, and I'm sure you'll agree, shocking. I ask you to follow your conscience and find Mrs. Kara Lamrock guilty of murder in the first degree.

"Your Honor, the prosecution rests."

"Thank you, Mr. Newton. Mr. Jennings, closing arguments, please."

Kimp reviewed his single page of notes, then slouched as he approached the center of the courtroom.

"Gentlemen of the jury, I, too, will be brief. I have reviewed the facts of the case and have spoken with Kara Lamrock. She's not the monster that has been portrayed by the prosecution. She has no record. She's never been in trouble. She's a kind and loving person. She has a loving husband, and a long productive future in front of her. Mrs. Lamrock is not guilty of these crimes. Please show compassion for this person. Her fate is in your hands. Thank you."

Judge Langston turned to the jury. "A capital offense has been committed. You, as citizens of the Southwest Division, must now decide the fate of the defendant, Mrs. Kara Lamrock. If you believe that the evidence leaves no doubt in your mind, then you must find the defendant guilty. The jury will begin its deliberations immediately."

Nathaniel believed that the longer the deliberation, the better for the defendant. In the case of Kara Lamrock, the jury deliberated less than an hour. Nathaniel could see that even Judge Langston was surprised by their speed in reaching a verdict.

Once again, the courtroom was filled to capacity.

Langston sat behind the bench, trying to look non-committal. "Has the jury reached a verdict?"

The hologram of the jury was visible throughout the courtroom. The lead juror stood and said, "Yes, Your Honor. We have. We have entered each of our votes into the court's system. You have it on your display."

Judge Langston's expression was grave. "Kara Lamrock, please stand and face the jury."

The clear tube that had imprisoned and protected Kara throughout the trial lifted, leaving her exposed. She looked bewildered. Nathaniel's heart broke as he realized that she didn't understand what was happening, and he watched helplessly until the bailiff roughly jerked her to her feet. He wanted so to change places with her. He would do anything to spare her from this horror.

"Please read your verdict," ordered Langston.

"We, the jury, by unanimous decision, find the defendant, Kara Lamrock, guilty of murder in the first degree."

The courtroom erupted in cheers.

"I will impose sentencing tomorrow at 4:00 P.M."

By the time the judge reached his chambers, his communicator was already ringing.

Langston actually smiled as he reported the verdict to his wife. He barely noticed the note that the bailiff had put in front of him until the bailiff called it to his attention. Immediately upon reading the note, Langston's smile disappeared.

Nathaniel watched as Judge Langston returned to the courtroom, his eyes wide, almost in horror as he bent over down and stammered to the bailiff, barely loud enough for Nathaniel to hear.

"It's highly irregular, but let him know that it can be done. I'll give the order myself immediately after tomorrow's sentencing."

Chapter 24

Velyn prayed that she would wake up and find that this had all been a nightmare. Kara would still be living happily with Nathaniel. She would see her that very day.

Unfortunately, what was happening to Kara was all too real, and Velyn began to sob uncontrollably. It was no nightmare. It had all happened so quickly. Her beloved Kara had been convicted of an unthinkable crime, one that she did not commit.

To a beautiful woman like Velyn, men had always been delightful companions. She was accustomed to their attentions and certainly not used to having to ask for favors. As she approached Malcolm's office, she knew that this was the biggest favor she would ever ask in her entire life. The thought of something happening to Kara was more than she could bear. She was convinced that Malcolm could make things right. Surely, he knew that Kara was not capable of what she'd been convicted of.

No one was sitting at Palya's station when Velyn arrived. The top of her desk was completely clear, except for a pen and a single pink envelope that was addressed to Velyn. Warily, Velyn picked up the envelope and opened it. She began reading, "Dear Ms.

Stevens, if it isn't too much trouble, would you please leave me your autograph." It was signed, "Your devoted fan, Palya."

In spite of Velyn's chaotic state of mind, she was touched by Palya's note. She picked up the pen and wrote, "To Palya. Best wishes always, Velyn Stevens."

Malcolm stood in his doorway watching her. His face was a mask hiding the thoughts that were racing through his mind. "Please come in, my dear. I've taken the liberty of ordering dinner for us."

Velyn managed a smile and held out her hand for Malcolm to kiss. "That was very thoughtful of you," she answered.

He led her to a table that looked like it had been set for royalty.

Velyn started speaking immediately as Malcolm poured wine into their goblets. "Malcolm, I came here to ask for your help."

Malcolm held up his hand, as if to stop her from saying anything. "First, we must toast your success. You've become the best-loved performer of the century. I must admit, that when you turned down my proposal of marriage in order to pursue your career, I believed that you would not become the star you are today." Malcolm raised his glass and his cold glare bore into Velyn. "I congratulate you," he said mockingly.

"Malcolm, you know that the reason I couldn't marry you had nothing to do with my career. I was still grieving for my husband. The time just wasn't right. I didn't mean to hurt you."

His face still a blank mask, Malcolm calmly answered, "Please, enjoy the dinner that I've had prepared for us. You said that you wanted to ask a favor of me. What is it, Velyn?"

"It's about my daughter, Kara. As you know, she's been unjustly convicted of capital murder. You have influence with the council and courts. You must be able to convince them that Kara is innocent and should be released." Velyn began to cry softly.

Malcolm made no attempt to comfort her. "Velyn, I'm not convinced of Kara's innocence. In fact, I've seen evidence that convinces me of just the opposite. There's nothing that I can do to help you." Malcolm did not even preface his last statement with, "I'm sorry."

Velyn looked up at him, shock in her tear-filled eyes. "Malcolm, you really don't believe that Kara's guilty?"

"I'm afraid that I do, my dear. But I'll be more than happy to pay for her memorial service should her punishment be termination."

Velyn was sick to her stomach. She stood up so quickly that she knocked over her wine glass. "How dare you? You monster! You know that she's not guilty. You're using Kara to get back at me because you think that I questioned your precious manhood."

Velyn fled from the office and didn't stop running until she was out of the building. She wanted to put as much space as possible between her and Malcolm. How could she have failed so miserably? She thought that she was going to throw up.

Velyn saw Nathaniel waiting in the executive parking lot. She ran to him as if she were being chased by a mob of vigilantes, but he quickly drove his rented transport over to her, jumped out, and held the passenger door open for her to get in. All her acting training deserted her, and she knew that Nathaniel could read on her face that she had failed her daughter. As Nathaniel drove away Velyn could certainly read the desperation on Nathaniel's face, a feeling that they both shared and one that was getting to be all too familiar.

KATHLEEN PAPAJOHN

Chapter 25

Malcolm felt gut-wrenching despair as he watched Velyn race from his office. Strangely, although he had anticipated feeling dejected after she left, this feeling of utter loss was a new experience for him. "What's wrong with me?" he thought. "I should be elated."

He looked outside his office door, but Palya was nowhere to be seen. Slowly, his sadness was beginning to morph into anger. He tugged absently at his right ear then picked up his communicator and said, "Palya, get in here immediately."

As if she had been waiting for his call, she was standing in his doorway as soon as he looked up, hanging back as if she thought there was something in his office that frightened her.

"Come over here and get on your knees," he ordered.

As he stared at her from the semi-darkness, Malcolm's anger was fueled by her hesitation. He was not used to repeating an order.

"Get over here now, you slut," Malcolm bellowed.

Palya still didn't move.

"What else should I expect from moon-trash like you? Where's your gratitude? I saved your parents from inevitable extinction in the mines and brought you here, where you've lived as if you were actually a decent person rather than the moon-scum that you are."

Palya started to cry. "Why are you saying these things? Malcolm, what have I done?"

Palya slowly walked over to Godfrey, her obvious fright growing with every step that took her closer to him.

"Behave like the slut you are, and I'll forgive your disobedience," Godfrey snarled.

Palya just stood there, looking at him, her eyes wide with fear. Godfrey ran out of patience. He balled up his fist, sprung to his feet and struck Palya squarely in the face, knocking her to the floor. Blood started oozing from the side of her beautiful mouth. Malcolm kicked her in the head with all his might. Her right eye began to swell.

"Finally, I'm getting rid of all garbage like you. All you leeches who are just feeding on my world. I, not that bitch that heads the council, will rule the Western Zone. In just three more weeks, I'll have an army that's unlike anything the earth has ever seen. In my brilliance, I've cloned an army in my image. These clones bow only to me and will help me rid the planet of all the undesirables. This world and the new worlds that we will settle will become second Edens. I will be the greatest leader in history. The citizens of my new world will be perfect specimens, uncontaminated by inferior beings such as you and your ilk."

Palya lay in shock. She had never seen this side of Malcolm Godfrey. "You're crazy," she whispered. Terrified, she feared for her life.

"Crazy? I'm brilliant! Who could ever conceive of such a perfect world and then make it a reality? Our settlements on Mars will be perfect, also. Margaret Owning will see to that. As captain of our first settlement ship, Margaret knows the 'right' kind of people to recruit. Of all my so-called associates, Margaret is the most loyal. She falsely believes that I saved her brother from the gallows. She'll do anything that I ask. Anything!"

Palya's face was a mask of horror. She looked at Malcolm as if convinced that he was insane. She was losing consciousness, but she started to crawl toward the door trying to get away. Malcolm stopped her with another well-placed kick, this time to her ribs.

"What's the matter? Am I boring you?" He kicked her in the face again, and blood poured from her mouth. "Does the cat have your tongue?" He laughed.

"Let me finish my story. You look like you can't wait to hear how it ends. Remember the boy that was killed near Patriot's Park? He was actually one of my clones. He escaped from the incubation facility. In another few days he would have grown into a soldier. He just couldn't follow instructions and stay put. That little bastard almost ruined everything. Tracking him down wasn't easy. Unfortunately, the reprogramming of the destructor that killed him went a little awry. If anyone had found out who and what he was, I could have been ruined. Nice of Mrs. Lamrock to take the heat for that little fiasco."

Malcolm looked down at Palya. He was disappointed that he no longer had an audience.

"Apparently, you've become bored with my little story. What a shame."

Malcolm stepped over Palya's lifeless body and crossed to his desk. He spoke matter-of-factly into his communicator. "Brader, get up here. I've got something for you to clean up." Malcolm pulled a white linen handkerchief from his pocket, bent over, and casually wiped Palya's blood from his shoe.

Chapter 26

For Nathaniel, each passing second was like an hour. Finally, his communicator buzzed. It was Sellers.

"Nathaniel, I have good news. Although I haven't been able to get in to see Judge Langston, I've gotten Mologor Graph to review the original hologram that I located at Interglobal. Judge Graph is very influential with the council and he's well-respected by his colleagues. Mologor got Langston to agree to look at the evidence before imposing his sentence on Kara. I believe that this new record will exonerate Kara and get her released. At the very least, we'll be able to get a new trial where you'll be allowed to provide proper representation for your wife. I'm leaving Judge Graph's chambers right now to bring the hologram to Langston."

"Thanks, Cushman. I owe you." Nathaniel felt as though his heart had resumed beating with this first glimmer of hope, but there was still a nagging sense of doom floating around somewhere in the back of his mind. "Please hurry. Langston plans to pass sentence this afternoon at four."

"I'll be at Judge Langston's chambers with the evidence before then. I want to personally see the look on Langston's face when I prove that his trial was a mockery."

Nathaniel waited outside the courtroom for what seemed like an eternity. He kept pacing back and forth, looking at his watch.

At 3:45 the clerk of courts told everyone to take their seats. *Where is Cushman?* Nathaniel worried.

At 3:50 exactly, Kara was brought to the courtroom. Nathaniel had to remind himself to keep breathing as he watched her. She appeared to be less in shock than she had been the day before. Her eyes scanned the courtroom as she desperately searched for Nathaniel. All she could see was the faceless crowd that ghoulishly waited to hear her sentence.

Guards led Kara to the defendant dock where, once again, a transparent, tube-like cell came down around her. She looked defenseless and stricken as Judge Langston approached the bench. It was fifteen minutes before the sentencing was scheduled to begin. Nathaniel looked desperately for Cushman, realizing that Langston was going to pass judgment earlier than scheduled.

Langston wasted no time. "Kara Lamrock, you have been found guilty of first degree murder. In weighing all the evidence, I find no mitigating factors; therefore, I sentence you to death by vaporization. The sentence will be carried out expeditiously."

Nathaniel had to grab the back of the bench in front of where he was standing to keep himself upright. He felt like all the air had left his body. His eyes flashed toward where his beloved Kara stood, terror evident on her face.

"No!" he screamed, that single word ripping through the courtroom's silence like a gunshot. He thought his head would explode from the pain of watching Kara being led away. How could things have gone so terribly wrong? He had seen treachery before, but nothing like this.

An audible gasp came from the spectators. In spite of public sentiment against her, no one expected the ultimate penalty to be imposed. Trey Thrasher rushed from the courtroom, anxious to deliver the grizzly news.

Nathaniel tried to ignore the buzzing of his communicator as he frantically fought his way through the crowd of spectators trying to get to Kara. Finally, he looked down and saw who was calling him.

"Nathaniel, it's Cushman. The news about Kara's sentence is already everywhere. Langston double-crossed us. As soon as I heard, I contacted Mologor. Even though it's unprecedented, Mologor Graph agreed to get the council to sign a stay of execution. I have it in my hands. I'm in the basement of the courthouse now. I'll get the stay up to Langston within minutes. Once he has the stay in front of him, there's nothing he can do but comply!"

Nathaniel almost cried with relief. "I'll be waiting on the first floor, right outside Langston's office."

Nathaniel couldn't hear Cushman's response over the roar that was coming from the first floor of the courthouse. He looked through the glass casement down to the public execution chamber below, where a large crowd was shouting as if they were at a sporting event. He saw that people in the crowd were straining to see something that was going on at the back of the auditorium. Nathaniel's breath went out of him when he saw Kara being led into the chamber. Guards surrounded her as she was dragged from the rear of the room to a raised platform located in the center of the chamber.

In a panic, Nathaniel raced for the stairs. When Nathaniel left the stairwell, a woman in the crowd turned to him as he tried to push past and said, "They ain't wasting no time on her, are they? I just wish I had time to get the rest of my family here. It ain't every day you see a bitch like that get her comeuppance."

Finally, Nathaniel saw Cushman. "Get out of my way, you fool!" Cushman was trying to push his way past the incompetent guard that stood outside Langston's office.

"Not so fast," said the guard. Two other guards were restraining Cushman. Both had their guns drawn.

While Cushman fought with Langston's guards, Nathaniel was pushing his way through the crowd. People were cheering now as Kara was being led to a platform where guards placed restraints around her ankles. She was being trapped in a concrete slab. Nathaniel screamed her name.

Somehow, over the din of the crowd, Nathaniel saw Kara look toward the sound of his voice. "Kara!"

"I love you," she mouthed silently as she reached her arm out to him.

The guards left her alone on the platform. Another transparent tube descended around her. A guard from the court's security force tried to restrain Nathaniel, but he broke free and rushed onto the platform where Kara was ensnared like a caged animal. He wrapped his arms around the cylinder as if he could protect her.

Unlike Nathaniel's, Kara's eyes were dry as she looked at him and smiled. Nathaniel's hand pushed on the outside of the cylinder as if strength alone would let him touch the woman he loved. She brought her hand up and placed it gently on the inside of the cylinder, exactly matching Nathaniel's hand. She had never looked more beautiful.

"I love you," she said quietly.

The light from the death flare was blinding. For an instant, Kara's face registered her agony. Before Nathaniel could tell her he loved her, she was gone.

In spite of the tube's searing heat, Nathaniel would not take his arms away. His arms and the side of his face were burned. His body slowly slid down the entire length of the cylinder as he fell to his knees in grief. It took five guards to finally pull him from the platform.

Chapter 27

Trey Thrasher was a veteran newsman. His first assignment had held dreams of future investigative journalism that would bring him fame as well as Pulitzer Prizes. He wondered how he had come to this. Even the makeup on his face, the makeup he wore for the cameras, felt heavy, like it was weighing him down, crushing his body along with his spirit. He had no wife, no children. He also had no hope of ever attaining either a normal family life, or the thrill that exploration of the facts could bring a newsman of his caliber. He couldn't remember the exact moment when his dreams died, when he had exchanged them for an easy life, a bigger living pod, temporary but pretty women.

He looked at his face in the mirror and didn't like what he saw there. No, he hated what he saw there. His head ached, and he had to look away. Finally, his coverage of Kara Lamrock's trial had opened the eyes of one who'd had them closed for so long. It had been like seeing the sun after being locked for years in a dark room.

During his career, Trey Thrasher had covered child molesters, drug dealers, and fraudulent con men who had unflinchingly taken the life savings of the helpless people who had trusted them with their life savings. He had covered car thieves and murderers of the worst sort--violent, evil men and women who should not have walked the same Earth as other people. In each and every instance, he had concentrated on the sensationalism of the story. Gory details were what the public wanted--his public. He never gave a second thought to the guilt or innocence of the people he covered. It was the story, just the story. But he had known all along that Kara Lamrock was different.

Now she was dead. No, not just dead. She was gone. He had known that something was wrong from the moment he saw her walk to the defendant's dock and then watched as the transparent cage came down around her. Here was a woman with no soul left. They, the system, had stripped her not only of her dignity, but also of her very essence. With one look, Trey had understood that she was innocent. He had felt guilty before, but never had he felt guilt like this. Because of his coverage of Kara's trial, coverage that was no more than exploitation, facts be damned, Trey Thrasher believed that he had finally crossed the line. He was beyond redemption.

Her face haunted him. The story, with its all-too-convenient evidence, nagged at him. After hitting "send" to submit his last words on her execution, he began to cry. It was a silent cry, the tears flowing out of his eyes but no sound coming from him. Stunned by his own tears, he wasn't sure if they were for Kara or for himself. The story was irrevocably over, yet he believed, no, he knew, that for him, it was just starting. The trial, the verdict, the execution, everything was just window-dressing for the real story. Suddenly, he felt better. He was a reporter after all. The facts were everything, and he was convinced that he had not seen all the facts in this case. He would find them, though. He promised himself that. He even knew where to start.

The offices--cubicles actually--for court-appointed attorneys were in the basement of the courthouse itself. Thrasher took the elevator to the basement and stepped off into a maze of gray, life-size, unlidded boxes. All the attorneys sat in their own cubicles in one very large and very drab room. There were no windows. Harsh light came from huge squares recessed into the ceiling.

Trey looked around and thought how awful it must have been for the attorneys who worked for the state. He couldn't imagine spending an hour here, let alone eight hours a day, four days a week. Each attorney had his own computer, but there were no 3-D holographs that he could see. Flat-screen monitors, some even black-on-green from before the war, sat in the shabby office space of each man. There were names on each of the cubicles, and instead of asking where he could find Kimp Jennings, Trey walked along the narrow corridors of the maze until he found him.

Jennings was sitting in his cubicle staring at a column of numbers currently displayed on his computer screen. He looked up at Trey standing in the opening to his cubicle. Trey couldn't help but feel sorry for Kimp Jennings. This young attorney was so green. According to the records, Jennings had only recently changed careers, something each citizen could do every twenty years if they wished.

Kimp Jennings had previously taught high school geometry. With his career change, he was looking at the next twenty years in a cubicle, unless he could get enough experience and exposure with successful trials to be picked up by a private law firm. That probably wouldn't happen, given the results of Kara Lamrock's trial. Hell, the ink was hardly dry on his graduation certificate from law school.

"What do you want?" Jennings asked. He looked at Thrasher, contempt evident in his voice. "More gory details? C'mon, what now? You want to know what color nail polish she was wearing when she was disintegrated? Leave me alone. I've got to document the number of hours that I worked on the case so that her husband can be billed."

"You've got to be kidding me! You're billing her husband?"

"The company, rather, the government doesn't work for free. You don't pay taxes any more, or is that something you overlooked, like you overlooked just about every rotten piece of so-called evidence that was presented in this farce? At least I want the bill to be accurate, although I'd hate to be the one who presents her husband with it. I don't even want to be in the same sector when he gets this." Jennings looked like he would have thrown his old computer if that were possible.

Trey leaned back against the tiny table in Kimp's cubicle. Jennings's reaction hit him full force, making him feel as if he had been physically assaulted. He concentrated on breathing to regain his composure. The fact that the government was billing for Jennings's work was not just astounding; it was offensive. Trey briefly wondered if the Supervisors were hoping for a violent reaction from Kara's husband when he received Jennings' bill. That would give them an excuse to restrain him, or worse. Trey knew he had been correct. Starting his investigation with Kara's lawyer was essential.

"Look, I'm not convinced that Kara was guilty, and I think that you may be able to help me."

"What for? She's gone. I couldn't help her when she was alive, and now it's too late. Nobody can help her now. I almost wish that she really *was* guilty. Then, maybe I wouldn't keep seeing her face every time I close my eyes"

"You and I both know that she didn't have anything to do with killing that kid. Yet, there's still a young boy that was murdered. What about him? Can you sleep knowing that the real killer is walking around, probably laughing his ass off? Doesn't that kid deserve some justice, too?"

Kimp looked Thrasher up and down. At least the contempt was gone from his voice. He took a deep breath and asked, "What do you want to know?"

Better, Trey thought.

It was his turn to size up Kimp Jennings. He wanted Kimp to trust him, but he thought that the best he could hope for was grudging information. He didn't blame him. Trey would feel the same way as Kimp felt if the tables were turned.

"I'm going to record this." When Jennings saw the small recording chip he sighed and turned away.

Thrasher thought better of it. He turned off the recording device and put it on Kimp's desk, right in front of him so that he could see that it was off.

"You're right," Trey said. "This will be off the record. In fact, it will be better for both of us if we keep this conversation confidential."

Jennings looked at the recorder and turned back to Trey. "Better for both of us, or better for you?"

"Look, I deserve that. I don't blame you for not trusting me. That trial was a circus, and I was the ringmaster. I'm sorry for that. All I'm after now is a little background."

"Trying to soothe your own conscience?"

"Yeah, something like that," Trey answered.

"Well, what do you want to know? Everything that happened in trial was recorded."

"How did Kara's case get assigned to you? Were you just the lucky attorney who pulled the short straw?"

"Usually, it works like that. If a defendant can't afford a private attorney, they are assigned a lawyer who is picked randomly from a pool of lawyers that works for the government. This time, Cilio Fernatti, Manager of Court Cases, picked me personally. I guess that they wanted me to get some trial experience, so I got assigned directly."

Trey was stunned. One thing about the government, it was run exactly like a successful business. Every policy was fully documented. Procedures were followed precisely. He had never seen an exception since the government had become stabilized. The system worked. The government made a profit year after year.

In fact, it ran like a clock. The system depended on each person following the rules faithfully. There was no redundancy. The fewer decisions that workers had to make personally, the less chance there was for mistakes to happen.

Jennings was looking at him quizzically.

Trey just shook his head. "Okay. Thanks for the information." He almost ran back to the elevator. He needed to get back to the office, and he needed some time to think. He knew that his next step would take him to the offices of the Manager of Court Cases, Cilio Fernatti.

Before he got to the elevator, he heard Jennings call after him, "Hey, Thrasher, there's make-up on your shirt collar. Looks really good. The shade suits you."

Chapter 28

From behind his bedroom door, Nathaniel heard Solis's voice, but it was unintelligible. The words all ran together until all he could hear was white sound. He couldn't discern meaning from anything that was said, nor did he try.

"Mr. Lamrock has not come out of his bedroom for two days. He has not washed and will not eat. I fear that he will die in there. When they came to sanitize the pod after Kara's death, Nathaniel attacked the cleaner that was in charge of the sanitization team. If I had not pulled him off the man, Nathaniel would have killed him. The only reason the man did not have Nathaniel arrested for assault is that he felt so sorry for him."

Nathaniel heard Velyn knocking softly on his door. "Nathaniel, it's me, Velyn. Please open the door. I must speak with you. Kara would have wanted us to be together right now."

Nathaniel didn't respond. He sat on the edge of his bed as if he were made of stone. No movement was possible.

"Solis, you may need to knock down the door. We can't let Nathaniel just wither away and will himself to die like this."

Before Solis could respond, they heard a click and the door cracked open. "Come in," Nathaniel whispered.

Nathaniel looked out his door and saw that Digger was also there, staring into space as if he were in another world. Velyn was listening to Solis and sadly shaking her head. Sympathy and shared sorrow was written all over her face.

Before she entered Nathaniel's room, Velyn turned to Solis. She placed her hand tenderly on his arm and said, "It was right of you to call me. Nathaniel loved Kara more than I have ever known a man to love any woman. He probably wants to die without her."

His room looked like a hurricane had hit it. In his rage, Nathaniel had turned over or broken everything. Velyn entered the room warily and closed the door behind her. She moved a piece of broken glass off the bed and sat down.

Nathaniel stood with his back to her, his mind going back to the day he had met Kara. He remembered that he had just been given a very disturbing new assignment. His partner and friend, Digger, was speaking with the woman that he had brought in from Interglobal to help them. According to Digger, the woman was a computer genius whom he had known for years. Nathaniel had to admit, that they needed help.

The first time that Nathaniel saw her, Digger had been leaning over, pointing to something on the computer screen that was sitting on her desk. They looked to be in earnest discussion, and Nathaniel didn't want to intrude. He could meet her later, or never, as far as he was concerned.

Digger walked away, and the consultant bent over her desk, absorbed by whatever it was that he had given to her. A few stands of dark, reddish-brown hair had escaped from the knot she had tied to the back of her head. Nathaniel couldn't help but notice that the back of her neck was so pale and so graceful. He thought that she must usually wear her hair down because the Phoenix sun would tan every part of a body that was exposed, even briefly. He found himself walking around the desk to get a better look at her and couldn't help but stare. The loose hair was the only thing that marred the perfection of the picture. It added vulnerability to her flawless beauty.

Nathaniel had sensed Digger looking over his shoulder, making him feel like he had been caught doing something wrong.

"What's up?" Digger had asked. Then he followed Nathaniel's gaze. As if he could read his mind, Digger said, "Yeah, I know. She's really something. But she's smart, too. I went to school with her. She was top of her class in almost everything. C'mon, I'll introduce you."

Digger had led Nathaniel to where Kara was sitting. "This is Kara Stevens. She's just been loaned to us from Interglobal to assist our team with data mining and research."

Nathaniel had forced himself to utter a few pleasantries, thinking, *Oh, no. Another brainiac.*

As he looked at her more closely, he noticed again how graceful the curve of her neck was. He had continued watching her out of the corner of his eye as he turned to ask Digger if there were any new developments. He knew he was being impolite, cutting her out of the conversation, but he didn't trust that he would be able to speak intelligibly if he had to face her head-on.

Nathaniel still couldn't believe it happened, but eventually he had admitted that he loved her, and to his astonishment, she had loved him, too. Kara had gone on to make Nathaniel's life bright and full of laughter. She banished his old ghosts so that he could lock them away in a place that he thought he would never, ever open again.

When Nathaniel looked at Velyn, he could see that his own grief was so strong it frightened her. Her red-rimmed eyes told him that her personal grief had hit her with the force of a hurricane, but that she was putting that aside in order to comfort him. Before she could say anything, he knelt in front of her, held onto her legs and put his head in her lap.

"It's my fault," he moaned. "I could have saved her. I should have just kept her from going with those police units that arrested her. I should have terminated all of them the minute they laid a hand on her. I even had a second chance when we were in court. I should have gotten her out of there. I should have killed every son of a bitch in the courtroom to save her. Velyn, I can't live without her!"

Nathaniel got to his feet and began pacing around the destroyed bedroom. He saw his own image in the mirror over the dresser. His eyes were cold and hard. He knew from the look on Velyn's face that he was terrifying her, but he couldn't stop himself. He thought that he would explode if he didn't give voice to the violent thoughts that were raging in his mind.

"I will still kill them. I will kill every single person associated with Kara's termination if it is the last thing I ever do."

Velyn sighed and looked at Nathaniel with compassion. It was obvious that her own heart was breaking. "Nathaniel, don't say such things. Here, sit with me. We need each other now. I'm moving into the spare bedroom. I'll take care of you." Speaking into the intercom, Velyn said, "Solis, check me out of my hotel and have my bags delivered here. And please make us some tea."

The door opened slowly, and Nathaniel looked up to see Digger. His eyes were puffy and red, and he looked as though he hadn't slept in days.

"Let's all go into the living room and talk," Velyn said softly.

As they sat together and drank their tea, Velyn reminisced about Kara's childhood. She was telling Nathaniel and Digger about the time a three-year-old Kara had been so proud of her floral arrangement, which was really only sticks and rocks, when the doorbell rang, startling them all. It was the Biltmore's limousine driver with Velyn's bags.

Solis carried them into the spare bedroom. He went to great lengths to hide his sorrow from the others, but even his eyes were moist.

"Nathaniel, Kara told me that she had a surprise for you. Did you ever learn what it was?"

"Surprise? No, Kara didn't have time to tell me anything before those goons arrived and arrested her."

Velyn looked worried, but then she shook her head. *This is no time to be questioning Nathaniel*, she thought.

"Excuse me for a moment. I have something I want to show you." She got up and went into her bedroom. In a few minutes she was back, carrying an over-stuffed scrapbook.

"This is Kara's baby book. I've kept it with me all these years. Everywhere I travel, it is always with me. I look through this book when I'm lonely, and I can always feel Kara's presence. Look through it with me now."

Velyn forced a smile. "You both should see this," she said as she opened the large blue satin cover of the scrapbook. There were pictures of Kara as an infant, a page with her baby footprint, pictures of Kara's first birthday. Nathaniel gasped as Velyn turned a page and revealed a long, dark curl.

"Nathaniel, what is it?" Velyn asked.

"Velyn, is that Kara's hair? How old was she when that lock of hair was taken?"

"It was her first haircut. I believe she was about three. I cried the day that they cut her hair for the first time."

"Velyn, I need to have that lock of hair. Does anyone else know that you kept this baby book?"

"It was my special secret," Velyn answered. "I always kept it with me. As long as I had this book, I knew that Kara was never far away."

Nathaniel jumped up and grabbed the lock of hair from Velyn. "Solis, get me an envelope," he ordered. "Digger, I'm going to need a weapon."

Digger didn't look surprised and, without comment, reached into his jacket and handed Nathaniel his own laser.

Nathaniel nodded, putting the gun into his waistband. He then took the envelope from Solis, put the lock of hair into it, and then put the envelope inside the pocket of his jacket, next to his heart.

Without a word, he turned and darted from the apartment, leaving everyone staring after him in puzzled astonishment.

Chapter 29

Nathaniel had long ago reconciled himself to the unholy alliances that he had made with his informants in the underworld. No matter how much progress society made, there were always those who chose to take another path. These antisocial misfits often ended up in places like this. Nathaniel stepped over an unconscious junkie and looked up at the rundown hive of living pods.

This living facility had been constructed over one hundred years earlier, and its walls held a century of grime. Once a polished and gleaming building, it had been home to young professionals and families. Since the end of the war, the entire neighborhood had disintegrated. It drew the socially abnormal like metal shavings to a magnet. The paint on the outside of the building was peeling and flaked like the skin of an old potato. The front door hung lopsidedly on one hinge. As he stepped inside the building, Nathaniel's sense of smell was assaulted by air pungent with the smell of vomit and human excrement. Roaches scurried across the floor, unaccustomed to the light coming from the open doorway.

Nathaniel took the precarious-looking stairs to the second floor and knocked on the first door. The number "2" in the "2A" that identified the pod, hung upside down in the middle of the battered door.

"Who's there?"

"Open the door, Billy," Nathaniel snarled. He heard the sound of three deadbolts being thrown back.

The door opened a crack and a dirty, unkempt man looked out. The door closed again and Nathaniel heard the sound of a chain lock sliding. Once again, the door opened. Billy Bargus, one of Nathaniel's former informants, stood grinning at him like the idiot he was.

Obviously nervous to see him, Billy said, "Come in, Nathaniel. Nice to see you, Nate. Get you a beer?"

Billy's hands were shaking as he held a home-rolled cigarette to his lips. Unreasonably, Nathaniel was fascinated by the ash. *How could an ash be that long and not fall off the end of the cigarette?*

"Billy, I'm not here to hassle you. How would you like all your outstanding warrants squashed?"

Nathaniel forced a smile. He purposely ignored the vials of synthetic morphine, Billy's drug of choice, that were scattered on the dirty table.

"Even the one that was issued because some junkie girl claims I beat on her? You know I wouldn't beat a girl for no reason. She asked for it, spitting on me the way she did." Billy's hands continued to shake. The ash grew even longer.

"Even that one," Nathaniel replied. "All I need is a little favor, an introduction."

Billy looked slyly at Nathaniel and wondered if maybe he could get more than a few cancelled warrants out of the situation. "I could really use a few bucks, Nate. People still take cash, you know. Not everyone lives on barter credits."

Disgustedly, Nathaniel pulled some bills from his pocket. He held them out to Billy, but quickly pulled them back, just out of Billy's reach. "I need you to help me find Axcardo."

Billy jumped back. He looked away so that he didn't have to look Nathaniel in the eye. "You're crazy, Nate. Axcardo's dead. He was put to death last year after he was convicted of racketeering."

Nathaniel grabbed Billy by the shreds of material that passed for his shirt and flung him against the wall, before punching him in the stomach. The remnants of his cigarette fell to the dirty floor.

Nathaniel's eyes bore into him. "We both know better, now, don't we, Billy? My sources tell me that Axcardo just got back from Venezuela. Now, if you want those warrants to disappear and to get your hands on this cash, you'll do as I ask. Otherwise, I can have the warrants served right now. It might do you some good to spend the next sixty years in rehabilitative confinement."

Billy started shaking even harder. "Nate, please. Axcardo'll kill me."

Nathaniel pulled his weapon and shoved it hard against Billy's temple. "Would you rather die here right now? If I were you, I'd be more worried about me, not Axcardo."

Billy felt the cold steel against his skull. He watched as Nathaniel put the money back in his pocket. "Okay. Put the gun away. I can't get in to see Axcardo myself, but I'll take you to one of his capos tomorrow. After I know that my warrants are cleared."

Nathaniel pressed the gun harder against Billy's head. "Do you actually think that you can bargain with me, you creep? You're in no position to negotiate. I'd just as soon end this right now."

Billy was shivering violently, even though the temperature in the squalid apartment must have been over a hundred. In spite of his miserable existence, it seemed that life was still precious to Billy, at least his own life. "Okay. Please. I'll take you right now."

Nathaniel pushed Billy toward the door with such force that it opened on its own when Billy hit it. "Get moving!"

He followed Billy as he reluctantly went down the dark stairway and out into the dirty street.

Billy's directions took them to a building in the middle of what was known in the press as the "Combat Zone." Strip clubs and slimy bars lined the littered street. When Billy knocked on the door of one of the less sleazy storefronts, a large, burly man incongruously dressed in an expensively tailored suit opened it. The man would have looked more at home in an exclusive salon than in the middle of the sordid part of town.

The man looked at Billy with distaste. "What do you want?" he sneered.

"This man wants to meet with Axcardo," Billy stammered. "I told him that Axcardo was dead, but he doesn't believe me."

"How dare you even utter Axcardo's name!" the man said furiously. "I'll have your head for this."

The man reached for Billy but Nathaniel was faster. He grabbed the man's arm and battered it against the half-open door. Nathaniel pushed the door open and roughly threw the man against the wall, gripping his neck and putting his own face close to the man's ear. Nathaniel pulled his weapon and put it to the man's temple. "Where's Axcardo?" he hissed.

"You're a dead man," the thug wheezed.

"I'll take my chances," Nathaniel said as he released him, keeping his weapon aimed directly at the man's head.

The man began to cough, taking several large gulps of air until he caught his breath. "It's your funeral," he said. "Follow me."

The man led Nathaniel down the hallway to a large door guarded by another man even larger and uglier than the first.

"This man wants to see Axcardo," the first man said condescendingly. It was if the man thought that this was Nathaniel's final request before he died.

The second guard looked first at Nathaniel, then at his gun. "Look into that camera," he instructed.

The second man then whispered something into his communicator. After what seemed like hours, but in reality was only seconds, the door clicked open. The man put his ear to his communicator, listening intently, then said to Nathaniel, "I'll need to take that," indicating Nathaniel's weapon.

Without hesitation, Nathaniel handed his weapon over and started to walk through the door, Billy close on his heels.

"Not you," the guard said to Billy. "You'll stink up the place."

Billy slithered out the door and didn't look back. As soon as he hit the street, he started to run.

Nathaniel stepped into a room that was beautifully outfitted with furnishings that looked like they were meant for royalty. It was if he were in another world where the squalid surroundings outside the building did not exist. A man stepped forward, and the first guard smirked, looking as if he expected Nathaniel to be terminated immediately. The guard's look changed to one of amazement when Axcardo walked up to Nathaniel and threw his arms around him, embracing him like he was his long-lost brother.

"It's been too long. I'm so happy to see you." Axcardo stepped back and looked at Nathaniel affectionately. "What brings you here?"

"It's good to see you, too, Axcardo, but I didn't come here to reminisce. I need a favor, a big favor."

By the time Nathaniel got back to his own living unit, it was well after 23:00.

"Digger, Velyn, sit down, both of you."

"Nathaniel, what's going on?" Digger asked suspiciously.

"Kara doesn't have to be gone. There are people who can bring her back. I've called in some old favors with some very old 'friends' and with the lock of hair that Velyn gave me, I can have Kara cloned." Nathaniel was speaking fast, his nerves completely frayed.

Digger's face registered the shock he felt. "Nathaniel, cloning's been banned for decades. If the authorities have even a hint that you're involved in cloning, you'll be executed on the spot. Your so-called friends will also be executed. Why would anyone take such a risk?"

Nathaniel was resolute. "Don't ask. I've taken care of everything."

Velyn threw her arms around Nathaniel and hugged him. She was afraid to try to speak, because if she was dreaming, she didn't want to wake up.

Digger began pacing back and forth. He looked as if he had seen a ghost. He stammered, "How? When?"

"How doesn't matter," Nathaniel answered. "When is right now. Negotiations have been completed. There's one drawback. Kara's entire genetic map is contained in the lock of hair you gave me. The problem is that Kara's hair was taken when she was only three years old. Using that hair as the source of her DNA will allow her to be exactly duplicated all right, but..."

"But what?" roared Digger. "Come on, Nathaniel. You're killing me here!"

"Once the cloning process is completed and the fertilized egg is implanted in a host, it will be only days until Kara is born. Kara's growth will be accelerated until she is the age she was when the curl was cut off. It's at that point that the normal aging process will begin. Kara won't be an adult for another twenty years."

Velyn's eyes were wide. "Are you telling me that I'll have my baby back? I can be her host?"

Digger looked concerned. "Velyn, Kara would be in grave danger if anyone learned of her existence. None of us can ever get near her, including you, including me, including Nathaniel. Once she's grown or out of danger, maybe."

It was Digger's turn to pace, his mind's turn to run wild. He had seen cloning first hand. He had even been the one to execute the people who flaunted the cloning laws. "What we need is to find a host that won't be connected with Kara to act as a surrogate, someone brave enough to do this."

Nathaniel called to Solis, "Bring me the communicator." Nathaniel walked into his bedroom and closed the door behind him. He began dialing. "Juan, this is Nathaniel Lamrock."

"Nathaniel, I'm so sorry for your loss. Is there anything that I can do?" Juan asked.

"Thank you, Juan. Yes, in fact there is something. May I please speak with Sha?"

KATHLEEN PAPAJOHN

Chapter 30

Digger watched in awe as Dr. Stroman took the vial containing the cells that carried Kara's genetic map, her DNA, and placed it in the small refrigeration unit that Digger had used to bring him Sha Nuala's unfertilized egg. Digger followed him down the hall to where a gynecologist colleague waited with Sha Nuala to re-implant the egg that was now-fertilized and carried a complete complement of Kara's DNA.

It was too risky for Nathaniel to be involved. There would be only a small window of time before Nathaniel would be watched. Nathaniel's past with the Internals ensured that the government would fear any vengeance that he might harbor as a result of his wife's execution.

Axcardo must have owed Nathaniel big time, because he had agreed to work with Digger in place of Nathaniel. Axcardo himself had been cloned several times before his latest incarnation. Axcardo was a career criminal who had his own cellular DNA stored in hiding places around the world, ready for use in the event that he was ever caught and executed. Digger knew that Axcardo's repeated execution was inevitable. Normally, Digger would have been one of the men who chased him down. To Axcardo, execution was nothing more than an inconvenience. Axcardo's men and good doctors like Stroman would ensure that Axcardo came back as a clone no matter how many times the government executed him.

Digger could not keep from smiling. Within days, Kara would again be a living, breathing member of the human race. He vowed that this time around, he wouldn't wait for Nathaniel to claim her. Digger would have a second chance, and he promised himself that he would make an adult Kara fall in love with him before she ever laid eyes on Nathaniel.

In order to make everything appear normal, Digger knew that Sha Nuala would have to present herself at one of Interglobal's many maternity clinics for her initial pre-natal examination. The visit would be necessary for Kara's embryo to be genetically altered, inoculated so that she wouldn't age past her adulthood prime, ensuring her immortality.

In a normal full birth process, Kara would receive the sub-dermal chip that would identify her to the Population Clock. Since Kara's birth would not be 'normal,' Digger would ensure that a documentation master who worked for the Internals would create a special, untraceable chip for Kara.

Juan brought a very nervous Sha to one of Interglobal's clinics the day after she had been impregnated with Kara's clone. Already, Sha carried a four-month embryo in her womb. Juan presented the nurse at the front desk with the permit that Digger had backdated and guided Sha into a chair in the waiting room. Within minutes a smiling *taman* nurse approached them.

"Follow me, please," the unit said to Sha. "I'm sorry, sir. You'll have to wait here."

Sha looked back nervously at Juan, who smiled encouragingly. The unit took Sha to a cell-like room, told her to undress, put on a flimsy examination gown, and lie on a cold, steel table. A small black instrument was waved over Sha's stomach. The *taman* looked at the read-out display and smiled.

"Everything is A-okay. Congratulations. You're going to have a little girl. Now, please bring your clothes and follow me. There's one more procedure."

The *taman* took Sha down the hall and through a door under a sign that read *DSDS Unit*. Sha saw that, once again, there was another cold, steel table in the center of the room. This time, the *taman* asked her to lie down and place her feet in stirrups that were located at the end of the table. Before Sha had time to even wonder what was happening, the *taman* had inserted a small tubular device into her. Sha felt a warm sensation between her legs.

"That's it," the unit said. "This will protect you from infection and make sure that the delivery is quick and painless. Your baby won't be identified as 'official' until the actual birth. The population clock will recognize her by the serial number that will been implanted in the infant after you deliver. But, she's been genetically altered prenatally so that she won't grow old."

The *taman* smiled reassuringly, "Before you know it, you'll be a lucky mama."

You don't know how right you are! Sha thought, knowing that Kara's birth would occur in a matter of days, rather than months.

Relieved that the ordeal was over, Sha quickly dressed and followed the *taman* back to the waiting room where Juan waited anxiously.

Chapter 31

Nathaniel entered his living pod and immediately called out, "Solis, I have it!" Nathaniel placed an employee access badge on the table.

Solis appeared from the atrium, looking sheepish. He closed the atrium door in time to keep Nathaniel from seeing Tandem. "Was it where I told you it would be?"

"Your directions were perfect," Nathaniel answered. "It's a good thing that you remembered that Kara left her badge in my downtown office. It would have disappeared along with all her other belongings when they sanitized the pod."

Solis looked sadly at the badge. "I miss Kara."

Nathaniel was startled by Solis's words. "You feel sad?"

Solis looked sheepish again. "I mean, I believe that I would feel sadness if I were human."

I don't have time to think about this right now, Nathaniel thought. *The last thing I need is an emotional* taman.

"I'm worried about Cushman Sellers," he told Solis. "He never followed through with the evidence he found, and I owe him a visit. I need to find out what happened. He could be part of the conspiracy."

Nathaniel dialed Cushman's private number.

"Interglobal Security. George Max speaking. How may I help you?"

Nathaniel was momentarily taken aback. "I'm calling for Cushman Sellers."

Max's reply shocked Nathaniel. "Sorry. Mr. Sellers is no longer employed at Interglobal. Is there some else who can help you?"

What the hell happened to Cushman?

To George Max he said, "No thanks. It's nothing important," and quickly hung up.

"Solis, we've got to get inside Interglobal. There's something very wrong. Are you sure that Kara's badge will provide the same access as her sub-dermal chip?"

"I don't believe that anyone would think to inactivate her access, at least not yet," Solis replied. "It's been my experience that security is most lax at companies that are providers of security."

It was 07:00 P.M. when Nathaniel and Solis began preparing for their secret outing. Nathaniel wore black slacks and a vest over a tight-fitting black sweater, and Solis was dressed in similar garb.

In spite of his size, Solis was swallowed up by the dark night. They left the personal transport vehicle that Digger had secured for their use and crept quietly through the grove. Nathaniel carried a small valise that he intended to use to bring out any evidence that he could find. Solis was watchful for infrared security light streams. To Nathaniel, the beams were invisible. More than once, Solis had to grab Nathaniel's collar and pull him back in order to keep him from walking directly into one of them.

They reached the edge of the grove and lay flat on their bellies. Interglobal headquarters was less than twenty feet away. The janitorial *taman* units had arrived and were just starting to take their cleaning supplies from their van. Solis silently crept up behind them, and the units never knew what hit them. In seconds,

Solis had dismantled the cleaning units' CPUs and put their power supply chips into his vest pocket. He waved Nathaniel forward.

"The cleaning *tamen* will not be a problem now," he told him.

Nathaniel helped Solis hide the units in their own cleaning van, and then they entered the building stealthily. Nathaniel instructed Solis to recall the data that he had stored in his memory during their last visit to Interglobal, when they had their first meeting with Cushman Sellers. On that first visit, Solis had recorded the location of security cameras, all entrance and exit locations, locations of all doors, locations of management offices, and the records room. Now, Solis recalled that information from his memory bank.

"This way, Nathaniel," he said.

Solis headed for the north end of the building. The corridors were not carpeted, and to Nathaniel, their footsteps were as loud as drumbeats as they made their way to the executive area.

"That door leads to the archive and records room," Solis whispered.

"Stand watch here, out of sight, and let me know if we get any company," Nathaniel said.

The archive room was dark, so Nathaniel switched on his illuminator. The light from the wand revealed the room's disarray. Cabinets were open and holograms were everywhere. Everything in the path of the wand's light beam was bathed in a light green glow.

What a mess, Nathaniel thought. *Someone must have been working in here earlier and left in a hurry without putting things away.*

Nathaniel shrugged and then started searching the first open cabinet. He noticed that someone had been inventorying its contents. Each hologram casing had a number and a corresponding entry on a log that had been carelessly left beside the cabinet.

Whoever was working here either left in a hurry, or is pretty sloppy about their record-keeping, Nathaniel thought. *Solis was right about the lax security.* He quickly scanned the inventory list, but there was nothing even remotely related to Kara or to the murdered boy.

Nathaniel opened a second cabinet. To his surprise, the cabinet was completely filled with miniature holograms. Each record was as small as a credit card and as thin as a razor blade. There were thousands of them. Nathaniel saw that everyone was labeled *DSDS*.

As Nathaniel stared at the holograms, wondering what so many identical records could mean, Solis entered the room. "I came in to let you know that I've scanned Cushman Seller's office. There's nothing in it. It's been sanitized."

"Sanitized?" Nathaniel asked anxiously. "What happened to Cushman? Why would they cleanse his office? What could have been so important that they ensured there wouldn't even be a trace of his DNA?"

Nathaniel heard a noise from the hall. "It's the security guards. They're on their way up here," Solis said.

"Damn! They got wise to us sooner than I expected. I haven't had time to find anything. I need something that I can use to bargain with Malcolm. Take a handful of these DSDS records and put them in the valise. We can review them later. Hell, there are so many in here, I don't know where to begin. It looks like we're not going find anything useful. Let's get out of here."

"Hurry, Nathaniel. We're out of time," Solis whispered urgently.

Nathaniel peered around the archive room's door and saw three security guards running down the hall toward them.

"We need to split up," Nathaniel whispered. "It'll be easier for us to get out if we're not together. I'll take Digger's transport and meet you at home. You take the cleaners' van."

Solis nodded. "Okay, Nathaniel. Now, go!"

Nathaniel sprinted out the door and down the hallway to his right. One of the security guards shouted, "You there! Stop!"

When Nathaniel kept running, all three of the guards chased after him. Solis remained hidden in the archive room. Once the guards ran past the door in pursuit of Nathaniel, Solis slipped out and went back the way that he and Nathaniel had come in. Solis was not worried about Nathaniel. Something in their past that Solis couldn't quite remember told him that it was the guards who should be worried.

KATHLEEN PAPAJOHN

Chapter 32

"Solis, I want you to break down that wall." Nathaniel indicated where boxes had been stacked against his basement's back wall.

Solis looked like he was becoming concerned with Nathaniel's mental state, but nevertheless he complied with his request. He thrust his fist through the wall. Three more of his punches brought the whole thing down. The air in the basement was thick with dust. The opening he had just made revealed another room that had been hidden behind the collapsed wall.

Nathaniel pushed past Solis and went into his secret hiding place. The walls of the room were filled with shelf after shelf of old military equipment. Evidently, Nathaniel and Digger were more alike than anyone thought. Like Digger, Nathaniel had been saving for a rainy day. Each shelf held a compartment that Nathaniel had sealed with Plexiglas to preserve its contents.

Nathaniel chose carefully. He handed Solis a pair of what appeared to be dark sunglasses. "Put these on," he ordered.

Solis placed the glasses over his eyes. The dark lenses were curved and protruding making Solis look like a fly. Suction kept the glasses firmly in place.

Nathaniel put on a second pair of the glasses. "These glasses were made for special occasions like this," he told Solis. "Trust what you see no matter what your mind tells you."

Next, Nathaniel grabbed a couple of small flat plastic oblong plates. They looked like barter credit cards. He stuffed them into his vest pocket. "These are actually grenades. They're undetectable to security devices yet they're lethal when activated."

Finally, Nathaniel pulled a proton pistol from one of the compartments.

"Here, Solis. Conceal this in your waistband."

Solis put both hands behind his back and just stared back at Nathaniel. "Nathaniel, I could never use this. I am a protector. This is an offensive weapon."

Nathaniel stared back at Solis, anger flashing in his eyes. "Solis, although you may be a protector, you must know that we are going to meet the enemy shortly. You must be prepared for anything."

Solis's entire body stiffened. He looked directly into Nathaniel's eyes. After what seemed to Nathaniel to be an eternity, Solis said, "All right, Nathaniel. I'll take the gun but I cannot promise that I will use it." Without another word, he tucked it into his waistband at the small of his back.

If any part of the old Solis is still anywhere in there, Nathaniel thought, *you'll use it, all right. You won't hesitate.*

Nathaniel activated the glasses that he and Solis wore, bringing them both into complete synchronization. In addition to clearly displaying everything in their path no matter how little light was available, the glasses allowed them to see exactly the same thing that the other was seeing.

Nathaniel started up the stairs but stopped when he remembered something. He turned quickly and went back into the hidden closet. He grabbed a dagger from one of the small tables and hid it in his boot. A silver crucifix dangled from a chain that was hung on a nail inside the shattered wall. Nathaniel removed the unique medal from the nail and placed the chain around his neck, the face of the crucifix facing inward. He did not want the image on the cross to witness the unholy things that Nathaniel thought he would have to do. He turned and followed Solis up the stairs.

Just before they left, Nathaniel put the valise containing the DSDS holograms on the floor and kicked it under the kitchen table. *I'll look at that these when I get back*, he thought. *They must contain some pretty significant information if just the threat of exposing whatever's on them got Godfrey to agree to see me tonight.*

When he and Solis met back at his living unit, Nathaniel had called Malcolm Godfrey directly. He had been surprised when Godfrey answered his own phone. *Where the hell is his secretary?* Nathaniel had wondered. At first, when Nathaniel told Godfrey that he wanted to speak with him privately, Godfrey had laughed.

"Pretty soon you won't be speaking to anyone," Godfrey had told him snidely.

"Really?" Nathaniel had answered. "Then I guess that you don't care what I do with these DSDS holograms."

That was all he needed to say. Nathaniel had been prepared to threaten him personally, but evidently, Nathaniel had uttered the magic words.

"Be here in exactly one hour," Godfrey had told him. Nathaniel still couldn't believe it was so easy. Could Godfrey really believe that he was so untouchable, that he truly was indestructible?

"It seems as if we never left," Nathaniel said to Solis as they stood in Interglobal's lobby watching George Max pretend to search for their names in the guest register.

This time, Max did not seem to trust them to find their own way. He looked Nathaniel and Solis up and down in disgust. "I guess Halloween's a little early this year. Where did you get those glasses? Is it too bright in here for you?" he asked with a sneer.

"Follow me," he ordered without waiting for a reply.

Nathaniel marveled that there were no metal detectors. Anyone could walk right into Interglobal carrying an arsenal of weapons. Solis had been correct. Interglobal was so proud of the security devices and sensors that they provided to their clients. That false sense of pride made them too smug to worry about their own security.

Max led Nathaniel and Solis down a stairway that was not on the architectural drawings of the building that Solis had saved in his memory bank. "Go to the end of the hall and through that door. Mr. Godfrey is waiting for you."

Max hurriedly disappeared back up the stairs to the security desk. Nathaniel and Solis walked uncertainly down the short hall. Nathaniel pushed open the door and they entered a small dark room. There were two other doors and a large hologram monitor on the opposite wall.

Nathaniel stopped dead in his tracks. Cushman Sellers sat on a chair behind a table in the center of the room. A single lamp shone directly on Cushman. He had obviously been beaten--beaten badly. His lips were bruised and swollen. His head hung down on his chest. Nathaniel started toward him when Cushman looked up. Recognition flashed in his eyes and he said urgently, "Don't come near me, Nathaniel. They've got me wired."

Nathaniel whispered to Solis, "Evaluate."

Behind the black lenses, Solis's hidden eyes were darting left and right, scanning everything and everyone in their vicinity. His analysis was displayed on the internal face of Nathaniel's eyepiece: "Twelve lightly armed individuals, all-human. Three proton batons held by individuals standing just behind the door on the left; nine side arms, each with fourteen rounds held by remaining human subjects behind the door on the right. No body armor. One additional human, unarmed. Eight ounces of plastic explosive in a sensory device attached to Cushman Sellers."

Nathaniel heard Malcolm's cultured and unnaturally welcoming voice. "Welcome, Gentlemen."

Malcolm's image appeared on the hologram monitor.

"Please, Nathaniel, won't you and your friend come in? Why don't you join Cushman at the table? I'm sure you both have a lot to talk about."

"Oh, my," Godfrey continued. "You didn't really believe that I would be here in the flesh, so to speak, did you? Really, you're more naïve than I thought. I gave you more credit, Nathaniel."

Cushman was violently shaking his head back and forth, indicating that Nathaniel should not come near him. Suddenly, both of the doors at the back of the room opened simultaneously, and George Max's security team entered the room. Malcolm was watching Nathaniel and Solis intently. The exertion of trying to warn Nathaniel had sapped the last of Cushman's strength and his head fell forward onto his chest.

Nathaniel started to edge his way closer to Cushman. His intention was to somehow free Cushman and get him out there.

"Who set up my wife? Come on, 'Mal.' Everyone knows that you're behind everything that goes on at Interglobal."

Malcolm bristled at the use of his nickname. "Why should I tell you anything?" Malcolm replied. "I thought Mr. Sellers was your source of information about Interglobal business." Malcolm laughed. "Don't worry. You'll be joining him shortly. Oh, that's right. Dear ol' Cushman had a little accident. I guess he won't be able to help you out after all."

Nathaniel was enraged. "Godfrey, it's over for you," he yelled. "I have evidence that will ruin you," he lied. "Your whole career, in fact, your whole life is a sham. When I take this evidence public, it will bring you to your knees. Interglobal will be ruined."

Malcolm's maniacal laugh rang throughout the room. George Max's men eyed each other nervously. Malcolm leaned forward and his holographic image glared at Nathaniel. "You fool! Do you think that you can destroy me?" He jumped to his feet, his eyes wild with rage. "I won't listen to any more of your foolish lies! You have nothing!"

Nathaniel edged even closer to Cushman. "What about DSDS? Does the council know about that little project?" Nathaniel was bluffing, gauging Malcolm's reaction.

Malcolm froze. The look on his face was the most hateful Nathaniel had ever seen. "You won't live long enough to use that information against me!" Malcolm laughed again, and then signaled to Max's security team. His voice almost a whisper, Malcolm calmly said, "Kill them."

Outnumbered twelve to two by George Max's security guards, Nathaniel and Solis should have been easy prey. But as soon as Nathaniel heard Malcolm's words, "Kill them," survival skills that he had learned long ago took over.

Max's guards pulled their weapons and began to advance. Nathaniel turned to Solis and hissed, "Engage!"

Solis reacted to Nathaniel's command instinctively, exactly the way Nathaniel had known he would. Before any of Max's guards could respond, Solis had pulled the pistol from his waistband and got off three quick shots, each with deadly precision. His targets fell where they stood. He continued firing until all his ammunition was spent.

Nathaniel had been well trained himself and had experience with killing weapons of all types. He pulled one of the grenades from his vest and tossed it at a man standing twenty feet from where Cushman was tied. The explosion shrouded the man, and the two on each side of him, in a blue phosphorous flame. Mortally wounded, the men's screams filled the room, acid from the grenade burning into their flesh. The rest of the security team was in turmoil. Nathaniel took full advantage of their panic and confusion.

Nathaniel pulled a long, saw-toothed knife from his boot and charged. He swung it at the man on his left. The blade sliced through the man's shirt and went deep into his chest. Nathaniel stabbed the man in the stomach, lifting him off the ground and using him as a human shield. When he no longer needed him, Nathaniel threw him down.

Out of the corner of his eye, Nathaniel saw Solis hit the man to his right with a shoulder tackle. His fist landed on the prone man's temple, crushing his skull. Another guard finally regained his composure and fired his laser directly at Solis's head. Through his glasses, Nathaniel saw what Solis saw. He watched the gun's laser beam come toward Solis as if in slow motion. Solis swiftly and expertly ducked before the beam could reach him and yelled to Nathaniel, "I'm out of ammunition."

Nathaniel dived for the guard that he had just stabbed, grabbing the dead man's gun and tossing it to Solis.

Solis rolled onto his side and caught the gun that Nathaniel had thrown him. He fired at the man who was shooting at him, hitting him squarely in the middle of the forehead before the man had a chance to get off a second shot.

Nathaniel was next to Cushman. "Don't worry. We'll get you out of here," Nathaniel told him.

"No, you won't Nathaniel. If you touch me, we'll all be killed. I'm dying anyway. I don't have much time. Listen carefully. Malcolm himself was behind Kara's execution. He used her as a scapegoat to keep from being investigated. Malcolm is planning a coup. He has a large secret cloning operation in Apache Junction. It's an underground facility. There's a secret subway that connects it to Interglobal's headquarters. Malcolm's cloning an army, and the boy that was killed was a clone. He escaped from the facility before he was fully developed. Godfrey is mad. He wants to rule the universe."

Nathaniel was covered in blood and sweat, and his eyes were wild.

The four remaining guards were converging on Nathaniel and Cushman. He heard Solis scream, "Nathaniel, there's nothing you can do for Cushman."

Solis grabbed Nathaniel's arm and began pulling him toward the door. Nathaniel resisted and tried to stand his ground near Cushman, but Solis was too strong. He pushed Nathaniel through the door in just in time to keep him from being sliced in two by a laser baton. Nathaniel turned to look at Cushman in time to see him smile and take his final breath. The guard's laser baton sliced through Cushman's neck, decapitating him.Nathaniel screamed in rage, trying to get away from Solis, trying to get at the man who had just killed the only father Nathaniel had ever known. Solis was too strong. He kept pulling at Nathaniel.

"Nathaniel, we've got to go!" he cried urgently.

Finally, understanding that there wasn't anything he could do for Cushman, Nathaniel ran toward the stairs that led to Interglobal's main floor. When they were no more than ten feet into the corridor, Solis heard what was left of George Max's security guards charging through the door after them. Nathaniel turned and threw his last grenade. The corridor and the room they had just left exploded. The guards blew apart like leaves caught in a dust devil.

Goodbye, Colonel. You were a loyal friend after all, Nathaniel thought. *You were my true father.*

With their weapons spent, Nathaniel knew that they could not make it out the way that they had come in. George Max would have the rest of his team waiting for them. He saw a door on their left and pushed through it. Solis followed and locked it behind them. They found themselves in an underground subway.

"This must be the subway that Cushman was talking about," Nathaniel said.

There was no way to go but forward. Nathaniel's ears were still ringing from the grenade's explosion. He couldn't hear anything other than the wild beating of his own heart as he and Solis raced deeper into the tunnel.

In his mind, Nathaniel saw the population clock register minus thirteen.

Chapter 33

"Nathaniel, you're losing too much blood," Solis said.

"It's nothing," Nathaniel said as he collapsed onto the subway's floor.

Solis tore open Nathaniel's sweater and found that Nathaniel was bleeding heavily. Solis grabbed the medical kit out of his backpack and sat Nathaniel up against the wall of the tunnel so he could expertly cauterize the wound.

"Stay here while I look around," Solis told him, as if Nathaniel were capable of going anywhere under his own power.

Solis walked a few feet deeper into the tunnel where there were ventilation grates in the ceiling. Reaching up, he grabbed one of the grates and easily pulled it loose; then, he hoisted himself up through the opening. As quickly as possible, he returned to Nathaniel.

He had to shake Nathaniel to get him to open his eyes. "Nathaniel, you've been hurt. I need to get you to a safe place where your wound can be attended to properly. There is a large circular fan about 100 yards ahead. Beyond the fan, I saw blue sky. We can get out that way. Do you think that you can walk?"

Nathaniel nodded weakly. Solis got his arms around a semi-conscious Nathaniel and lifted him up through the opening where the grate had been. Once Nathaniel was through the grate, Solis followed and began dragging Nathaniel toward the fan.

When they reached the fan, Solis quickly short circuited it and removed it from its casing. They were almost at eye level with the ground. Solis climbed through the opening and pulled Nathaniel after him.

Interglobal's headquarters were about a quarter-mile away. Solis and Nathaniel had emerged from the tunnel in the middle of Interglobal's orange grove.

"We can make it back to the vehicle," Solis said with relief. "Everything's going to be okay."

Solis lifted Nathaniel onto his back and began running to where the *tamen* cleaners always parked their cleaning van. He put Nathaniel into the passenger seat and got behind the wheel.

"I need to get you to the safe house as soon as possible," Solis didn't understand how he knew how to operate the vehicle, but somehow, he instinctively knew how it worked. He expertly put the van in gear, whirled it around and headed deeper into the desert.

Digger was already at the safe house when they arrived. "What the hell happened to you two?"

Solis laid Nathaniel on a sofa. He started rifling through the medical cabinet. "Nathaniel was hit by shrapnel when he blew up Malcolm's conference room. I need to remove it and stitch up his side," Solis told Digger.

"Did you two do what I think you did? How could you be so foolhardy? Nathaniel, you know that Godfrey is looking for any excuse to remove you. Permanently!"

Nathaniel refused anesthesia. He wanted to stay alert. He groaned as Solis removed the shrapnel and started to take stitches. "Digger, we had no choice," he groaned.

Nathaniel told Digger everything that had happened since he and Solis broke into Interglobal, including the DSDS holograms that he had removed in his valise. He told him that Cushman was murdered by Max's henchmen. He told Digger that just before Cushman died, he said that Malcolm had a secret cloning facility in Apache Junction and that he intended to overthrow the government.

"Cushman also told me that it was Malcolm himself who set Kara up. Godfrey's mad, and by that, I don't mean 'angry,' I mean 'insane.' I'm going to kill the bastard." Nathaniel tried to get up, but Digger restrained him.

"Take it easy, Nathaniel," Digger said. "I'll help you give Malcolm Godfrey exactly what he deserves. We'll give him a first class ticket on his own private elevator to hell. But first, I think that we'd better get our hands on that valise of yours. I'll leave right away and get it from your pod before Malcolm's boys have a chance to regroup and go there themselves. Also, I need to find out if any of my informants know the location of Interglobal's cloning lab. I thought that criminals like Axcardo were the only ones who dared to use cloning, but there have been rumors of a large-scale cloning lab for years. What you've just told me confirms the rumors."

"Thanks, Digger," Nathaniel said. "There's one more thing that I need you to do. When you get to my pod, go down to the basement. You'll see the remains of what used to be the utility closet wall. Behind the wall there's a room filled with compartments that contain old military equipment."

Nathaniel took a deep painful breath and then continued. "In the top compartment on the left wall you'll find a small gray box. Inside that box there's a blue microchip. Bring me that chip."

Digger nodded his understanding. All business now, he rose to leave.

"Oh, the valise with the holograms is under the table, and there's also a couple of things that I'd like you to get for Solis."

As soon as Digger had the list of all that Nathaniel wanted from his pod, he told him, "I'll be back within twenty minutes. Just stay here and try to get back some of your strength. You're going to need it."

Solis went to the utility kitchen for some water. He came back to Nathaniel with a pill in his hand. "Here, Nathaniel. Take this. It won't take away all your pain, but it will help, and it will not make you sleepy."

Nathaniel took the pill gratefully and turned to Solis. "Solis, my friend, I'm going to ask you for a huge sacrifice."

"Okay, Nathaniel, but first we need to clean up. It is not sanitary for either of us to remain in this condition. We are both covered in blood other than our own."

Without another word, Solis lifted Nathaniel and carried him to what Nathaniel recognized as a century-old shower room. The floor and walls were made of white tile. One wall contained showerheads that were about six feet apart. Hundred-year-old lockers stood along one of the other walls. A long wooden bench was in front of the lockers. Solis placed Nathaniel on the bench and asked him if he could stand.

Nathaniel nodded and stood up slowly. He undressed, then stood under one of the showerheads and turned on the faucet. Solis did the same. The white tile floor soon turned crimson as the warm, soothing water poured over them, washing away the sweat and blood.

Solis leaned forward, and placed both of his hands high on the wall of the shower to support himself. He hung his head and let the water beat down upon him as if pondering what he had done that day.

As he watched Solis, Nathaniel felt a stab of guilt. Never had he seen Solis look like that. His face registered a combination of puzzlement and shame. Although he already knew what his answer would be, Nathaniel asked what was wrong.

"Nathaniel, I never believed that I was capable of such violence. Where did I learn this deadly behavior?"

Nathaniel just looked at Solis. He knew that Solis had no wartime memories, memories like the ones that invaded Nathaniel's mind and still kept him awake at night.

Finished, Nathaniel and Solis dressed in the clean clothes that Digger had left for them and then returned to the control room.

Solis waited until they were back in the control room to ask, "What is it that you want, Nathaniel. You know that I'll do anything for you."

"That's just it, Solis. The reason that you'll do anything for me is that you've been modified to serve. You've had a protector chip installed in your memory. Do you remember anything before you had that chip inserted?"

"No, Nathaniel. Sometimes I see shadows of the past that frighten me, but I struggle to put the thoughts out of my memory."

"Solis, you were once a destructor unit. You were actually deployed in the final corporate war. We served together, and you were one of the few units that survived. After an incident that I don't need to go into now, The Company disabled you. You were placed in inventory and forgotten about for more than half a century, until Kara found you and replaced your destructor chip with a protector chip. Kara reprogrammed you to serve us."

Solis was silent. He just stared at Nathaniel, his face registering disbelief. "I was a destructor? That's where I learned these lethal skills?"

"Yes, Solis, but you have been a protector unit ever since Kara found you. I'm asking you to let me turn you back into a destructor again."

"Nathaniel, how can that be? I can't be a destructor. I can harm no one unless they are a direct threat to you. I hold no personal malice towards any man."

"I know, Solis. That's why I need you to become a destructor unit again. You'll report only to me and follow only my orders.

We can't hope to prevail over Malcolm's troops with our meager force. That is, unless we have superior warriors. You would become our superior warrior."

Nathaniel knew that if Solis had a heart, it would have broken. He hung his head. "Nathaniel, can I have a few minutes to analyze your request?"

"Of course, Solis. But please, think fast. Digger will be back soon. We'll be engaging the enemy tonight."

Solis went into the utility room. He stood at the one-way window and looked out over the desert. He was motionless, as if lost in thought, for twenty minutes. Nathaniel knew what was going through his memory circuits. Solis would be leaving a life that he had come to love. Nathaniel knew about Tandem and that Solis would be wondering who would care for him. Solis had lost Kara. He must be asking himself if he would also lose Tandem, his toy soldiers, and Nathaniel. Nathaniel was suffering these worries right along with Solis.

Finally, his mind made up, Solis returned to the old control room.

"Nathaniel, you are my friend. If you believe that it is best that I become a destructor, then that is what I will be."

Nathaniel was relieved. If Solis had not agreed, Nathaniel would not have known what to do. "Destructors don't have friends," Nathaniel responded sadly. "As soon as this is over, I guarantee that I will return you to who you are now." Just then, Nathaniel heard Digger return.

"Solis has agreed to become a destructor unit. I'm going to replace his protector chip with the destructor chip that you got from my pod."

Digger visibly paled. "Nathaniel, don't you remember how violent those destructor units were? Every soldier feared them. As a matter of fact, Solis himself was responsible for the destruction of an entire town."

"That's why we need a destructor," Nathaniel responded forcefully. "We need that power and that ruthlessness. We'll never be able to fight against Malcolm with the men that we have."

Reluctantly, Digger had to agree with Nathaniel; even though he didn't want to see Solis become one of those "things" that he had hated so much. "Is this the chip you need?" Digger asked. He handed Nathaniel a small box containing a shiny blue microchip.

"Yes, that's it," Nathaniel replied. "I appropriated this chip from one of the D-4-B units before it was dismantled."

Digger couldn't believe his ears. "Nathaniel, the chips that those units carried were only the second release. They were manufactured before the Mars *taman* revolt," Digger said worriedly. "The chip's main program leaves its footprint behind even after it's been removed. You may never be able to return Solis to the way he is right now if you use one of those chips."

Nathaniel looked down at the chip in his hand. "Unfortunately, Digger, we haven't got a choice. Let me worry about Solis. He's under my command," he said sternly.

"I am ready," Solis said to Nathaniel.

"Solis, please get up on the steel table in the medical room. I'll be right in."

Solis looked up when Nathaniel entered the room. "Will this hurt?" he asked.

"I don't think so," Nathaniel answered. "I'll shut down your primary CPU before I remove the protector chip and then I'll install the destructor chip. You shouldn't know what's going on. You won't feel anything. Are you ready?"

"Nathaniel. I need to ask a favor of you."

To Digger, Solis's eyes looked as huge as platters.

Digger had come in and was standing behind Nathaniel. "Wait," he said. "Before you start the operation, you need to see some of the things that I brought back from your pod."

Digger placed Nathaniel's partly open valise on the table beside Solis. "There were a few things that Nathaniel thought you might want, in addition to the holograms from Interglobal."

Digger unzipped the valise all the way. A small furry head popped up. Tandem jumped out onto Solis's chest.

Solis reached up and gently stroked the kitten as it started to purr. "Tandem," he whispered. For a moment, Nathaniel thought that he saw tears in Solis's eyes.

Digger reached into the valise and took out a small wooden box. "Nathaniel thought you might want these too."

Solis looked at his toy soldiers and then back at Digger. "Thank you, Digger," he said sincerely.

With his free hand, Solis held the box of toy soldiers to his chest. "I'm sorry that I kept these from you, Nathaniel. I'd planned to tell you about them when the time was right."

Nathaniel looked at Tandem, the soldiers, and then at Solis. He was heartbroken and had to turn away until he could get his own emotions under control. He turned back to Solis and said resolutely, "I promise that I'll take care of your things until you return. Nothing will happen to Tandem."

"Thank you, Nathaniel. You might want to start by putting Tandem in the other room where he'll be safe from me."

Nathaniel picked up Tandem and the box of soldiers, and took them to the control room. He returned to the utility room, closing the door behind him.

"Ready?" Nathaniel asked him.

Solis hesitated for only a second. His light blue eyes looked resignedly at Nathaniel. "Ready," he replied somberly.

Nathaniel started the shut-down process. Solis's eyes slowly closed. In minutes, he was disabled. Nathaniel made an incision in Solis's chest. He removed one of his man-made ribs, exposing the motherboard that was located behind the processor rib cage. He picked up surgical pliers and carefully removed the protector chip from Solis's motherboard and placed it in the gray box that had previously contained the chip that Digger had brought him. Just as carefully, he inserted the destructor chip, and then replaced the rib that he had removed at the beginning of the process.

When he was done, Nathaniel started the CPU's boot up sequence.

At first, Nathaniel didn't believe that he had successfully changed the chip. Then he saw Solis's chest begin to rise and fall, simulating breathing. He watched the incision that he had just made begin healing itself. In seconds, all evidence that a scar ever existed was gone.

Solis sat up. His eyes snapped open. Nathaniel gasped when he saw the emotionless, stone-cold expression on Solis's face. Solis looked back at Nathaniel through pupils that glowed red as burning coals. He looked first at his right hand, then at his left, clenching and unclenching his fists.

In a disturbing voice that seemed to rumble from somewhere deep in his chest, Solis said, "Solis reporting. Ready for battle, Lieutenant Lamrock."

KATHLEEN PAPAJOHN

Chapter 34

Nathaniel stood, watching over Digger's shoulder as he stared at the workstation's display that currently showed a blueprint of Godfrey's cloning lab. After some not-so-friendly persuasion, Digger had convinced his source to reveal the whereabouts of Godfrey's cloning lab. Digger reported that his informant, Rudy, told him that there were rumors of a large underground facility located thirty miles east of Phoenix. He was more than happy to give Digger the lab's exact coordinates. The underground structure was just east of Apache Junction, latitude 34 36 39, longitude 112 16 20.

Digger had surveyed the location remotely, using the same type of technology that was used by the population clock. The clock's scanner was capable of identifying all carbon-producing units by recognizing and counting the unique identification chip that had been imbedded in every human. It matched each chip it found to entries in its own Human Population Census database that contained a unique record for every human living on earth.

Digger's first scan of the cloning lab's coordinates used the same parameters as the population clock. It identified an underground superstructure but found only thirteen people whose identification matched the clock's database.

"This doesn't make sense," Digger said. "Malcolm would never trust protection of any of Interglobal's facilities to a force that small. Some of Malcolm's people must have no internal identification chip at all. I need to run a second scan."

This time, he changed the scan's parameters to count carbon-producing units without any sub-dermal identification. The count was 1,056 humans.

"That's more like it," Digger said. "Malcolm would believe that this number would be sufficient to guard his facility."

"Try the scan one more time," Nathaniel suggested. "This time, count only carbon producing units with sub-dermal identification chips that do not match the population clock's database."

Digger changed the parameters and ran the scan again. The number displayed on the scanner's computer screen was 50,553.

Stunned by the high volume of hits, Digger turned to Nathaniel and declared, "Cushman was right when he told you that Malcolm was creating his own secret army! These can only be clones that Godfrey has outfitted with false identity chips. He must intend to load the false identification numbers into the World Population Database to make it appear that his clones are legitimate human beings. After all, as originator and manager of the Population Clock, Interglobal controls all the records. He obviously has plans to try to take over the Council--probably the entire Western Zone. Why else would he need that many units? We have to stop him before he starts another global war!"

Digger had contacted only his most trusted colleagues, and they had been arriving singly all night. They patiently sat in the control room. Nathaniel knew that they were waiting for Digger to join them and explain what this was all about. Nathaniel also knew that, like him, each man in that room owed Digger a debt. Most owed him their lives. All of them would probably follow Digger to hell if need be. Finally, Digger entered the control room with Nathaniel beside him.

It was just past midnight. Marty was standing by the medical room door, carefully watching Solis. She looked as though he frightened her. Tandem seemed to have taken a liking to Marty and was rubbing up against her legs. Bunker, obviously jealous, softly growled at Tandem. Nine of Digger's most trusted associates sat on small, uncomfortable chairs that Digger had placed randomly around the old control room. Solis was still on the table in the medical room.

Digger looked around and shook his head. "Not much of a force to fight Malcolm's army," he said so that only Nathaniel could hear him.

Digger stood before the small gathering. "I really appreciate each of you coming," he told them.

When each of the men started to speak, Digger raised his hand to silence them and to introduce the man standing beside him. "This is Lieutenant Nathaniel Lamrock. Nathaniel and I fought together in the war, and I trust him with my life. He'll be in charge of this operation. We'll be outnumbered, and I will not hold it against any of you if you choose to leave."

"What're we up against, Dig?" asked a shaggy-haired young man who Digger had introduced as "Surfer," his Special Ops moniker.

"We're going to hit Interglobal's secret research facility in Apache Junction, where illegal cloning has been going on."

The man called Surfer exhaled in what became a whistle. "What you're talking about is a complex operation. Why isn't this official Internals business?" he asked.

"I have reason to believe that Interglobal has gotten to one or more of the Internals' higher-ups. The mission would be compromised if the mole finds out what we're up to," Digger answered. "If word of what we're planning leaves this room, we'll be walking into an ambush."

"So we can't expect any help from the Internals?" asked Hatchet, another operative.

"That's right," Digger answered. "We're on our own. So again, if any one wants to back out, there's the door. No hard feelings."

When no one made a move to leave, Digger continued. "The lab itself is a huge underground complex. Simon Brader, Interglobal's chief of security, has over a thousand men guarding the facility. Our only edge is that we'll have superior weaponry. The arms that you'll be using haven't been manufactured since the war. Interglobal's forces will be carrying only conventional weapons. We may not have them outnumbered, but we'll certainly have them outgunned. Follow me downstairs, and I'll show you what we have."

Nathaniel and the men followed Digger downstairs where he opened what appeared to be a bay door leading to a large loading dock. Inside the room was row after row of weapons and armor. Digger began identifying the capability of each weapon in his arsenal. Most of the items had been used in the corporate war. Digger had managed to hide the arms before the Council had ordered all weaponry destroyed. Some of the armaments in Digger's collection were over a hundred years old. Although the weapons were old, they were still technologically superior to anything currently in existence. Each had been meticulously cared for and was in perfect working order. Digger had told Nathaniel that these weapons would give his team an advantage over Malcolm's force.

"There are eleven combat suits with very special features. Each of you will wear one. The suit is made of a soft, lightweight textile containing nano-muscle fibers that simulate actual human muscle tissue. This will increase your strength by a factor of ten." Digger continued demonstrating the suit's characteristics. The suit itself covered each man from head to toe. Only the face would be exposed, and even that would be partially covered by the helmet's faceplate.

"When the suit's on-board computer senses an incoming projectile, the normally pliable material becomes rigid, deflecting the incoming round. Once danger has passed, the material will become soft again, allowing you freedom of movement. For hand-to-hand combat, the suit is outfitted with wrist blades and retractable sonic spears as back up to additional hand-held weaponry that you will have."

Digger looked around at each man. "Some of you have used these suits before. To the rest of you, this will be your first experience with this type of armor. Believe me; it saved thousands of lives in the war. Each of you will be a recognized node on our local and wide area combat network. The drop down eyepiece provides a seven-inch display that allows you to take in all supporting data without taking your hands from your weapons. There won't be need for verbal communication because the helmet is outfitted with sensors that register cranial cavity vibrations and transmits them as instructions to the armor itself, or communicates your thoughts to other soldier-nodes on our network.

"There is an internal audible alarm that will sound if you are laser-targeted by the enemy. A sensor picks up directional signals from laser-guided weapons. If you hear that alarm, immediately fall and roll, or you're toast."

Digger didn't mention the suit's final feature because he didn't want the men to think about some of the life-threatening possibilities that their involvement in this mission could bring. The body armor contained a physiological monitoring system that continually sent statistics about the soldier back to the network's hub. Medics that were miles away could access a soldier's core temperature, skin temperature, heart rate, and hydration. If a medic saw anything wrong with a soldier, he could treat him remotely. If no heart rate was detected, the soldier was classified as a statistical loss. Unfortunately, for this operation, there would be no medics. Marty would be manning the control desk alone.

Digger asked the men to return to the control room. "Think long and hard about joining me. It won't be a cakewalk, and there is a possibility that some or even all of us may not survive. I'll be up in a minute to get your answer."

Digger took Nathaniel aside. "We have eleven body armor suits. There are enough to outfit you and me plus the men in the control room. I want Marty to stay here to monitor our vital signs. Our group will be able to do a lot of damage, but we still don't have the numbers to give Malcolm's men much of a fight. Even though Malcolm's force won't have the same level of technology that we do, there's still over a thousand of his merry men. You were right about needing a destructor. I only wish that we had more than one."

"Solis is as good as a dozen destructors," Nathaniel said confidently. "Malcolm's people will have had a glimpse of hell when Solis gets through with them. You told me that you have one other piece of equipment that you haven't showed the men upstairs. Where is Solis's battlewagon?"

Digger took Nathaniel to the back of the warehouse. The battlewagon hung, suspended by a hoist that was attached to the ceiling. It was obviously too heavy for any mortal to lift. It would take the strength of a *taman* that had been specifically designed for that purpose to wear the suit and still be able to maneuver.

The battlewagon was its own stand-alone man-shaped weapons platform. The suit had all the same characteristics of the human armor that Nathaniel, Digger, and the others would be wearing, plus a few of its own special added attractions. Each arm of the suit contained specialized weaponry. The left arm had a retractable earth-penetrating bunker-buster missile system. The right arm contained an atomic assault rifle and an atomizer canon that could disintegrate everything in its path. There was an anti-matter gas-cooled Gatling gun, affectionately nicknamed the "meat grinder," on the right shoulder. The gun fired five thousand rounds per second. A fusion pack that could melt any form of metal in less than a second was situated at the battlewagon's waist. For close combat, the left hand piece contained a sonic pistol. The right contained a hand-atomizer. The *taman* would be able to enter target coordinates mentally. The onboard computer would identify the coordinates as a red zone. On a thought-command from the *taman* wearing the battlewagon, the atomizer canon would disintegrate everything in the designated red zone.

All of the suit's weaponry had been designed using RRF, or Rapid Return Fire, technology. With RRF, the battlewagon would identify the exact origin of all incoming projectiles and respond with direct rapid return fire from any of the on-board weapons back to the originating offensive source with precise and lethal accuracy. Any one unlucky enough--and stupid enough--to target the battlewagon would be taken out instantly.

Finally, the suit's backpack contained fireflies. They were slightly larger than an average-sized honeybee. Fireflies operated independently. Each was fitted with a micro-camera and light that illuminated the tiny spy-in-the-sky, making it look like a firefly. Everything that an individual firefly saw was transmitted back to the battlewagon via a unique communication frequency. A microprocessor gave each firefly the intelligence to lock onto and pursue its own target. Small enough to fly through windows and even cracks under doors, fireflies could lead destructive energy waves from the battlewagon to their targets with complete precision.

Nathaniel went back upstairs to the medical room and leaned over Solis, who was still lying on the table as Nathaniel had instructed. His flame-red pupils gave Nathaniel chills. He had seen those eyes before in the corporate war and had hoped that he would never have to look into them again.

"Solis, it's time. Come with me," Nathaniel ordered.

Nathaniel took Solis into the warehouse and watched as Solis lowered the black battlewagon from the hoist and climbed into it. There was nothing human-like about this once-gentle *taman* anymore. The pupils of Solis's eyes glowed blood-red from behind the battle helmet's black faceplate. Painted on the helmet was the image of a skull, making Solis look like one of the four horsemen of the apocalypse. An anonymous someone had written the word *Adios* on his breastplate.

Nathaniel could hear Digger upstairs where he had returned to the control room.

"Please follow me back to the warehouse," he told the men. When they reached the first floor, Digger stopped and turned to the group. "Okay, who's with me?" he asked.

Surfer looked at him closely. "This is a suicide mission, isn't it? Even with the advanced weaponry you showed us, how can we fight a thousand-man force?"

Digger grinned and opened the bay door. "Here's how," he replied.

The large door opened slowly revealing Nathaniel standing beside the battlewagon, with Solis manning the controls. Encased in the battlewagon, Solis stood over twelve feet tall. Digger heard one of the men whisper as if in awe, "That's Solis, the Destructor!"

"No," Digger avowed. "In this case, Solis is the Equalizer!"

Digger looked over the group of men, each of whom was a personal friend. Nathaniel knew that no one would be there unless Digger had personally witnessed each man's bravery first hand, and on more than one occasion.

Digger asked again, "Who's with me?"

This time, no one spoke up. They looked at each other and then at Digger.

Surfer stood up and said, "I think that I can speak for each of us. We're with you Digger. All the way!"

Solis began walking toward the door. The floor shook with every step he took; the ancient battlewagon creaked, as if to protest having to move after all its years of rest.

Nathaniel grimaced and said, "We'll never be able to sneak up on the facility. They'll hear Solis coming from a mile away."

Solis stopped in his tracks. He turned toward a stack of oil drums that was in the corner of the warehouse. Easily lifting one of the barrels, Solis sat it on the floor, then poked his finger through the top, popping it open as if it were a can of beer.

He looked over at Nathaniel and said, "Here, apply the contents of this barrel to all my joints. It will reduce friction and eliminate the unwanted sounds."

Nathaniel and Digger looked at each other and smiled before Digger went to find a ladder.

Marty was busily passing out body armor when Digger tapped her lightly on the shoulder. "I want you to stay here," Digger told her. "Monitor everyone's vital signs. If I don't come back, take Tandem and Bunker and leave Phoenix. Don't go back to your living pod."

"Don't talk like that, Digger," Marty replied. Her voice caught in her throat as she told him, "I know you'll be back. I just know it."

Nathaniel left Solis waiting on the loading dock as he and Digger donned their own battle gear. Digger gave Nathaniel a final smile before he lowered his own faceplate. Everything was ready.

Digger and his men left the safe house and got into their transport vehicles. Since Solis's battlewagon was too large for a standard transport, he got into the bed of an oversized dump truck that was so large, one of its tires was three times as high as an average man. Nathaniel got into the truck's cab and started the ignition.

Together, Nathaniel and Solis followed Digger and his men. As they pulled away from the safe house, Nathaniel wondered if any of them would ever return.

Chapter 35

Across town in the Nualas' North Phoenix living pod, Sha moaned in pain. She had gone into labor three hours earlier and now her contractions were only minutes apart. Afraid to go to a government clinic to have her baby, Sha had asked her sister, Ea, to act as midwife. Juan had just completed the birthing space and had finished none too soon. At Ea's insistence, he sat outside the door listening to Sha's moans.

At eleven o'clock, Sha went into the active phase of labor. Ea came to the door and said to Juan, "It's time."

Juan went into the birthing chamber and stood by Sha's head, mopping the perspiration from her forehead. Sha held her breath. She felt the urge to push and began to bear down. She felt a burning sensation in her groin. Ea called Juan to join her at Sha's feet as baby Kara's head emerged. Juan watched in wonder as Ea took the baby. Kara took her first breath and immediately started to cry.

When baby Kara was placed on Sha's stomach, she looked directly into Sha's eyes. Sha looked down at her and was overwhelmed by the love that she felt for this child. Skin to skin, the baby snuggled into Sha. Kara had made her second transition to life outside the womb.

Chapter 36

Digger heard the metallic shuffling of equipment and the sound of men groaning. He sweated beneath his own suit of armor. His heart was pounding. Suddenly a loud hissing sound filled the early morning air; then Digger heard a dull thud as Solis's flare hit its mark. In its light, Digger could see the facility. From somewhere behind him, Solis fired another flare. It was then that Digger spotted the sand mounds that were obviously not part of the desert's natural terrain.

Underground bunkers, he thought.

He heard another projectile fly over his head, aimed directly at the roof of the cloning facility. The explosion that followed created a huge fireball. Digger and his men put their heads down and covered themselves as much as possible to escape the flying debris. Solis had done his job well. There was a gaping hole where most of the facility's front wall had been.

Digger's battle instinct told him to expect the worst. Then he heard the shushing sound of a missile launched from the facility. He turned and yelled to his men, "Stay down! Incoming!"

Fusion beams blasted the earth all around where Digger hid with his men. Chisel-like, pointed sonic spears started to fall all around him. For several seconds Digger's arm couldn't move because the normally flexible material of his armor had stiffened to repel one of the sonic spears. He watched as the spear hit his body armor, causing a spark and bouncing off.

A blood-curdling war cry came from the depths of the desert in front of him. In the light of the flares, Digger watched as hundreds of Brader's men charged out of their bunkers towards Digger's position.

Behind him, more craters opened. Bloodthirsty, screaming men continued to pour from them. Digger and his men were surrounded. Brader's men charged Digger's force from all sides, like a hoard of locusts. Digger thought that there must have been thousands of them. Out of the corner of his eye, he saw one of his men get hit by a fusion missile and go down. Surfer turned and returned fire.

Digger saw that Hatchet was surprised by the appearance of Brader's men behind them, and he was relieved when he saw that Hatchet had enough battle experience to scrap the original plan that was for Hatchet was to hold back, waiting to charge in a second wave attack. Instead, Hatchet and his men immediately joined the battle. They rose from their hiding places covered in dust, like zombies from their graves. Guns blazing, they looked like demons with a score to settle. Hatchet used his personal battle-axe with precision, slashing and chopping his way through the enemy to stand with Digger.

With Hatchet covering his flank, Digger's men were able to meet the frontal assault with everything they had. Still, the force they faced was overwhelming.

Adding to the chaos, a summer monsoon swept in. Lightning pierced the night sky, ripping the air itself apart. Heat from the desert floor rose to meet cold air aloft creating violent bursts of energy. Thunder cracked, sending shock waves through Digger and his men.

Suddenly, Digger saw Solis standing at the top of a nearby berm on his right flank. He was walking slowly and seemed to materialize out of the smoke and flames like a horrible apparition from hell. Hundreds of lightning bolts, like an electrical avalanche, streaked the sky behind him. The sun was just about to rise, and the battlewagon's large frame was silhouetted against the blood-red sky of morning. Another image took shape beside Solis. Digger knew that Nathaniel was with him, giving Solis the commands that caused the destruction that was now raining down on Brader's force.

Solis opened fire with the meat grinder in a 180-degree arc, aiming directly at the enemy in front of Digger. Without having any time to turn and run, they were chopped down like wheat harvested by a grim reaper.

Solis next focused on the enemy that was flanking Digger's position. Every round that Solis fired hit its mark with precision. It took only minutes to secure the area. By the time Digger turned around, more than six-hundred of Brader's men lay dead.

Solis let the fireflies loose. Thousands of tiny lights filled the sky, flitting this way and that. They swarmed Brader's remaining men as they vainly tried to hide from the lethal beams that followed the fireflies and tore into their flesh.

Brader had about four hundred remaining men who continued to fight. Digger stood and motioned his men forward. Blasts from his men's atomic assault rifles ripped through the enemy combatants in front of him. Digger knew that most of them had never seen weapons of war like the ones that he and his men carried. The smell of charred flesh filled the air. The earth could not absorb the amount of blood that poured from the dead and dying bodies, turning the desert into a pond of blood.

The world grew quiet. A desert breeze blew dust over the corpses that lay all around him. Digger looked up and saw green, narrow streams of light. He knew that the vibration sensors and tripwires that he had not seen before the initial assault had finally been activated.

"Digger, watch out!" Nathaniel yelled as he ran up to join him.

Nathaniel's warning came just in time. Digger ducked as a deadly beam flew past his head. The sniper who had shot at him exploded as Nathaniel took deadly aim and fired directly at the man's head.

Even behind the face mask, Digger could see Nathaniel's eyes. They were frenzied, half-crazed. Digger had loved Kara most of his life. He always knew that he would have been willing to give his life for hers if she ever were in danger. He thought that no one could ever hate the men responsible for her death more than he did. That is, he had thought so until that moment. He had never before seen hatred like the hatred that he saw in Nathaniel's eyes.

The look on Nathaniel's face looked somehow inhuman. It was a face that was twisted into something so intense, Digger had to look away. The mixture of hatred and pain that he saw on that face was too much for his own mind to process. He knew at that moment that Nathaniel the man was gone. The being that remained, a creature so intent on revenge that he could scarcely be called a mortal man, was someone Digger had never seen before, even in the worst of times.

Behind them, Solis moved slowly through the carnage, killing any of the enemy that he found still breathing, even the wounded who were crawling through the dust, trying to escape. Solis was a killing machine, showing no mercy as he walked through the smoke. He lifted his left arm and fired the bunker-buster. Pieces of earth and debris flew all around Digger and Nathaniel. The ground opened, revealing the facility's labyrinth of tunnels.

Digger watched Solis with dismay. "Why is he doing that?" Digger asked incredulously. "Those men are no more threat to us! Why is he killing them?"

Nathaniel looked dispassionately back at Digger. "I hold everyone associated with Interglobal responsible for taking Kara from me. Solis is just an instrument of my vengeance. He is following my orders. I told him to secure the area, and that is what he is doing."

"Well, make him stop!" Digger ordered in disgust.

Reluctantly, Nathaniel turned to Solis and held up his hand. Solis stopped firing and stood where he was, as if at attention.

Now, it was Nathaniel's turn to lead. Digger and his remaining men, covered in the dust and blood of battle, followed Nathaniel through the breeched wall and into the facility itself. They entered a rat's maze of tunnels that had been carved out of sheer rock. Brader's force was making a last ditch effort to defend the lab. Digger dodged a knife thrust and used his own wrist blade to disembowel his attacker. The resistance was light, and Brader's men retreated quickly.

Begrudgingly, Digger had to admit that Brader had almost outwitted them. His men had been battle-hardened fighters. Without Solis, Nathaniel, Digger and all his men all might have been dead.

***

The battle was obviously over, but Nathaniel heard an explosion, and the tunnel walls around them began to disintegrate. *Solis*, he thought. Hurriedly, Nathaniel turned and ran back to where Solis was preparing to launch another atomic grenade at the building.

"Stop!" Nathaniel screamed just in time to prevent another assault on what was now Digger's hard-won position.

Solis turned at the sound of Nathaniel's voice and began slowly walking toward him. The assault rifle imbedded in the sleeve of his suit's left arm began to turn and whirr as if it were measuring the distance between them. Solis kept coming. He was close enough for Nathaniel to see the cold emptiness in the blood-red eyes staring back at him. The rifle seemed to move on its own and was aimed directly at Nathaniel's head.

"Solis, it's Nathaniel," he cried. "I order you to stand down."

231

The assault rifle continued to whirr.

"Solis! Attention! Lieutenant Lamrock speaking! Report!"

Finally, recognition flashed in Solis's eyes. He stopped dead, as if he had been unplugged. Then he slowly lowered his weapon.

"Unit Solis reporting. Mission incomplete sir," Solis said.

From his quizzical look, Nathaniel knew that Solis didn't understand. There were still humans left alive. Solis's mission had been to terminate all humans. *He's wondering why his controller is telling him to halt the mission before it was complete.*

The red eyes still stared malevolently at Nathaniel, but Nathaniel was relieved that at least Solis had complied with his order to stop killing. Uncertainly, Nathaniel took a step closer to Solis. He hardly recognized this thing that used to be a gentle giant.

"Solis, when this is over, I promise you will feel better. Right now, I need you to give me an analysis of the facility."

Solis turned toward Malcolm's cloning facility. He activated his internal situation analysis program and issued the first command, *Perform non-destructive element detection.* The scan began its first step, a quantitative image analysis. Next, a nuclear microprobe searched for scattered particles. Finally, the program used a micro-beam to scan each level of the facility and identify all heat and activity, human and otherwise. As the analysis program executed, the structure's coordinates and thermal images from each level were displayed on the screen that appeared on Solis's faceplate.

In seconds, the words *Scan complete* appeared. Solis issued the next program command, *Report.*

A read-out appeared on his screen along with a robotic voice. Solis turned up the volume so that Nathaniel could also hear it.

Seven subterranean levels. Level one destroyed – no activity. Twenty-seven carbon producing units on level two. Nathaniel knew that nine of these were Digger and his men. *Level three, no activity. Level four, one thousand carbon-producing units. All but three, at rest.*

Clones and their keepers, Nathaniel thought.

Level five, one thousand two hundred twenty-six carbon-producing units. Eighty-five alert. Level six, fifty-five heat producing units. No carbon production noted in these units.

Nathaniel thought that these must be *taman* units.

The droning, robotic voice of the analysis program continued. *Level seven, two active carbon producing units moving rapidly toward the rear of the facility. DNA analysis shows one of the units to be Malcolm Godfrey. Both units are agitated. Additionally, there are forty-seven thousand immobile carbon producing units.*

Solis turned and faced Nathaniel. "Analysis complete."

"Good job," Nathaniel told him. "Now, I want you to remain here. I do not need you to destroy anything else. I will return as soon as we search the facility. Do not, I repeat, do not harm anyone unless you are fired upon. Do you hear me?"

Time stood still as Nathaniel waited for Solis to respond. Solis continued to look at Nathaniel with what appeared to be both disappointment and blood lust at the same time.

"Solis, acknowledge!" Nathaniel repeated.

Solis's eyes glowed red as he stared at Nathaniel. Nathaniel had fought bravely since before sunrise. He had not dreaded the coming battle. In fact, he had welcomed it. For the first time that day, when he looked into Solis's eyes, Nathaniel was afraid.

Solis continued to stare fixedly at Nathaniel.

"Acknowledge!" Nathaniel repeated louder.

Finally, Solis reluctantly nodded.

Nathaniel sighed in relief. Without another word, he turned and raced back to join Digger.

By the time Nathaniel caught up with Digger, the remnants of Brader's defense force had scurried away like rats. Some of Digger's men were standing around. Others were sitting on the hard concrete floor, waiting for their adrenaline to subside. One man whispered something to his comrade, and they both laughed.

Hatchet looked up as Nathaniel came in. "I only count eight of us left. Who got it?"

"Big John went down early in the battle," Digger said sorrowfully.

"I know his family," Hatchet told him. "I'll let them know that he won't be coming home."

Digger nodded gratefully then turned to Nathaniel. "So what are we looking at here?"

"Solis ran a scan of the facility," Nathaniel told him. "There are seven levels. Hostiles can be expected on each floor. The majority of clones are on the bottom level."

Digger looked through the smoke filled tunnel to a bank of elevators. He strode over to his men.

"Attention. I want you to form two groups. Take the elevators, and each group search an entire floor. Be careful. There are more hostiles in the building. If you find Godfrey, I want him alive. Report back here to me in a half hour."

Digger's men started to move toward the elevators. They seemed relieved to have something to do. Digger turned to Nathaniel.

"What do you say we take a look ourselves?"

***

Seven floors below where Nathaniel and Digger stood, Malcolm was keying the final destruction sequence that would set off an explosion that would destroy the structure with everything, and everyone, in it. As soon as he hit the last key, a blaring alarm began to sound throughout the facility.

Digger's team seemed to be road blocked at the elevators. "They're not working," one of the men said to Digger as he came up to them. Then they heard the alarm. On the wall, strobe lights flashed and nine individual green cubes lit up. An earsplitting alarm continued to blare.

"What the hell is this?" Digger asked.

The first cube went dark.

Nathaniel turned to Digger's crew. "Go outside and wait for further instructions," he told them.

Reluctantly, the men started to leave the facility.

Nathaniel spoke into his communicator. "Solis, what's going on? Did your analysis find a detonation device in the building?"

Several seconds went by before Solis responded. Nathaniel was stunned that Solis would keep information like the existence of a self-destruct system to himself. Many thoughts ran through is mind. *Is he capable of anger? Could he be getting back at me because I did not let him complete what Solis saw as his mission? Does Solis believe that he is not obligated to volunteer information?*

"You did not request that information," Solis replied.

A second cube went dark.

"Digger, put a clock on that thing," Nathaniel shouted.

"Solis, I'm asking now. Is there a detonation device in the building?"

Again, Solis's response was slow. "Affirmative. My analysis reveals that there is a large amount of atomic explosive material. The trigger has been activated."

Exasperated, Nathaniel asked, "Why the hell didn't you let us know before this?"

"You did not ask," Solis answered matter-of-factly. "And I was not personally compromised."

A third cube went dark. "These things are going out at sixty-second intervals," Digger called to Nathaniel.

"The whole thing's going to blow," Nathaniel yelled loud enough to be heard over the ear-piercing siren.

Digger screamed into his communicator, "Everyone out. Now! Get to the transporters and get out of here."

***

235

Seven floors below where Nathaniel and Digger heard the first alarm, Malcolm turned to Brader. "That should take care of them," he snarled.

They both took off running down the narrow corridor. By the time they reached the silo, Malcolm was breathing so hard that he had to key in the combination to the vault door twice before he got it right.

"Start the system!" he yelled at Brader as they rushed into the silo together.

Just inside the door, a single airship outfitted to carry eight passengers stood in a tall shaft pointing at an angle to the top of the facility. Brader hurried to a keyboard just to their left. He typed in a series of commands and confirmed passwords that were known only to him.

Password invalid appeared in green luminous letters on the display. Brader typed in the password again. This time, the shaft seemed to shutter, then there was a loud scraping sound as the roof of the shaft began to screech open.

Malcolm climbed the narrow white mobile stairway that led up to the airship's pilot compartment. He climbed into the compartment and pulled the canopy shut over him.

It seemed to take forever for the ceiling to yawn open.

Brader ran up the mobile stairs. He pulled on the handle to the transparent hatch that covered the passenger compartment. It wouldn't budge.

"Malcolm," he yelled. "The hatch is stuck. Press the release from your side."

Like a bad child, Malcolm smirked and waved bye-bye to Brader. "Sorry, Brader, I've got the last ticket for this trip."

The plane's engines began to fire and the airship slowly began to rise, knocking the mobile stairs over and away from it. Brader hit the ground first, followed by the steel stairway that fell on top of him.

The airship's nose eased through the opening at the top of the shaft, and the aircraft banked left, accelerating into the early morning sky.

***

Nathaniel and Digger waited to make sure that everyone was out before they raced out of the building themselves. Nathaniel knew that when the facility went, the desert in all directions would go with it. They ran toward the transport vehicles. They were about two hundred yards behind the rest of the team.

"Solis, get out of here," Nathaniel yelled into his communicator. *We're not going to make it*, he thought. "Solis, where are you?"

Abruptly, Nathaniel felt like he was being pulled onto a high-speed ski lift. From out of nowhere, Solis grabbed Nathaniel under one arm and Digger under the other. He accelerated to over a hundred miles an hour. In seconds, he had carried Nathaniel and Digger two miles away from the facility. Solis stopped on the other side of a small mound and quickly used his body to cover both of them.

The ground trembled as if a violent earthquake had hit. Thunder rolled from beneath the sand as, just yards behind them, the desert hiccupped and then crumbled into itself, dropping the desert floor at least ten feet. They were two miles from ground zero when the explosion erupted. A wind, as strong as a category-three hurricane blew across the desert creating one of the largest dust storms Nathaniel had ever seen. Nathaniel felt the heat of the blast even through the protection of Solis's armor.

KATHLEEN PAPAJOHN

Chapter 37

Nathaniel and Digger staggered through the safe house door, battle-worn and drawn. Digger went into the utility room to get himself some water. Solis followed, looking like he was eager to repeat the battle all over again. He clenched his fists, pacing backing and forth between the utility room and the control room.

Even without his battlewagon, the apartment suddenly seemed too small to contain Solis. Marty sat in one of the chairs that Digger had left out for his men. She had manned the control desk, but looked as if she had participated in the battle herself. Her eyes were wide as she looked accusingly at Nathaniel.

"It's bad enough that you and Digger are so ragged-looking and completely covered in dust and blood, but to see Solis looking like he's ready for more is just too much." She picked up Tandem and Bunker and went into the bathroom, closing and locking the door behind her.

"Digger, your assistant is having some kind of meltdown," Nathaniel told him.

"Marty, come out of the bathroom," Digger called tiredly.

"Not until that monster is gone," Marty called back determinedly.

"Solis isn't going to hurt you. Nathaniel's taking him to the medical room right now. He'll take care of him. Come on, Marty. It's been a rough day."

Marty hesitantly peeked around the bathroom door. "I still don't trust him," she murmured, but she slinked out of the bathroom anyway, obviously curious to see what was happening to Solis.

For the second time in twenty-four hours, Nathaniel started the update process. This time, Solis wouldn't close his eyes. He looked accusingly at Nathaniel as his CPU began to shut down. Even after he was disabled, his red eyes still stared into Nathaniel's. At least the light had gone out of them. Nathaniel carefully removed the destructor chip from Solis's motherboard replacing it with Solis's protector chip. He returned the destructor chip to its original container. With that done, he restarted Solis's CPU by initiating the boot-up sequence.

At first, nothing seemed to be happening. Then, slowly, Solis's eyes started to fade from bright red. Nathaniel relaxed only when he could see recognition in Solis's light blue eyes.

Solis sat up and looked around. His first words were, "Where's Tandem?"

"He's right here. He's been waiting for you."

Solis smiled as Tandem rubbed against him and purred. "Did I do all right?" Solis asked.

"You did just fine, but I'm really glad to have you back."

Digger poked his head in the door and said urgently, "Nathaniel, come in here. You've got to see this!"

Nathaniel left Solis and Tandem to join Digger in the control room. There was a news flash coming in on the hologram. Trey Thrasher's face was genuinely grave as he reported the morning's events.

"I've never seen anything like this. Bodies are everywhere. There were so many deaths that the Population Clock could not handle the input. At 5:17 this morning the system locked up. It froze, unable to continue tracking all human life on earth. This man is alleged to have caused all this violence and mayhem."

Nathaniel's picture flashed onto the screen. The hologram rotated 360 degrees so that every side of Nathaniel's countenance could be seen by the viewing public.

Thrasher continued, "As you know, Nathaniel is the husband of Kara Lamrock, the woman who was convicted of murder and executed just three days ago.

"We have the new head of security for Interglobal in the studio with us. George Max was appointed Chief of Security after Simon Brader was killed in this morning's attack. Mr. Max, do you have any idea why Nathaniel Lamrock would go on such a rampage?"

George Max looked solemnly into the camera. "I believe that it's obvious that Nathaniel Lamrock was out to exact revenge on the Company for the conviction and execution of his wife. In his deranged mind, Lamrock holds Interglobal responsible for the court's decision. It's only by the grace of God that, at the last minute our CEO, Mr. Malcolm Godfrey, escaped from the research complex."

Once more, footage that graphically depicted the extent of the destruction was displayed.

A picture of Nathaniel replaced the carnage that was being aired on the hologram. Trey Thrasher, was pleading with the public to be on the lookout for Nathaniel. For some reason, Trey's plea lacked his usual enthusiasm.

It was the words that Trasher said next that Nathaniel couldn't believe. It seems that Trey Thrasher was not quite through with his interview with George Max. The camera was once again live, close up on the face of George Max when Trey asked his next question. "Mr. Max, before I let you go, I have another question. Yesterday, my station got a look at some evidence that was used to convict Mrs. Lamrock. Our experts tell us that the video, the one that the prosecution used as its most important evidence at her trial, had been altered. My staff found traces of DNA that belongs to Simon Brader on the video. They also tell me that it is obvious from their findings that the video was altered and that those findings are absolutely conclusive.

"Additionally, internal Interglobal records that we got hold of put Kara Lamrock in a totally different facility at the time that the rogue *taman* was altered. That is, Kara Lamrock was nowhere near the lab where it was alleged that Kara altered the *taman*. According to your own company's records, it is impossible that Mrs. Lamrock could be in both places at the same time. It seems that the surveillance footage that Mr. Brader said tracked Mrs. Lamrock's every move was also altered.

"What do you have to say about all this?"

George Max didn't even blink. He had been told that the truth may have gotten out. He was ready with an answer.

"Trey, thank you for bringing this up. Our security department has come to the same conclusion that your staff did. We didn't want to release the information until we were sure, but we also believe that Mrs. Lamrock was innocent of any crime. In our opinion, Mr. Simon Brader orchestrated the frame-up to cover his own mistake. Unfortunately, since Mr. Brader is already dead, further action in this situation is impossible.

"I can assure you however, along with every person watching this broadcast, that Interglobal has taken every step possible to be sure that nothing like this ever happens again. We have already begun building a memorial to Mrs. Lamrock at the plaza by Patriot's Park. Hopefully, this memorial will remind us of the terrible things that can happen when we rush to judgment. In fact, we are urging the council to consider abolition of the death penalty. Even though Mrs. Lamrock was innocent, I hope that the public will remember that her husband, Nathaniel Lamrock, is still guilty of the murders that happened this morning."

George Max was not through, but Trey quickly cut him off. "I have one more question, Mr. Max. Another tragedy happened this morning. It seems that Cilio Fernatti, Manager of Court Cases, committed suicide. Would you care to comment?"

Nathaniel watched George Max's smile fade. From where he stood, it looked like Max's whole face was crumbling in on itself.

"Oh, and it also appears that Manager Fernatti left a suicide note."

George Max could hardly speak. He eventually managed to reply, "We have no comment at this time."

Trey looked at George Max as if he was something nasty that Trey had just stepped in. Trey let his own face display what he was truly feeling for the first time ever, on camera. He proceeded to dismiss his guest abruptly.

"That will be all, Mr. Max. Thank you for your time."

For a change, Trey didn't even try to hide his feelings or mask his disdain for this man. He quickly turned his back on Max and went to the next story, another Elvis sighting. For the first time in his long career, Trey Thrasher looked proud of the job he had done.

Disgusted, Nathaniel asked himself how in the hell Malcolm could have gotten away. No one could have survived that blast. Then he remembered seeing something out of the corner of his eye as they were racing away from the battlefield.

At least Kara has been exonerated. Nathaniel owed a huge debt to Trey Thrasher, a debt that he vowed to repay some day.

Nathaniel turned to Digger, who was still staring at the holograph in shock. "That bastard had an escape plane! He must have planned a way out right from the beginning. He left nothing to chance. He even had a plan in place in the event that his secret cloning lab was ever uncovered."

Digger was starting to regain his composure. He looked at Nathaniel and then reached over to switch off Thrasher's annoying voice when Nathaniel stopped him from turning off the hologram.

"Wait, Digger!" Nathaniel grabbed Digger's arm. "That building that they're showing is where I met with my informant."

Trey Thrasher's smug voice droned on. "In an unrelated story, Billy Bargus's badly beaten body was found today in his rat infested lair. Authorities got a tip that Billy was a runner for one of the Western Zone's biggest drug lords, Axcardo. When they went to pick him up, this is what they found. Obviously, his nefarious employer was disappointed with him and this bloody corpse is the result."

The camera panned around the filthy, bug-infested room where Billy Bargus had lived the last days of his pathetic life, to show Billy's badly beaten body.

"Evidently, Billy must have stepped out of line and this was the price he paid," Trey said.

"What's wrong, Nathaniel?" Digger asked nervously.

"Billy Bargus was my informant. He's the one who brought me to Axcardo. From the looks of it, someone roughed him up pretty good before they killed him. Billy never was a hero. He would have given them any information they wanted."

"What do you mean?" Digger asked.

"Billy would have spilled his guts. We have to assume that Malcolm knows about Kara!"

Digger looked like he was about to get sick.

"Malcolm's not stupid. How long do you think it will take him to put two and two together? Nathaniel, it's public record that you were the one who got the Nualas their baby permit. He'll suspect that Kara is with them. It's one of the first places that Malcolm will look."

Nathaniel was close to panic. "We've got to warn the Nualas and get Kara out of there!"

Digger shook his head. "*You* can't do anything, Nathaniel. Your face is all over the news. You'd lead Malcolm right to her."

"Then what do you suggest?"

"You've got to send Solis. The flight to Mars is scheduled to leave in two days with the first set of colonists. We've got to get the Nualas and Kara on that ship. I've still got the connections that can get me the paperwork and documentation that will be needed to get them out of here."

Nathaniel was beside himself. "Malcolm will find them first. He'll get to them before they can get on the flight."

"Solis will just have to hide out with Kara and the Nualas for the next couple of days until the ship is ready to leave. Believe me. I still have enough pull to get passes for all of them. No one has connected me with you yet. The Nualas will have to board with Kara. Solis can board separately. The Nualas can reunite with Solis after take-off. Once the ship is out of Earth's atmosphere, there's no way that Malcolm can get it back, even if he suspects that Kara is on board."

Digger looked around. "Also, it won't be long before they find this place. We need to destroy everything. I have incendiary charges already in place. I'll set them off when we leave. We can't let them find any evidence that we were here. I have some contacts in Morenci, an old mining town east of here. My people can hide us until we can figure out how to expose Malcolm, but we need to leave right away."

Digger turned to Marty. "Marty, pack all the food and water that you can carry. We're going on a little vacation."

Nathaniel looked up and saw Solis standing in the doorway listening to his conversation with Digger. "Don't worry, Nathaniel. I will take care of Baby Kara and the Nualas."

Solis bent down, gently put Tandem in the valise and looked up at Nathaniel. For a minute, Nathaniel thought that he saw tears in his eyes.

Nathaniel walked over and put his arm around Solis. "Solis, you're my best friend, the brother I always wanted. I've trusted you with my life, and you've never failed me. Now, I'm entrusting Kara and the Nualas to you. Here is the address. Their living pod is on Happy Valley Road, just two miles west of the desalinization plant."

Solis took the address from Nathaniel. "I am your best friend?"

"You are my brother. Be careful."

Marty carefully approached Solis. Seeing his gentleness with Tandem, she didn't understand how she could ever have been scared by him. "Solis, please take the keys to my personal transport. It's yours. I won't need it anymore."

Solis took the keys and smiled. "Thank you, Marty."

Nathaniel turned to Digger. "I need to secretly transfer all my assets into Solis's account. I've accumulated a lot of wealth over the last century, and I want Solis to have it in case there is anything that Kara might need. It's imperative that the transfer goes through right away. Can you help me?"

"Of course," answered Digger. "It'll take about twenty-four hours for your funds to make their way through the maze of accounts that I have set up just for such a purpose. I'll get Marty working on it right away."

Digger gave Solis directions to another safe house where he could hide the Nualas and Kara until they were ready to leave.

"You've got to hurry, Solis. I'll have passes waiting for you at the spaceport. Don't try to contact us under any circumstances. We'll find you when things cool down."

Nathaniel could hear Tandem purring. Solis nodded, picked up the valise and went out the door.

Nathaniel watched sadly as the door closed behind him. He knew that it could be years, maybe decades before they would meet again.

"Now, we have to do something with you, my friend," Digger told Nathaniel. "That ugly mug of yours is plastered all over every newscast. Besides that, as soon as the population clock is fixed, Interglobal satellites will be able to find you by locking on to your imbedded census chip."

"What do you have in mind?" Nathaniel asked warily.

Digger handed Marty a laser scalpel. "Marty, please take Nathaniel to the nuclear reactor building. Remove his serial number chip and put it in this canister. Seal it, then hide it deep in the reactor. The radiation won't hurt you, but it will keep any human from going inside to snoop around. The walls of the reactor building are so thick even satellite scans won't penetrate them."

Digger looked over at Nathaniel. "When you get back, we'll cut your pretty locks, maybe even shave your head. That should change your appearance enough until we get to Morenci. My documentation 'specialist' has obtained a replacement chip for you. He also hacked into the population database and you will have an entirely new identity."

Marty took Nathaniel's arm. "Let's go, Nathaniel."

They walked out of the safe house and crossed the parking lot that was between Digger's safe house and the reactor building. When they got to the reactor building, Marty motioned for Nathaniel to sit at what used to be a computer terminal station in the operations room.

"Let me see your arm, Nathaniel," she said, gently taking his arm and exposing the small scar that was the only sign of his inoculation. In less than a minute, Marty expertly removed the serial number chip from Nathaniel's arm. She then placed the chip into the canister that Digger had given her, closed the lid, and sealed it shut.

"Now, wait here. I'll be right back." Marty walked through the operations room, stepping over old computer printouts and other remnants of a long-passed technology, but then she hesitated. Obviously reluctant to go into the reactor vessel, she stopped and looked timorously over her shoulder at Nathaniel. She took a deep breath and pushed open the vault door leading to the reactor. The nuclear rods were long gone, but Nathaniel knew that the invisible killer, radiation, was all around her. He watched anxiously as she disappeared into the bowels of the reactor.

***

Because of the intense radiation to which she was now exposed, Marty's environmental adaptation chip activated. The chip protected *taman* units by morphing the units' physical makeup so that they could adapt to any climate. Marty held her breath and walked deeper into the reactor vault where even more radiation assaulted her. Marty's man-made nerve endings tingled as the heat from the radiation particles attacked her outer skin. She was aware that the effects of radiation had never been tested on her environmental chip, and the thought that she might be irreparably damaged fleetingly crossed her mind.

The chip sensed the intense heat immediately. It incorrectly interpreted the heat source as close proximity to the sun rather than emanating from the radiation. The excess artificial tissue that protected Marty from normal climate changes had given Marty's torso a matronly appearance. Now, programming encoded in her environmental chip determined that this sub-dermal tissue was no longer needed, and it began to burn it away. The liquid in individual hair follicle sacks beneath Marty's scalp began to boil. This liquid had been designed to determine her hair color. In Marty's case, the liquid had made her hair light brown. Now, the chemicals in the bubbling liquid reacted with the radiation and started to turn Marty's hair from its nondescript shade of brown, a hair color that was often described as "mousy" to a vibrant shade of auburn.

Kneeling on the reactor's hard steel floor, Marty reached beneath her and placed the canister containing Nathaniel's serial number chip on a platform beneath the catwalk that crossed over the rod basin. She made a mental note of precisely how many paces she was from the vault's entrance and then turned to leave.

***

When Marty walked back into the operations room, Nathaniel jumped up from the chair and assumed a defensive posture because he didn't immediately recognize her. The Geiger counters in the operations room were going wild.

"Stay away from me, Nathaniel. I need to go to the decontamination chamber immediately to wash off."

Nathaniel backed away from her as she ran into a shower-like stall beside the reactor room's entrance. By the time she emerged, the Geiger counters were silent.

"Thankfully, that old technology still works," Marty said with evident relief. "Now, let's get you back to Digger."

When Marty and Nathaniel entered the safe house, Digger's jaw dropped. "Marty, what the hell happened to you?"

"It was the radiation. I was hot."

"You're still hot! Take a look at yourself in the mirror."

Marty looked quizzically at Digger, then turned and went into the bathroom closely followed by Digger and Nathaniel, who crowded into the small room behind her. She looked as though she didn't recognize the woman she saw in the mirror. Her thick waist was gone, and she no longer had mousy brown hair. She shook her hair loose from its barrette and it fell over her shoulders in long red waves. Looking sheepish, she turned to Digger.

"You're right. I really am hot," she said.

Digger laughed. "I just got an assistant that looks like last month's Playboy centerfold." He smiled and picked up the razor that was on the sink.

Marty was still looking at herself in the mirror. It was evident that she was confused but pleased.

"OK, Nathaniel, your turn for a makeover," he said almost too gleefully.

Chapter 38

The Nualas lived in a quiet middle class neighborhood in North Phoenix, the perfect setting to raise a child in obscurity.

Solis entered through the only window in the dark, attached garage. Anyone other than a *taman* would have been blinded by the absolute darkness in the garage, but Solis didn't need his superhuman sight to know that danger lurked within the house. The hair on his arms stood up and he felt a chill at the base of his spine.

In order to protect Tandem, he placed the valise's carrying strap around his neck freeing his hands and carrying the bag on his back. He felt his way along the wall, moving ahead quietly, an inch at a time. Finally, he reached the back of the garage where he saw that the door to the Nualas' living pod had been wrenched off its hinges.

A man clad completely in black crouched in the middle of the living room. Although his back was to Solis, Solis still could make out that the stranger was looking at something on the floor.

When Solis entered the room, the man looked up, startled by his presence. He tried to run, but before he could get away, Solis grabbed him around the neck in a deadly grip. Solis looked past the struggling man and saw the bodies of Sha and Juan Nuala lying side by side. They would remain forever together in death, as they did in life.

Solis's eyes began to smolder. He glared at the twisting, squealing murderer in his grasp. Solis felt unfamiliar stirrings of anger at this monster. "Where's the baby?" he growled.

The assassin tried his best to answer, but no sound could escape his throat as Solis tightened his grip with hands that gripped the neck like a vise. The best the assassin could do was croak incoherently. Solis lifted him off his feet, picking him up so that they were eye to eye. He loosened his grip slightly so that the man could answer.

"Where is the baby?" he repeated.

The man struggled, but when he realized that Solis's grip on him was getting looser, he mustered enough courage to spit out an answer. "What baby?"

The man had miscalculated when he thought that he might have a chance to fight Solis off. The words he had just uttered so defiantly were the last two words that this killer would ever utter. Solis's hold tightened on the man's neck until there was no more breath coming from him then tossed the lifeless body aside like a rag doll.

Solis scanned the pod, recognizing that there was no life in the three bodies lying in front of him. His analysis told him that a carbon-breathing unit was in the next room. Carefully, Solis pushed open the door to the Nualas' bedchamber. There, hidden under the bed was a baby. Solis looked down at the child and his eyes changed from red to a deep shade of blue.

"Kara," Solis whispered almost reverently. He gently lifted the child and cradled her in his arms. Tandem was still safely tucked away in the case that Solis carried on his back. "Don't worry. I am here to take care of you now."

Chapter 39

Nathaniel told Marty to stand behind him as he knocked on the door. Digger was parking his transport around back where it would be out of sight. A cheery-looking, gnome-like woman opened the door.

She immediately began talking non-stop. "Come in, come in. We've been waiting for you. You must be tired and hungry. Just leave your things there. Yegman will take them to your rooms. My name is Gwendolyn. Please call me Lyn. I have some red tea brewing. It'll pick you right up."

An exceptionally tall man, whom Nathaniel assumed must be Yegman, towered over Lyn. Yegman was gangly, with arms that hung down to his knees. He picked up the bags, grunted something that sounded like "hello," and started down the corridor toward the back of the house. From his extreme height, Nathaniel knew that Yegman had been raised somewhere other than Earth--somewhere with a lot less gravity.

A moonchild, he thought as he ran his hand over his own newly bald head.

Digger came up behind them. He looked Marty up and down as though seeing her for the first time. "I'm still trying to get used to the new Marty," he said with a smile. "Marty, are you actually blushing?"

"Of course not. You know that *tamen--tawomen*--don't blush," she answered brusquely. She held out an envelope, the one containing the DSDS holographs, but Digger ignored it.

"Lyn, we'll need a place to stay for at least two weeks. It has to be someplace with secure communications."

"We're all ready for you Digger."

Lyn had worked with Digger before. She didn't even question why Digger needed to hide out. If he said he needed something, she would make sure that he got it.

"There's an old mine about eight miles north of here. It hasn't been used since before the war, but it's close to Route 666, the Devils Highway. The road is almost never used anymore so you should be able to get in and out without being seen. I've stocked it with plenty of food and water and made sure that the encryption devices and communications equipment still work. Yegman has installed hologram receivers so that you'll know what's going on in the rest of the world.

"You and your friends can stay here tonight. In the morning, Yegman will take you out there."

Digger leaned over and kissed Lyn on the cheek. "Thanks, Lyn. I knew that I could count on you."

Lyn started to giggle. "Oh, Digger. You'll never change," she said affectionately.

"Right now, we all could use some rest. Marty, you go with Yegman."

Nathaniel was watching Marty when Digger kissed Lyn. If he didn't know that *tamen* were emotionless machines, he would think that she was jealous.

She stood with her arms crossed, tapping her toe on the floor.

Petulantly, she shrugged at Digger. "Whatever you say, boss."

Chapter 40

Velyn was only half-listening to her agent.

"I don't know why you want this gig, but I pulled some strings and it's yours. It wasn't easy. The entertainer that I had already booked for the trip is furious, and the Cosmos is really hot with anger! I'll have a lot of damage control to do. The trip alone takes six months. You do know, don't you, that even after all that time in space, when you finally do get there, you won't find any luxury hotels. It's going to be like old Earth's Wild West up there. There aren't even enough *tamen* to take care of essentials. I just can't see you cooking your own food and making your own bed, Velyn."

"Don't worry about me, Herv. In my prior life I was used to hard work, plus I'm taking my own entourage with me. I really need to get away--the further, the better. Besides, I'll have a captive audience for six months. What more could a girl ask for?"

Velyn forced herself to exchange a few more pleasantries and then hung up as soon as she could without making Herv even more suspicious than he was already. She knew that she couldn't get near Kara, but at least she could be on the same planet with her. She would have to pack quickly. She planned to stay at a hotel near the spaceport tonight so she could be one of the first to board tomorrow.

Memories of Kara as a child kept pushing their way into her mind. *I love you, my darling little girl*, she thought as she threw her makeup into her travel trunk. Finally, she closed the trunk and called one of her *tamen* to take the baggage down to the lobby.

"Has any one heard from Apollo?" she asked. The *tamen* just looked at each other and shrugged.

I certainly hope that he gets to the spaceport on time, Velyn thought. *What could be keeping him?*

As Velyn left her room and closed the door behind her, she knew she was closing the door on a life that she had loved. She shrugged. *So what! None of it matters anymore. Kara's the most important thing now.* Velyn realized that Kara had always been the most important thing in her life. She had to lose her before she had realized the obvious.

A message was waiting for Velyn when she checked into the Spaceport Hotel. "You can retrieve your message in booth number three." The *taman* behind the registration desk looked bored, obviously unimpressed by celebrities, since virtually every guest of the five-star hotel was famous for something or other.

It seemed that each of the guests wanted something different, and the hotel catered to every need, whether real or imagined. Even the message booths in the lobby guaranteed their privacy with their mirrored one-way windows and an encrypted communications system. Paparazzi were always on the lookout for a story, but the Spaceport Hotel took great care that they were not welcome in the hotel. The hotel had become a haven for entertainers that were constantly being harangued by the press.

Velyn stepped into booth three and closed the door. She keyed in the access code given to her by the registration clerk. She gasped as a pre-recorded hologram of Solis appeared.

"Velyn, this message will erase itself as soon as it's finished. The Nualas are dead."

Velyn was so stunned by Solis's statement that she thought her heart would stop. How could it continue to beat? There was only one thought that was screaming in her head. *Kara. What about Kara?*

"Kara is safely hidden away at a safe house with me. I am in possession of travel vouchers that Digger left for us. Again, Kara is safe. Here is the bad news."

The Nualas are dead and there is still more bad news? What could be worse than the death of the Nualas?

"Malcolm knows that Kara is alive and that she was cloned, but he believes that the cells used to clone her were harvested when she was still a baby. He does not realize that Kara was cloned from class one tissue that was taken when she was three years old."

Please God. Please God. Please God. Maybe Malcolm will be looking for a baby!

"Kara is growing so fast, that by the time I see you, she will be a toddler."

Solis was about to tell Velyn that the only hope she could cling to was true.

"The only thing in our favor is that Malcolm thinks that she is still a baby."

Thank you God. Thank you God. Thank you God.

"That's the good news. The bad news is that Malcolm has convinced the authorities that finding baby Kara is the key to finding Nathaniel Lamrock. The authorities are scrutinizing every baby that boards the ship. The order to the security agents is that every female child under the age of two be held until proof of identity is produced. The authorities are testing the children's DNA to determine if one of them is Kara.

"Already, Kara has almost matured to the age of three, but I am afraid that with the Nualas dead, they will be looking for me. The authorities will think that it's suspicious for a single man like me to be traveling with a small child. If another couple could take Kara, I believe that it would be safer. I was instructed not to contact Nathaniel or Digger under any circumstances. I am here in the hotel, in room 723. What should I do?"

Solis's image began breaking up. He was turning to snow in front of Velyn's eyes. She looked at the empty space where his hologram had been. Even though the message had self-destructed, she remained sitting in the booth trying to gather her wits. She realized that she hadn't taken a breath since she recognized Solis on the hologram.

Solis wants me to tell him what to do? That's crazy. He doesn't know how to get in touch with Nathaniel or Digger? Oh God, what am I going to do?

Velyn jumped. She was suddenly startled by someone knocking insistently on the door. She stood, opened the door, and stepped back into the lobby, only to be almost knocked over by a young man who flung his arms around her. She finally extricated herself from his grasp and took a step back.

"Velyn!" Leo cried, "I can't believe it's you! I told Andrea that it was you going into this booth. The desk clerk told us that you'll be playing in the ship's lounge during the trip. I can't believe it! I can't tell you how bad Andrea and I feel about Kara. We're both so sorry about your loss. At least she was exonerated and had time to tell her husband the surprise."

Andrea hung back, obviously embarrassed by Leo's show of emotion. She shyly stepped forward and reached out to take Velyn's hand.

"It's good to see you again, Velyn. I never had a chance to properly thank you for all that you did for us. I'm so sorry about Kara. Trey Thrasher did a special tonight that said people everywhere are petitioning The Council to abolish the death penalty. They want to call it 'Kara's Law.'"

Velyn could hardly speak. Her mind was still reeling from Solis's message. Through her haze, she finally realized that Leo was still talking to her.

"That's right. 'Kara's Law.' And Velyn, Andrea and I are going to Mars, also. I have a permit to prospect some land there. Andrea and I plan to build a cabin, and I'll be able to mine hematite and scapolite. Once there are regular flights between Earth and Mars, we'll be able to send the ore back to Earth. It should bring in a good profit. If I'm right, there ought to be enough ore on my land to support us for the next twenty years."

As if she were watching herself from a great distance, Velyn heard herself responding to Leo.

"Twenty years? Did you say that you will be on Mars for twenty years?"

"That's right, at least twenty years. We'll be in on the ground floor, so to speak. We want to start a family. I don't know yet what the rules will be on Mars about letting settlers have their own kids, but Andrea and I will be ready."

Even through the haze, Velyn had picked up on something that Leo had said when he first started talking to her.

"Leo, what do you mean about the secret that Kara had for Nathaniel?"

"Didn't she tell you?" Leo asked. "She found his sister, Rosemary. Kara told me that Rosemary is Captain Margaret Owning!"

"What?" Velyn almost yelled. Then, realizing that she was drawing attention to herself, she said quietly, "We won't be able to contact Nathaniel for two years, at the earliest. Kara never told him about Rosemary. Are you sure that she said that Rosemary is Margaret Owning?"

"Oh, yes." Leo said. "Kara said that the family resemblance was so strong, that there's no doubt."

Velyn thought for a minute and started to nod in agreement. "Of course, with all that was going on, I didn't notice. Kara was spot on. The problem is that there is no way to let Nathaniel know until the shuttle system is in effect. That will not occur for another two years!"

Oh, dear God, one more thing to add to the list. This piece of information is just going to have to wait. First things first. What am I going to tell Solis?

Leo was looking at Velyn. It would be obvious to anyone, even to him, that something was terribly wrong.

"Velyn, I think that you better tell us what's going on."

Velyn looked thoughtful. She took a deep breath. "I need to ask you and Andrea a favor, a big favor. It may be dangerous."

This time it was Andrea that spoke up. For the first time since Velyn had known her, Andrea's face was set and her voice strong. "Tell us Velyn. We will do anything you need us to do. Anything!"

Leo looked at Andrea in surprise and then nodded at Velyn. He, too, showed more determination than Velyn had thought he was capable of. She had misjudged them both.

"Just tell us what you need us to do," he said, his voice strong with resolve.

Chapter 41

"You have to understand that Kara cannot be connected with Velyn in any way." Solis's protective instincts were focused like a laser on Kara's safety and survival.

Leo sat on the hotel's small bed with an open map in front him. "Of course, I understand," he acknowledged. "Andrea and I are happy to take Kara aboard with us."

Leo motioned to Solis. "I plan on purchasing a small parcel of land here." He pointed to a spot on the map. "I know that it's far away from the main settlement, but I'm very handy with tools and building materials. I can build a cabin that will house all of us comfortably. There's plenty of natural fuel that will provide warmth in the winter. There's also an underground water table that I can tap into with just a shallow well."

Solis sat next to Leo on the bed and stared at the map. He loaded the coordinates of where Leo planned to establish his mine into his internal CPU and began to analyze the area. His analysis showed a large ore deposit just beneath the Martian surface squarely under the spot that Leo had indicated. In fact, the deposit was much larger than the small parcel of land that Leo intended to acquire.

"There are large mineral deposits all over this region." Solis drew a large circle around the point where Leo indicated his mine would be.

Leo studied the landmass within the circle that Solis had drawn and then said, "Solis, I'm not a rich man. We've saved just enough to purchase five acres along the east side of Terra Meridiani.

I believe that there's enough ore to provide us with a comfortable living. With all the construction that will be going on, hematite will be in high demand. We can send the scapolite back to Earth once they get the shuttle going. It's quite valuable in the gem market. Maybe in a few years we'll be able to expand and buy more land, but right now, the area that I marked is all that we can afford."

Solis shook his head and looked thoughtfully at the map. "Once it is generally known that hematite has been found here in large quantities, this land will be very expensive. Right now is the time to buy it. Would you consider a partner, Leo? I believe that I may have the funds to purchase all the land in this area."

Leo couldn't hide his astonishment. "That's over 800,000 acres, more than a thousand square miles! How could anyone afford to buy that much land?"

"If you would accept me as your partner, I believe that I may just have enough funds to complete the transaction with enough left over to cover our operating expenses until we can get on our feet," Solis answered.

Leo stuck out his hand and said, "Man, you got a deal. Andrea is never going to believe this!"

Smiling at his good luck, Leo shook Solis's hand vigorously.

Solis smiled also. He was relieved that he could help secure a good future for Kara.

"Good. I am pleased that you agree. I will take care of the purchase today. Here is Kara's boarding pass. It is in the name of Alizarin Davis. You should have no problems boarding the ship. Tomorrow, please have Andrea in the lobby at precisely 5:03 A.M.

Kara, I mean Alizarin, will be waiting there. I will be very near, watching her. I intend to remain hidden until after Andrea picks her up. We will not be able to speak again until after we are in deep space.

KATHLEEN PAPAJOHN

Chapter 42

As Solis walked up the ramp and got in line with the others that were boarding the space transport, he never took his eyes off the couple two positions in front of him. The man carried what appeared to be a backpack filled with mining equipment and hardware of various types. The woman held the hand of a beautiful little dark haired girl. Solis watched intently as they showed their papers to the steward at the door.

The steward looked closely at the little girl and then looked down at a picture that he had been given by his boss. He was supposed to screen all small children before they boarded the ship. From where he was standing, Solis could see that the picture was of a baby no more than a year old. From his viewpoint, Solis could also see that Andrea was nervous. His sharp hearing picked up the sound of Andrea's heart racing in her chest. Solis feared that the steward would also hear the hammering.

Andrea picked Kara/Alizarin up and held her so that she faced back over her shoulder, away from the steward.

Alizarin saw Solis and waved. Solis's logic told him that she was just a little girl, incapable of deceit, not knowing the danger she was in. In spite of his desire to watch over her, he forced himself to look away, praying silently that she would not call out to him. He bent over, pretending to tie his bootlace so that she would not be able to see him.

The man waiting in line in front of Solis turned to him and said, "You must have a way with kids. That little toddler over there really likes you."

Solis peered discretely around the man only to see Alizarin laughing. She was bending and squirming over Andrea in such a way that Andrea was having trouble holding her. The child could still see Solis.

"I do love children," Solis told the stranger nervously. "That one is especially cute. I hope to have my own someday."

The steward studied the child again and then, to Solis's relief, he must have decided that the baby in the picture he was holding did not match the child in front of him. He returned the boarding passes to the woman. "Cabin 352A. Down the stairs and then through the doors on your left. Have a pleasant trip," he said.

When his turn came, Solis handed the steward his boarding pass. The steward hardly glanced at him. To the steward, Solis was just one more single man looking for a new start and expecting to find riches in a new planetary home.

"Cabin 353B. Down the stairs. Have a pleasant trip."

Solis smiled and took back his papers. *Digger must have great connections to get papers this good.* He picked up his valise and heard Tandem's soft meow. By the time Solis reached the stairs that led to his cabin, the steward was already scrutinizing the papers of the next traveler in line.

***

At Lyn's safe house, insistent knocking on his door woke Nathaniel. He was instantly alert.

"What is it?" he asked irritably. It had been a long night. Thoughts about Kara had kept sleep away until just before dawn. Not being able to see or talk to Kara was almost unthinkable, yet he knew that she would be safe with Solis, and that gave him some comfort. He promised himself that he would be on the next flight to Mars.

"The newscast has started. Margaret Owning is speaking. You told me to wake you, so don't be so cross. Digger has already powered up the viewer," Marty said.

"Sorry, Marty. I'll be right there." Nathaniel jumped up and pulled on his pants.

Digger was already staring at an image of Margaret Owning. Margaret appeared to be exactly what she was--the captain of one of the largest space transports in Interglobal's fleet. Her blond hair was pulled back severely into a single, golden-blond braid that was so long, it appeared that she had not cut her hair in decades. She carried her slim frame almost regally, as if she were used to having her orders obeyed without question.

Captain Owning was speaking. She was doing a voice-over while the hologram displayed a backdrop of Olympus Mons. The Martian mountain was sixteen miles high, three times the height of Earth's Mount Everest.

The hologram's display returned to the live press conference. Margaret Owning captured Nathaniel's full attention. She finished speaking and was ending the press conference by responding to a final question asked by one of the reporters.

"I will captain the return trip to Earth after the first Martian year, which is about twice as long as an Earth year. The Company plans to institute regular flights to Mars every twenty-six months."

One of Margaret's aides came up behind her and whispered in her ear.

"I'm sorry, gentlemen," she said. "It's almost time for take-off."

Without another word, Margaret turned and started to walk toward the ship, her long, blond, trademark braid hanging visibly down her back. The camera panned from Margaret to a small number of colonists waiting to board. Nathaniel held his breath, hoping for a last glance at Kara. He was disappointed when he did not see her in the crowd waiting to board.

When the last person had boarded, Margaret walked up the ramp, turned and waved to the newsmen who crowded behind the barriers, each trying to get a last minute quote from Captain Owning. Margaret entered the ship and the hatch closed behind her. Within minutes, the hologram showed emissions from the space transport's heat surge as the ship rose through Earth's atmosphere and headed off into space.

Nathaniel turned and looked at Marty. If it were possible, he would have sworn that her skin actually paled. She looked as though she had seen a ghost.

"Marty, what is it?" Even Digger had noticed that something was wrong. He was looking down at Marty and Nathaniel had never seen Digger with such a look of concern on his face.

It took several seconds before Marty was able to speak. She turned to Nathaniel and said, "Did you notice Captain Owning's eyes--her gray eyes?"

For a minute, Nathaniel didn't seem to understand what she was saying. Then Digger's head snapped up, and he stared at Nathaniel.

"Nathaniel," Digger said almost in a whisper, "I believe I know what Kara was going to tell you. Have you ever looked closely at Margaret Owning? She bears a striking resemblance to you."

Nahaniel was stunned. *Rosemary, after all these years, could it really be you?*

Before Nathaniel had time to react, the scene on the hologram shifted to Patriot's Plaza. It was crowded with more people than Nathaniel had ever seen. The camera panned the faces of people standing completely still. Each person was holding a single lit white candle. The camera panned again to show a memorial surrounded by stuffed animals, balloons, and streamers that read, "We're sorry," "We love you, Kara," and "Down with Capital Punishment."

Digger turned the viewer off just as Marty said, "Since neither of you had time, I took a look at some of these DSDS holograms. Would you like to know what DSDS stands for?"

"Okay, Marty," Digger said resignedly. "You've got your captive audience."

"It stands for 'DNA Soup Delivery System,' a procedure that is mandatory at all Interglobal prenatal clinics."

Both Nathaniel and Digger responded at the same time. "Godfrey's DNA!"

Chapter 43

Solis stood on a hill overlooking the Martian panorama below. It bore little resemblance to his previous home on Earth, or even to the lush greenery of the main settlement where most of the Mars colonists planned to build their homes – and their futures.

The site below him was desolate and harsh. In the distance, majestic snow-capped mountains towered over the barren landscape that itself, seemed to swallow up the one tiny mining cabin.

At first glance, the red dust looked like dried Oklahoma clay, but it was dust after all, and it was everywhere. Although Solis did not view Mars the same way, he knew that Leo and Andrea saw only beauty in the austere, rocky, reddish-brown landscape.

Despite the high technology that lay within his circuitry, Solis was not a complex being. He just wanted to go home. He longed for things to be the way they had been before, when his only job was to care for Nathaniel and Kara, his charge who was now a child with a new name--Alizarin.

Solis wanted life to be simple again. The need to return to Earth and his old way of life was overwhelming. It was doubtful if a human man would not succumb to the sadness that Solis was feeling. In spite of his own wishes, Solis had promised Nathaniel that he would care for Alizarin. That promise, with all the responsibility it entailed, rested squarely on his shoulders. He had strong shoulders.

Solis knew that he could face whatever lay before him, but he worried how Alizarin would be able to endure the harsh conditions that he knew would have to be faced.

As if Alizarin could read his mind, she handed Solis a bouquet of twigs and small sticks and said in a soothing voice that was older than her years, "Don't worry, Solis. Everything is going to be all right. I promise." She reached up and tightened her grip on his finger, trustingly looking up into his clear blue eyes. Then, absently, she tugged at her right earlobe.

Solis loved the feel of her tiny hand in his. With Tandem cradled in his other arm, he smiled down at Alizarin, and they began walking toward their new home.

ABOUT THE AUTHOR

Born in Boston, Kathleen has lived in Phoenix, Arizona for the past twenty years. She was co-Salutatorian of her Rio Salado College graduating class (1995) with her late husband.

She has spent her professional life working with computers-from teaching computer programming to her last position as Chief Information Officer for a major weapons manufacturer.

Although her novel, *Maligned*, is fiction, much of the technology in the story is inspired by her work, and by the work of her late husband who was a member of the intelligence community prior to founding his own computer consulting firm. Kathleen is also the author of a number of short stories.